AUTOMATED MANHUNT

He can't get very far. A man on the lam doesn't make much sense these days. He can't use the ultra-highways without using his TV phone-credit card to rent an electro-steamer. If he does use it, they have him. He can't buy anything without it, including food or shelter. He can't even have it on his person or the police will get a fix on him and track him down, no matter where he is. And you simply can't live in the world as it is without a credit card.

The
Towers
of Utopia

Mack Reynolds

Part One
Barry Ten Eyck

Barry Ten Eyck came briskly into his inner office in fine mood, tossed his briefcase to his old fashioned steel desk and called over to his secretary cum Man Friday, "Miss Cusack, I shall allow exactly four crises this morning. No more."

Carol Ann Cusack looked down at her notes. She was a tallish brunette with unusually dark blue eyes. She had a strong face, a wide warm mouth, and glossy, quizzical brows, and was well liked by the staff for her quick humor.

She said, "I have nine. No, ten."

"Four," he said again, severely. "No more. Turn the others over to Jim and Bat. A good Demecrat must learn to delegate authority. Besides, they need the experience."

"Mr. Cotswold is on vacation."

"That's right, he is. Then turn the last six over to Bat Hardin. He has strong, broad shoulders whilst I am failing by the minute."

"Yes, Mr. Ten Eyck."

"When are you going to begin calling me Barry, Carol Ann?"

"When I am no longer your secretary, Mr. Ten Eyck. The Head Chef, Monsieur Daunou, has tendered his resignation again."

"What! Pete can't do this to me." He glared at her.

Somehow, in spite of his position as the Demecrat of Shyler-deme, Barry Ten Eyck's glares didn't come off. Not, at least, when he was dealing with his immediate staff. A tall, lanky, easygoing and good-natured type, especially when not under pressure, when he could get as tough as the occasion warranted, he wasn't exactly typical as young Meritcrats went, believing in a highly informal administration.

"What's the reason this time? Too many complaints about his latest soufflé creation?"

Carol Ann shook her head. "I wouldn't know. He seemed to be in some sort of huff."

Her boss slumped down into his chair. "Good grief, the budget doesn't allow for any pay increases, if that's it. I'll see him later. You don't get a chef like Pierre Daunou just any day in the week. Have you got the computer report on this week's take?"

Carol Ann said, "That's the next crisis. It's down to four hundred and seventy-five thousand pseudo-dollars."

He stared at her. "It is? That's not much above our breakeven point."

"No, sir."

"What happened—in particular?"

"That's the next crisis. We lost two hundred and three resident families."

"And took in how many?"

"Eighty-three. Some of them, of course, renting from the owners."

Barry Ten Eyck winced, got up from his desk and looked out the window and over the acres of parks and trees that surrounded the hundred-and-nineteen-story, aluminium-sheathed, twin towers of the apartment building which he managed.

He muttered, barely audible, "The building is less than ten years old. What gets into people that they can't stay put in an apartment worth some $40,000 that they've been given practically free?"

Carol Ann said dryly, "They haven't got anything else to do but move around. They get bored."

He took a breath and turned to her. "What's the current occupancy, Miss Cusack?"

She flicked a switch, said something into a desk TV phone screen. She looked up and reported, "Four thousand and fifty-two, including Mr. Vanderfeller's penthouse."

He grunted. "Which is empty most of the time. It'd be our most lucrative occupancy if we had some high-living playboy in there."

Carol Ann said, "Which brings us to your third crisis."

He looked at her.

"Mr. Cyril Vanderfeller is in residence. He wants to see you soonest."

Barry Ten Eyck groaned. "This is my day. And it started so sun-shiny. What is there about the old rich that they all like to make like Meritcrats? I'll work in a visit to him some time this afternoon."

"He said soonest."

"Miss Cusack, I'm the Demecrat of this deme and if I started letting people like old man Vanderfeller order me around it'd soon get to be such a habit on their part, I'd never get any work done. What else is wrong today?"

"You've used up your four crises."

"I'm feeling masochistic. Let me have it. Deal me brutal blows."

She looked at her notes. "There's a petition being circulated by the Gourmet Club. They want a Moroccan restaurant."

"A Moroccan restaurant. What in the hell is a Moroccan restaurant? What do Moroccans eat?"

Carol Ann shrugged. "I wouldn't know. Dates?"

"Ha, ha, Miss Cusack."

"At any rate, they'll bring up the request at the Deme-Assembly this afternoon."

"Oh, good grief, is that today?" He thought about it. "A Moroccan restaurant. We have French, Italian, Mexican, Spanish, Chinese and Japanese restaurants,

3

besides the four auto-cafeterias. Now they want a Moroccan restaurant. I'll wager there aren't fifty people in Shyler-deme who'd ever eat in it."

"Yes, sir."

He sighed plaintively. "I am put upon, Miss Cusack. I suffer needlessly. Dial me a Moroccan cookbook. I'll have to learn *something* about it."

He stared unhappily and unseeingly at a far wall while she activated the TV phone library booster and dialed cookbooks and then sub-categories until she got down to Moroccan cookbooks.

She said, "There are only seven in English."

"Any one'll do," he said gloomily. He looked down into the booster screen and began idly flipping pages with the button.

One of her desk screens lit up and spoke. She said to him, "Mr. Hardin."

He activated one of his phone screens. "Morning, Bat. What spins?"

The face in his screen was that of Bat Hardin, his Vice-Demecrat and second in command. Hardin was a hard-working type in his late thirties and bore a perpetually worried expression. He had crisp, short hair, a dark complexion and his features were so heavy that he would never have been thought handsome by average contemporary standards. He was a good team man, always available when things got rugged.

Now he was looking at his chief strangely. "I've just been talking to Stevens. Listen, you'll never believe this. There's been some more burglaries."

Barry stared at him.

Bat said doggedly, "Three more. Last night. On the eighty-third floor this time."

"God dammit!" Barry Ten Eyck came to his feet. "Meet me in Security."

Bat's face faded even as he said, "Great."

Barry Ten Eyck said to Carol Ann, "I'll be over in Stevens' office."

4

The Security offices were immediately across the corridor from those of the Democrat. Barry Ten Eyck met Bat Hardin at the door.

Barry said disgustedly, "Same pattern?"

"Evidently." Bat Hardin was a medium sized man with a military carriage. Barry had heard that he had fought in the Asian War and for a time had been a police officer in a mobile town.

The door identified them and immediately opened.

Stevens looked up from a phone screen he was scowling into.

"What in the devil is all this, Stevens?" Barry said.

Stevens held up his hands in a gesture of helplessness. "Three more burglaries. This time on the eighty-third floor." He was a sour man, tight of face and not exactly unpopular with the rest of the staff; a better description was that he was avoided, at least socially. He was competent at his job and Barry Ten Eyck appreciated having him. Competent men were at a premium, especially these days when you didn't have to work if you didn't want to, because of that confounded Negative Income Tax so many people seemed to take as a free ride from the cradle to the grave.

Bat said, "The last three were on the sixty-second floor. You said the only way it made sense was for the crook to live on the same floor."

"That's the only way it does make sense," Stevens said stubbornly. "And even that doesn't make very much sense. This whole thing is impossible."

Barry drew up a chair. "All right. You're Security. Tell us about it."

Bat sat down too and held his peace, although he was characteristically chewing away on his under lip.

Stevens said, "Look. Shyler-deme is a building with five thousand apartments. Given full occupancy, we have some twenty thousand tenants, give or take a few hundred. Okay. Every tenant, man, woman and child, has an I.D. which is identified by our TV computer check. Outsiders to this building can come onto the ground floor and never be checked. But the moment

5

anybody enters an elevator, he's checked through his TV pocket phone I.D. card, or, if it's a child, his electronic tag which he usually wears around his neck. Everybody. If he isn't an inhabitant of this deme, his phone buzzes and the computer check asks for his business."

"All right, all right, Steve, all this is basic," Barry said.

"No, let me give you the whole picture," Stevens said in irritation. "What it amounts to is that nobody, but *nobody*, can go either up or down an elevator, unless he's cleared for it. Any visitor has to be checked before he can go up to an apartment. And once he gets into the building proper, he can only go where he's scheduled to go. He can't go from one floor to another. There are more than ten thousand spy lenses, computer-checked, in this building. If an outsider comes in the living areas of Shyler-deme, he's monitored. He goes to the floor and apartment he's checked through for, and nowhere else. When he leaves that apartment, he leaves the building—or we in Security are immediately informed."

Bat said slowly, "Then it has to be somebody who lives in Shyler-deme."

Stevens looked at him. "Even that doesn't make sense. Even a tenant can't go somewhere he doesn't belong. If you live on the thirty-eighth floor, in Tower-Two, you can't go to the sixty-second floor just for the Dutch of it. You have to have some reason. If you have a friend, or relative, sure, you can have it cleared out. But you can't simply roam around. Sure, you can go to any of the public floors, like the Swank Room nightclub or the Chink restaurant up at the top of Tower-Two, but you can't go onto residential floors without checking it out with our Security computer monitors."

Barry said, "However, the burglaries took place."

"Yes. But it's impossible."

Bat said, "How about the staircases?"

"The doors are locked, except for emergencies, and

6

there hasn't been one since this building was opened. They're for extreme emergencies. Who needs staircases any more? We have our own source of power and three different sets of motors. If one set breaks down, another immediately takes over."

Bat said, "But couldn't our bad-o have cleared himself to visit some acquaintance on, say, the eighty-second floor and then, afterward, opened the door to the stairs and made it up to the eighty-third floor and pulled his romp?"

Stevens shook his head in exasperation. "No. He can't open those doors. They can only be opened here in Security. You know that."

Barry growled, "Whoever's behind this must be a jazzer."

Stevens looked at him. "As far as I'm concerned he's a crazy."

Bat said, "How do you know the same guy is involved?"

"Because the burglaries duplicate each other."

Barry said, "What'd the crook get this time?"

"The same as before. Nothing."

The two other men looked at him questioningly.

He said sourly, "In one apartment he ransacked the whole place but only lifted a small collection of coins."

"Coins?" Barry said.

"Money. You know, coins. Like they used before the Universal Credit Cards."

"Oh, of course. What was the collection worth?"

"So little as to be meaningless. In another apartment he took three books. Old books, printed on paper. Once again, practically valueless. And he took a small painting from there, too. And in the third apartment it was some junk jewelry. Nothing valuable."

Bat said slowly, "Do you have any idea where the loot might be fenced?"

"Fenced?" Stevens said in disgust. "Even if there were any fences any more, it's not worth being fenced. I keep telling you, whoever this clown is he isn't stealing anything worth taking."

They looked at him in frustration.

Barry muttered, "If it gets around that burglars are prowling the deme with us unable to do anything about it, we'll lose residents like dandruff." He looked at Stevens unhappily. "How could this guy know which apartments are empty, and then, how could he get in?"

"Both are impossible, so far as I'm concerned."

Bat said, "How about patrolling the floors?"

Stevens was still disgusted. "With the ten human relations officers I have? Public protection is automated these days, Hardin. Besides we here in the office, ten men have to do for everything, including traffic control down in the car pool and the transport station. And what could a man do that a spy lens can't? I've activated every mini-spy lens in the deme, except in private apartments, of course."

"Any ideas at all?" Barry said.

Stevens shook his head. "It's such a ridiculous thing, all six of these burglaries. I get the feeling it isn't being done by pros but possibly by kids. You know, juvenile delinquents, as they used to call them."

Barry Ten Eyck ran a weary hand slowly down from his forehead over his mouth. "Could kids get up and down delivery or disposal chutes, enter apartments from inside, rather than coming through the door?"

"Or come in through windows?" Bat Hardin added.

"No," Stevens said disgustedly. "Not by any method I can think of." He looked at Bat. "Through windows on the eighty-third floor? They'd have to be human flies. Besides, they'd have to break the windows, and none of them were broken."

Barry Ten Eyck stood up with a sigh. "Doggonit, it beats me." He looked at his Vice-Demecrat. "Bat, I'm turning this over to you. Working with Steve, here, of course."

"Oh, great."

"Come on back to my office, I've got another thing or two."

Stevens sat looking after them sourly as they left.

8

As they crossed the corridor, Bat shook his head. "Human Relations officers," he said. "What a mealy-mouth expression for cop."

Barry chuckled. "You're out of the times, Bat. And did you notice it was public protection, instead of law enforcement? We live in an age of gobbledygook, saving face, status symbols, ridiculous titles. How long have plumbers been calling themselves Sanitary Engineers? But I think tops was reached over in England where lavatory cleaners are now called Amenities Attendants."

The door to the Demecrat's offices opened before them and they passed through.

"Yeah," Bat said. "Back before the First World War if you asked a man what class he belonged to, nine times out of ten he'd stare at you and say, 'I'm a working stiff.' But I was just reading the other day that back as far as the middle nineteen-forties one of the big polling outfits went around asking what class a person considered himself to belong to, upper, middle or working class. It turned out that eighty-five percent of the American people considered themselves to belong to the middle class."

They went into Barry's inner office, Barry saying, "I'll bet it still applies, even though half the country is on Negative Income Tax, which is actually just relief."

"It applies all the way up the line," Bat growled. "Take the term scientist. It used to have a connotation of a man working in research. Now a guy who's no more of a chemist than to be doing up drugstore prescriptions calls himself a scientist."

Carol Ann looked up and said to Bat, "Morning, handsome."

He looked at her in mock criticism. "I won't make nasty cracks at you if you promise not to make 'em at me."

"Handsome is as handsome does," she told him.

Bat looked at his superior. "Holy smokes," he said. "The girl's beginning to develop a kindly streak."

Barry said to his secretary, even as he slumped into

9

his chair, "Get me Larry Brooks, the Demecrat over in Victory-deme."

When his equal number in one of the other three high-rise demes in the pseudo-city of Phoenecia faded in, his face questioning, Barry said, an air of self-deprecation in his voice, "Look, Larry, don't think I'm around the bend but you haven't been having any burglaries, have you?"

The Victory-deme manager looked at him wide-eyed. "Burglaries! In this day and age? You think my Security Division is senile?"

Barry sighed. "All right, all right. You haven't heard any rumors about them in Hilton-deme or Lincoln-deme, have you?"

"Of course not. Do you mean to tell me you've had a burglary in one of your apartments?"

"Six of them in the past week," Barry said glumly. "I'll bring it up at our next council meeting."

"Mayor Levy will want to know about it."

"I'll have more details by then—I hope," Barry muttered. "See you, Larry."

The last thing Larry Brooks said before fading out was, "Burglaries, yet."

Barry Ten Eyck got up and looked at his second in command. "All right, Bat, it's yours. See what you can do. Carol Ann, I'm on my way up to old man Vanderfeller to see what's spinning with him. Don't bother me unless you have to."

"To hear is to obey," Carol Ann said.

Barry Ten Eyck entered one of the staff express elevators and said, "Hundredth floor."

A robot voice said, "Yes, Mr. Ten Eyck."

He bent his knees automatically to accommodate to the acceleration. However, shortly he said, "Stop at the eighty-third floor."

"Yes, Mr. Ten Eyck."

At the eighty-third floor the compartment came to a halt and the door opened. He stepped out and looked

10

up and down the corridor. He brought out his pocket TV phone and said, "Mr. Stevens, of Security."

Steve's sour face faded in.

Barry said, "Well, did you get a report on this?"

"On what, Barry?"

"On the elevator stopping on this floor and my getting out?"

"What the hell, Barry! You're the Demecrat of this deme."

"All right. How many others, on the staff or otherwise, can come and go anywhere in the building, at any time?"

"Why, actually, only Bat Hardin and your Second Vice-Demecrat, Jim Cotswold. Even repairmen are checked out. If you're going to use computers and TV spy lenses in the way of automating security, you've got to go whole hog, Barry. A mouse couldn't move around this building without my knowing about it."

Barry Ten Eyck sighed. He said, "All right, Steve," and deactivated his phone and returned it to his pocket. He got back into the elevator compartment and ordered the hundredth floor again.

At the hundredth floor he switched over to Cyril Vanderfeller's private penthouse elevator, saying, "Penthouse, please."

"Yes, Mr. Ten Eyck," the elevator said.

At the entrada, the building manager was met by the Vanderfeller butler, who had obviously been forewarned as soon as the elevator had started up to this rarified ultra in swank housing. He was dressed in black, with anachronistic tails on his coat, and wore that expression of an undertaker so common to the butler trade.

He said, in seeming deep gloom, "Good morning, Mr. Ten Eyck."

Barry said, "Good morning, Jenson. I believe Mr. Vanderfeller is expecting me."

However, he had to go through more routine than that.

Jenson said, "Yes, sir, I shall take you to Mr. Abernathy."

"The appointment was with Mr. Vanderfeller."

But the other evidently didn't hear him. He led the way to the office of the private secretary of the scion of the Vanderfeller family.

One of the scions, Barry Ten Eyck thought, as he followed. One of many. He had read somewhere that there were some two hundred and thirty of the family now, each sporting fortunes probably of magnitudes inconceivable to such as Barry Ten Eyck. Information about the Vanderfellers seldom got into the mass media. They were hardly interested in publicity; to the contrary, it was said that such old rich as the Vanderfellers paid out millions of pseudo-dollars a year to keep their names from public appearance. Vaguely, Barry knew that the original Amis Vanderfeller had made his pile during the Civil War, a bit on the shady side, though not illegally. It seemed as though he had been sharp enough to scrape up a thousand dollars or so and to take an option on a warehouse full of condemned military rifles. When the conflict started, even condemned rifles were in demand and he unloaded them on a grateful Confederate government at an astronomical profit. This had been put immediately into cotton and shipped over to England before the Federal blockade was strong enough to prevent speedy blockade runners from getting through.

That had been half a dozen generations ago. The development of the railroads from coast to coast and the advents of World Wars One and Two hadn't hurt the family fortunes any. By the third generation, the brighter descendents had pooled their interests and gotten the family monies into trusts and foundations where they would be largely safe from governmental tax depreciations. And also safe from stupid speculations on the part of the less brilliant of the clan—of which it was rumored there was a sizable number.

Currently, the family was in a score of enterprises. Cyril Vanderfeller himself, who in Barry's opinion had delusions of grandeur about his abilities, devoted most of his efforts to international construction projects, largely hotels and apartment buildings such as Shyler-deme, and to mobile town sites. It was said that he had an apartment in every building owned by Vanderfeller and Moore Constructions, one of the top two hundred cosmocorps in existence.

The butler murmured into the identity screen on the door to secretary Abernathy's office and they waited for several minutes until it opened.

Barry Ten Eyck took a short, weary breath. Undoubtedly, Abernathy was in the process of impressing him by the need for him to wait. Very well; he was as impressed as he was going to get.

The door finally opened into an ultra-efficient looking office, though not overly large, considering the extent of the penthouse. David Abernathy looked up from a TV phone screen on his desk and came to his feet to shake hands.

"Morning, Ten Eyck," he said. His handshake was exactly right. So was David Abernathy exactly right. Exactly, down to the last fold in his Byronic revival cravat.

Barry shook and said, "Good morning, Abernathy." Was there the faintest of frowns present, in view of the fact that he hadn't mistered the flunky? The hell with it.

Barry said, "Miss Cusack tells me that Mr. Vanderfeller wanted me to drop by."

"Yes, that is correct," the other said stiffly, reseating himself. "He told me to summon you."

Summon him, yet. Barry Ten Eyck was not directly under the authority of Cyril Vanderfeller, although Vanderfeller and Moore Construction owned the Shyler-deme complex. However, nobody with good sense and desire for advancement earned the enmity of a Vanderfeller.

"Let's go," Barry said. Damn it, was this going to take all day? He had plenty to do.

Abernathy ignored that and turned to a desk phone

screen into which he spoke softly. Finally, he stood. "Mr. Vanderfeller is in his escape-sanctum," he said loftily, and then led the way.

Barry had been through this before on several occasions, but the rigmarole didn't improve with age.

They finally stood before a huge double door. There was no identity screen evident upon it, but undoubtedly a micro-spy lens was somewhere located in the hand engraved woodwork. The door looked as though it had once graced the home of some medieval Florentine but to Barry Ten Eyck's jaundiced eye it was as out of place in this ultra-modern decor as a walrus in a goldfish bowl.

The door smoothed open and they stepped through into what would seem a quarter acre of Victorian-era library. From past experience, Barry knew the books were real, largely first editions or other rarities, and largely not only unread but uncut.

Cyril Vanderfeller, somewhere in his late fifties, stood by one monstrous window looking out over the extent of Phoenecia, the three other demes rearing to approximately the same hundred and ten floors boasted by Schyler-deme. The term deme had been taken from the old Greek, the unit which made up the city of Athens as reconstituted by Solon. They were set in almost an exact square, roughly a square mile of wooded and grassed areas about each and with another approximate square mile of Common land and buildings in the middle. There was an excellent view of the golf course from here, Barry knew.

Cyril Vanderfeller turned. He affected a "hail fellow well met" air, dressed with great informality and kept his face and form appearing, at least, in the best of health.

"Barry!" he said in warmth. "Long time, no see, my good fellow." He advanced with his hand out.

Barry shook and said, "Good morning, Mr. Vanderfeller."

The older man took his place behind an ornate wooden desk, barren of course of any phone screens in

14

view of the fact that this was an escape-sanctum. He had gestured to a nearby straight chair although the room was amply provided with comfort chairs. The secretary remained standing and kept his trap shut in the presence.

Vanderfeller put the tips of his fingers together, leaned his elbows on the desk, very businesslike. "My time, of course, is limited, Barry, so I'll come immediately to the point."

"Yes, sir." Barry's own time, evidently, was meaningless compared to that of the tycoon. Well, maybe the other was right. He probably could have bought or sold all the pseudo-city of Phoenecia out of petty cash.

"My boy, I'm on an informal tour of our demes in my capacity as a member of the board. Sort of a quick check-up, you understand. I'll be here only a day or two. However, Abernathy and I have been checking out your administration of Shyler-deme. I was somewhat surprised to note that income from all sources has dropped below the half million a week level."

Barry Ten Eyck nodded. "Yes, sir. For the first time last week."

"Why?"

"Occupancy has fallen off, sir. At present four thousand and fifty-two apartments, ranging from mini-apartments to duplexes with as many as twenty rooms, are occupied, but that is barely enough to make our breakeven point through our maintenance fees and our sales and services to them."

Vanderfeller looked at him severely. "My dear boy, when this deme was opened, approximately eight and a half years ago, every apartment was speedily taken. In fact, some of the residents had been waiting for six months or more to move in. Do you mean to tell me that nearly a fifth of them have tired of their homes— their own *homes*—and simply moved out?"

Barry said unhappily, "It's not a unique phenomenon, Mr. Vanderfeller, as you must know. Most of the empty apartments are owned by people on NIT, and there's a high level of ne'r-do-wells and weirds among those whose only source of income is Negative Income Tax."

Vanderfeller maintained his severe expression.

Barry recrossed his long legs. "Sir, as you know, when the Asian War ended, several things came to a head. There was a danger of economic collapse, since, if we admitted it or not, the economy since the Hitler War had largely been based on war or the threat of war. By that time we were spending more than a hundred billion a year directly or indirectly on the military. You couldn't simply pull that big a prop out from under without substituting another one. At the same time automation, the computer economy, hit with a vengeance. All of a sudden there was precious little need for employees in the primary labor fields."

"Yes, yes," Vanderfeller said impatiently.

Barry went on doggedly. "That's where Negative Income Tax came in. Oh, they had other names for it, such as Guaranteed Annual Wage or even Incentive Income Supplement, but what it actually amounted to was a dole and it wasn't all philanthropic. It kept consumer buying up and the economy needed that badly. But NIT wasn't enough to keep the economy booming. Something was needed to take the place of war industries. Mass construction was the answer and it fit in with other problems, such as the falling apart of the cities, air and water pollution, slums and ghettos and so forth. So the government embarked on the biggest home construction and highway development—most of it underground—in history. Every person was guaranteed a residence, be it a house, an apartment, or a mobile home. Every citizen now has a right, once in his life, to obtain a home. The government ponies up the entire amount and then, over a period of thirty years, deducts it from the citizen's credit balance automatically through the National Bank computers."

"Of course, of course," the older man said testily. "A corporation such as Vanderfeller and Moore is granted an appropriate sum to build a deme such as Shylerdeme, some five thousand apartments of varying size. The price will range anywhere from one to two hundred million. The average apartment sells for forty thousand, thus paying for the building, eventually. The complex remains in the hands of the corporation and the profit is made by selling commodities and services to the tenants who are what amounts to a captive pool of customers. They buy almost all of their food, their clothing and their other necessities through the ultra-markets in the underground areas of the deme. They rent their electro-steamers from our car pool, they pay for their entertainments such as theatres, sport spectacles, night-clubs, auto-bars, swimming pools. They have literally scores of ways provided for spending their income, be it government NIT, or earned salaries, or dividend income. But what has all this got to do with the drop off in tenancy, my boy?"

Barry said, "Sir, they simply don't *care* enough about their apartments to give a damn, if the urge hits them to move. You seldom appreciate something you haven't put anything of yourself into. Theoretically these people own their apartments and are paying for them, but in actuality they never *see* the money and most of them haven't worked for it. It's simply deducted from their usual monthly checks.

"All right. The population of the country now is roughly three hundred million. Most of them live in pseudo-cities such as Phoenecia and in demes, the units of the pseudo-cities. A deme such as we're in now will hold twenty thousand people. They prefer demes because of all the facilities available. Those who don't like this anthill type of life often get mobile homes—they used to call them trailers—and join one of the mobile towns. Comparatively few, these days, like individual homes but some do, and build off by themselves or in small communities.

"But the thing is, these people get restless and kind of go through fads of where to live. When Phoenecia was built the fad was for living in the mountains. There was a lot of talk about the benefits of the altitude, the scenery, the clear air and so forth. There was no trouble at all in filling the apartments. But in a couple of years, living on the sea became all the rage and, currently, living out in the desert areas such as Arizona and Utah. And Mexico and Central America are beginning to draw people."

Vanderfeller said in indignation, "But to simply *abandon* their homes?"

And be lost as customers to Vanderfeller and Moore? Barry added silently.

Aloud, he said, "They don't always abandon them. Last week we lost two hundred and three resident families, or singles, but gained eighty-three. Sometimes they rent their places. Sometimes they sell their equities, usually precious little, to each other. If somebody here in the mountains can locate another family, say on the seashore, who wants to swap apartments, they make a deal. Of course, both continue to have the same sum deducted from their credit balance. The government continues to collect whether they leave or not."

"But from what you say," the tycoon said aggressively, "some simply leave without finding a new tenant."

"That's right. They go off and possibly buy a new apartment somewhere else, this time in the wife's name. If they move again, they can get still another in the name of one of the kids, if they have children over eighteen."

"What can you do about it, Ten Eyck?" the older man snapped. "You're the Demecrat of Shyler-deme. It's up to you to prevent the building's income from simply melting away."

"I'll do what I can, sir. Obviously, we're working on it. One thing we might do—other Demecrats have—is lower the maintenance charge. That'd make remaining here more desirable."

Vanderfeller glared at him. "Lower the maintenance rate!"

"Yes, sir. As you know, theoretically the tenants own their own apartments; but they have to pay us a

18

monthly maintenance fee. It averages about a hundred dollars."

The older man was indignant. "Our income is low enough, young man. We take in some four hundred thousand dollars a month toward expenses from this source. Every bit you cut is a drain on profits."

"Yes, sir, but it's one way of keeping tenants. Other demes are doing it, which is one of the reasons our people move to them. For a family on NIT to pay only fifty a month maintenance, instead of a hundred, means another fifty pseudo-dollars in their credit balance."

"What else causes them to move?" Vanderfeller demanded.

"They like new buildings, with new gadgets, new improvements, or supposed improvements. I scanned some ads the other day. New demes have Tri-Di screens that occupy one whole wall of the apartment. The figures are projected life size. That's a big pull. Another new development is an auto-bar that has a list of two hundred drinks available. You can do a lot of fancy guzzling with a device like that in your apartment. The ones we supply as standard equipment can be rigged only for ten different drinks of your choice. One thing we might do is upgrade our bar services."

"Bring it up with Central Management," Vanderfeller muttered. "But it sounds expensive."

Barry shrugged. "Any renovations of that magnitude usually are. All five thousand of our apartments would be involved."

Vanderfeller stood, by way of preliminaries to dismissal, and made an effort to regain his jovial air of good fellowship.

He said, "Well, Barry, my boy, it's your problem. But we of the board of directors will be expecting upbeat reports from Phoenecia in the near future."

Barry stood, too, and repressed a sigh. "We'll do what we can, sir," he said. From the side of his eyes he could see Abernathy, out of view of his superior, make a face of disbelief.

The bastard.

19

He took the penthouse elevator down to the hundredth floor and there switched to the general elevator banks of this tower. He dropped down to the fifth basement level and made his way in the direction of the kitchen offices of the Restaurant Division.

Doors opened before him as he progressed. He spoke a word here, a word there to the technicians he encountered. Barry Ten Eyck made a point not only of knowing every member of his deme's staff but knowing them intimately enough to be up on problems, family matters, health and welfare. It paid off.

He said, in passing, "Hi, Chuck, how's Doris?"

"She's better. If she'd just lay off that candy."

He called to another, "How was the vacation, Slim?"

"Tiring. I'm glad to be back."

The door of his Head Chef's private office smoothed open before him, and he entered.

Pierre Daunou was standing looking at a large control screen. He grumbled, "Triple deck-aire sandwiches," before turning to see who his visitor might be.

Barry Ten Eyck said, "Hi, Pete."

Pierre Daunou would never fail for employment. Were there ever a surplus of first rate chefs, he could always get a job in Tri-Di shows as a stereotype chef. He was roly-poly, apple cheeked, small of mouth and with a tiny French mustache of yesteryear. Ludicrously, in this ultra-modern atmosphere, he even wore a white apron and a tall chef's white hat.

"*Bon soir*, Barry," he said. And then, meaninglessly, he snorted, "Triple deck-aire sandwiches." He made a Gallic gesture of disgust.

Barry sank into a chair across from his head of the deme's Restaurant Division. He said. "What about triple decker sandwiches?"

The chef plopped himself down into his own swivel chair behind his littered, phone screen desk. He flicked up a hand. "Five years I spend attending the *Cordon Bleu* in Paris. Ten years I spend here and there as an apprentice and then as an assistant chef. Fifteen years of study. And now what do I do?"

"You're the best chef in Phoenecia," Barry said soothingly.

"I am the best chef for five hundred kilometers around!" the other said in quick contradiction. "And what do I do? I design triple deck-aire sandwiches for idiots without palates!" He flicked his plump hand in the direction of the control screen he had been consulting when his superior had entered.

"Hamburgers, hot dogs, fried steak, fried chicken, triple deck-aire sandwiches, french fried potatoes, ice cream. Do you realize, Monsieur Ten Eyck, that those seven items compose half of all orders filled by this department?"

Barry chuckled. "I'm surprised it isn't even higher."

The Head Chef slapped a palm down on the desk. "For the sake of those who do not want to eat in their own apartments and have their food sent up directly to the auto-tables in their dining coves, we have here in Shyler-deme four auto-cafeterias and six other restaurants. Monsieur Ten Eyck, we even have an alleged French restaurant, designed by I, myself. At great trouble I reproduced the interior of *Le Chalut,* a superlative little two-star restaurant in which I was once employed in Provence. Outdoing even myself, I created masterpieces of cuisine such as *Rognon de veau flambé* and *Lamproie bordelaise.* And what do they order when they are graced to enter my French restaurant?"

Barry was looking at him apologetically. He cleared his throat.

"Hamburgers! French fries! Triple deck-aire sandwiches!"

Barry said soothingly, "Some of us appreciate your efforts, Pete."

The chef gave his flick of a hand gesture of disgust. "A handful!"

Barry said, "Ah, Pete, Miss Cusack tells me you're a bit dissatisfied again."

"A big dissatisfied!" the other snorted. "Ha! I tell you Monsieur Ten Eyck, this time I am through. What is the use of my years at the *Cordon Bleu,* the greatest

21

school of *haute cuisine* the world has ever seen, if I wind up here in this shining automated kitchen equipment mass producing triple deck-aire sandwiches for clods? No. I have made savings. I shall return to Common Europe and open a tiny *boîte* in Italy, Switzerland, possibly France itself and I shall be appreciated, Monsieur Ten Eyck. Gourmets will come from a thousand kilometers about to dine well on the products of the kitchen of Pierre Daunou! Never again will I even think of the words triple deck-aire sandwich!"

Barry Ten Eyck sighed. "I wish you'd think it over, Pete. As you know, I consider you the best man on my staff. The Restaurant Division goes like clockwork. I'd hate to see you leave."

The other puffed out his cheeks, only slightly mollified. "You have my notice Monsieur Ten Eyck. In two weeks, Pierre Daunou will leave in search of employment where his arts are appreciated."

Barry stood. "Well, as I said, I'll hate to see you go. I hope you'll change your mind." He turned to leave, then turned back. "Oh, Pete. Do you know anything about Moroccan cooking?"

"Moroccan cooking? I know everything about Moroccan cooking. I once worked at the *1001 Nights* restaurant in Tangier. But there is very little to know. The number of dishes is limited, though at the best some are superlative. Ha! *Treed.* One takes three plump pigeons, eh? One takes salt, two teaspoons. One takes saffron, a pinch, ginger a teaspoon, pepper, the same. One takes a chopped tablespoon of chervil, the same of parsley. One takes three pieces of cinnamon bark and three large onions, in large pieces. One takes five hundred grammes of olive oil and 800 grammes of flour."

Barry had raised a hand to head the other off, but it was too late.

"One puts into the pot the pigeons, the salt, saffron, ginger, pepper, chervil, parsley, cinnamon, onions and the olive oil and makes it to boil. Of the flour one makes very thin pastry sheets about eight inches across.

22

Thin, thin, as thin as strudle pastry. You know strudle pastry? Ha! One puts about thirty of these sheets of pastry on a plate, one over the other, making a circle about eighteen inches across. When the pigeons are cooked, one removes the cinnamon and puts them with the onion onto the pastry. All is covered with ten or twelve more sheets of pastry. Over this one pours a very little liquid from the cooking pot. And thus it is ready to serve."

"Sounds wonderful," Barry said.

"Wonderful? Ha! *Treed* is the oldest of all Arabian dishes, *mon ami*. It is said that when the Prophet Mohammed was asked what he liked best in the world, he answered that he loved his wife above everything but after her he liked *treed*. But why do you ask of Moroccan cuisine?"

Barry shrugged. "The members of the Gourmet Club want a Moroccan restaurant. I understand that a couple of them just got back from a vacation to Marrakech, or somewhere in Morocco, and are evidently all keyed up about a Moroccan restaurant in Shyler-deme."

"Ha! The Gourmet Club," the Head Chef snorted. "About thirty-five members. If there were thirty-five hundred perhaps I would remain, for their sakes."

Back in his own office, Barry Ten Eyck slumped down into his chair and eyed the busy Carol Ann Cusack speculatively.

He said finally, "Miss Cusack, what do you say we retire from stooging for the cosmocorps of Vanderfeller and Moore, buy ourselves a small mobile home, start collecting NIT and take off for Costa Rica? We'll get out from under before they fire us for incompetence."

She didn't look up. "No, thank you, Mr. Ten Eyck," she said.

"Well, why not? Half of the rest of the country doesn't work. Why should we?"

"Because living on Negative Income Tax is somewhat short of the good life."

"Oh, I don't know. If you live in a swanky apartment in a deme, NIT doesn't go very far. But I've been hearing about Costa Rica. You can do very neatly there on two sets of Negative Income Tax. What do you say we give it a try?"

"I don't think my husband, Sid, would approve, Mr. Ten Eyck."

"Oh, your husband, your husband; every time I propose to you, you bring in your husband."

"Was it a proposal this time? It sounded more like a proposition. Did you see Mr. Vanderfeller?"

"Can't you tell? Why'd you think I wanted to run off to Costa Rica?"

"I thought it was my fair young body. Did you see Mr. Daunou?"

He nodded wearily.

"What's wrong with our temperamental chef this time?"

"He hates to see clods eating triple deck-aire sandwiches. He wants to cook *treed* instead.

"*Cook* treed? I thought that was something you did to a coon."

"Please, Miss Cusack, leave us not be facetious. *Treed* was the Prophet's favorite dish—next to his wife."

"It's *Mrs.* Cusack, I keep telling you."

"I like to keep up the illusion I've got a young, beautiful, voluptuous girl as a secretary, rather than an old, beaten-up, married broad."

Carol Ann sighed and said, "While you were out, Mr. Wonder, down in Transportation, called."

"What'd Dick want?"

"Another seventy-five seater electro-steamer."

"Oh, wizard, with our budget melting away by the minute. Why?"

"He thinks it would make a profit. We've got enough residents now working over at the Dodge-Myers Complex on all four shifts to make it worth while running a bus service."

"Oh? We have?" Barry thought about it. "How far is the Dodge-Myers set-up, Miss Cusack?"

"A hundred and seventy-five kilometers. According to Mr. Wonder, the Shyler-deme employees there would save fifteen or twenty minutes time a day, if they had their own bus running back and forth for each shift."

"Well, it's worth looking into. Have you ever seen the Dodge-Myers Complex, Miss Cusack?"

"I applied for a job there, just before taking this one. It's tucked away, up in the hills, and most of the buildings are underground. One of the most modern industrial complexes in this vicinity. No smoke, no industrial mess, the nearest homes at least five miles away. All in the newest tradition."

"So it's to be assumed that our people will continue to work there. I'll take it up with Dick Wonder later. Has Bat come up with anything on the burglaries?"

"Not that I know of, Mr. Ten Eyck. I haven't seen Mr. Hardin since he was in here with you earlier." She turned to answer one of her phone screens. "Here's Mr. Hardin now."

Barry activated one of his own screens. "Hi, Bat. What spins?"

Bat Hardin's face was registering shock. "Barry," he said, "listen. The burglar's been at it again."

"This soon! And in broad daylight? Same as before?"

Bat Hardin said strangely, "Not exactly. This time he didn't do so well in selecting an empty apartment. He was jumped by the resident, evidently, while prowling the place. It was Lawrence McCaw's mini-apartment on the fiftieth floor."

"Good grief, what happened?"

"The burglar killed him."

Barry Ten Eyck winced. "Oh, Lord," he said. He shook his head and began to come to his feet, "What tower?"

"Tower-Two," Bat said. "You coming up, Barry?"

"I'll be right there."

Half way to the door he called back to Carol Ann,

"Get Mayor Levy and the Security Chief over at Administration. Tell them ... well, tell them what happened. You know as much about it as I do."

He hurried out into the corridor and to the elevator banks. The fiftieth floor, in Tower-Two. Devoted entirely to mini-apartments. You would think a prowler would be more ambitious. Damn few who lived in mini-apartments had anything worth stealing. But that was the big mystery, wasn't it? This burglar didn't seem to steal anything worth stealing. Barry wondered if the man was some sort of kleptomaniac.

Two of Stevens' human relations officers were posted outside Apartment 508. Barry nodded to them wordlessly and hustled on through.

The tiny apartment was jam-packed with Bat Hardin, Stevens, Doctor Bert McCoy, of the Shyler-deme hospital, one more of Stevens' men and, sprawled on the floor and now covered with a bedsheet, what was obviously the remains of the late occupant of the apartment.

Barry stared down at the corpse. He said, "He's
"Very. Several knife wounds in the abdomen and up into the heart region. You wish to see him?"
dead, Doc?"

"Good grief, no." Barry looked around at them. "Did any of you know him? What did you say his name was, Bat?"

"Lawrence McCaw. No, I didn't know him. With anywhere from fifteen to twenty thousand people in Shyler-deme at any given time, you never get to know more than a fraction."

The doctor, an efficient, straight-standing type, shook his head, as did the Security officer.

Stevens, who was staring down at the sheet covered figure glumly, said, "I knew him slightly. He was more or less a recluse. Almost an escapist. You seldom saw him in the public rooms."

"Who found him?"

Stevens stirred. "I did. Pure luck, actually. Almost intuitive, I guess you'd say. I had a strange feeling that our burglar friend was on the prowl again and I was checking the spy lenses. Just on an off chance, I activated several of the apartment lenses on this floor."

Barry Ten Eyck's eyebrows went up.

"I know, I know," Stevens said sourly. "It's supposedly illegal for anyone save proper government authority to invade the privacy of a home. But you know what the situation was. At any rate, I gave a quick check-out on several apartments. The fourth one I tried, I saw McCaw, there, sprawled on the floor. I made a beeline up here. His door was partially open. And there he was."

Barry looked at the Security officer. "Go on out and tell those two guards not to let anyone in here and above all not to tell anyone what's happened."

"Yes, sir." The man left.

Bat Hardin said, "You notify Levy and Ben Snider?"

"I had Carol Ann do it. I imagine they'll be over shortly." Barry rubbed his hand down over his face and muttered, "We've got to keep this bottled up long enough to find whoever did it. We've got to, or residents will be moving out of this building like rats. Burglaries and murders!"

One of the guards stuck his head in the door. "Here comes Mayor Levy and Chief Snider."

The doctor had been putting equipment back into his bag. He said, "One thing before I leave. If I have the story correctly, supposedly the apartment was being burglarized when the occupant here, McCaw, interrupted the thief. However, if so, the wounds were strangely located. By them and the position of the corpse, I would have said the opposite situation applied."

Barry scowled at him.

The doctor said, almost defensively, "It would appear, rather, that the victim was the one surprised. Perhaps I am wrong."

Barry looked at Stevens. "Steve, how do you know this was one of the burglar's jobs?"

"Same pattern," Stevens growled. "Two other apartments on the floor have been prowled. And look at this place. It's been ransacked."

Mayor Emmanuel Levy came bustling in, closely followed by his Chief of Security of Phoenecia, Ben Snider. Both were heavy-set though energetic men.

"What in the world is going on here? A killing! We haven't had a killing in six months and that was more of an accident than . . ." Levy began.

His eyes fell on the covered body and he sucked in air.

Later, when they had talked it out from every angle, and the whole thing had been turned over to Security routine, Barry Ten Eyck had the mayor for lunch in *Le Chalut,* Shyler-deme's French restaurant. It was, as Head Chef Daunou had described it, a perfect replica of a Provence restaurant, complete to placards on the walls advertising *Pernod,* various cheeses of Avignon, Carcassonne and Les Baux, the wines of *Côtes de Provence.*

Levy, whose short, wide figure indicated he was far from immune to good food, looked about appreciatively and said, "I don't believe I've been in here before, Barry."

Barry Ten Eyck said, "The chef just finished it a couple of months ago. It was his pride and joy."

"Was?"

Barry said, "He's leaving me. Fed up with automated cooking."

"How long have you had him?"

"Oh, he's been here a couple of years. Almost as long as I have."

"Let him go, my boy."

Barry looked at him. "He's the best chef in Phoenecia."

The mayor nodded. "And if he's been here two years, he's already set up the plant so that he's redundant. I assume you have a restaurant staff of some twenty persons. I'll wager that at least half of them could take over your Head Chef's job and would, besides, take only half the pay he receives. You know that much about deme management, Barry. Once a kitchen is set up there's precious little to change."

"That was Pete's complaint," Barry said. "He isn't able to practice his trade—his art, as he sees it. The kitchen is programmed for the dishes our residents want and he can't introduce anything ... Say, that reminds me. Pardon me for a moment."

He brought his pocket phone out, activated it and said, "Chef Daunou, please."

When Pierre Daunou's petulant face faded in, Barry said, "Pete, I'm here with Mayor Levy in *Le Chalut* for lunch. What was that dish you were telling me about? The special one you created."

It was all but pathetic to see the beam come over the roly-poly man's face. "Perhaps the *Rognon de veau flambé?*"

"Yeah, thanks, Pete, that was it. Is it on the menu, today?"

"Monsieur Ten Eyck, it is always on the menu, and always perfect. That is one thing for which admittedly one must give the automated kitchen credit. Once a perfect dish is created, it never fails to produce it, over and over again, in perfection. Ah, Monsieur Ten Eyck . . ."

"Yes?"

"With my compliments, will the mayor and you have a bottle of *Châteauneuf-du-Pape* to accompany the veal?"

"With greatest pleasure, Pete."

Still beaming, the chef's face faded.

"Poor bastard," Barry muttered.

The mayor took up where he had left off. "Larry Brooks, over at the Victory-deme, had the same difficulty. That is, overly tempermental personnel in the Restaurant Division. The Head Chef was a Hungarian, his second a Bavarian. While they were setting up the operation they didn't do so badly, kept themselves busy, but once the basic programming was accomplished it was one headache after another. Continual

29

bickering. One wanted to cook everything with paprika, the other sauerkraut, or some such. Larry eventually let them both go just this week. No trouble at all. Everything as smooth as butter. No, I tell you, Ten Eyck, let this chef of yours go. You'll never miss him."

Shortly, the center of the table sank, to return with their dishes. The bottle of wine was there, and a single rose in a vase. Barry suspected that Pierre had given his personal attention to their order, which was on the far-out side in this day of automation; one no longer expected personal attention in a restaurant.

"I say," Levy said, after exactly one forkful of the veal.

"Ummm." Barry poured wine. "Are you sure I ought to let this chef go?"

Emmanuel Levy laughed. "No, not sure at all."

They ate in silence for a moment.

Finally, Phoenecia's mayor looked up, slightly quizzical. "I hear from Abernathy, Cyril Vanderfeller's man, that you've been having an inordinate number of vacancies."

"Yeah," Barry said. "And these burglaries and the killing aren't going to help any. Everything seems to be happening to me. Everything. If I woke up tomorrow pregnant, I wouldn't be overly surprised."

Levy chuckled dutifully. He said, "It was that silly Gallagher's fault."

"Gallagher? The Democrat who preceded me?"

"Ummm. Let go for incompetence. When Shyler-deme opened he wanted to fill up the apartments overnight, evidently as an indication of what a fireball he was. He gave Shyler-deme no theme. And these days, if you want to keep your people, you need a theme."

"Theme?" Barry said. Mayor Levy was, of course, a former Democrat himself. You didn't become the mayor of a pseudo-city without long years of managing a deme yourself. And there were a lot of things you learned on the job that they never taught you in the colleges devoted to deme and pseudo-city management.

"Yes, of course. You decide, perhaps, to specialize

30

on elderly, retired folk. You set up your public rooms, your parks, even your restaurants and bars, to cater to their needs. Shuffleboard, rather than tennis courts, chess tournaments, extensive card rooms, bingo rooms. Your hospital is staffed with specialists in the diseases of the older elements. You screen families with noisy children, and refuse to sell them apartments. Or, perhaps, your theme is young marrieds *with* children. You go in big for nurseries and playgrounds, that sort of thing. Or, particularly if your deme has a goodly percentage of mini-apartments, you go in for young singles, perhaps of the swinger variety, as we used to call them when I was a boy. Lots of dances, lots of sports, plenty of nightclubs, entertainment, entertainment, entertainment."

"I'm afraid it's a little too late for me to switch to one of these themes," Barry said unhappily.

"Yes. That's where Gallagher fell short. If you're going to have a theme for populating your deme, you must decide upon it before selling the apartments. He let in anyone and everyone. Old, young, singles, couples, even, so I understand, a sizable number of both escapists and weirds."

"How right can you get?" Barry growled. "I spend half my time fielding complaints about the services and public rooms. The young married people want one thing, the oldsters another, the singles still others. Today, one group sent around a petition demanding one of the public rooms be converted into a Moroccan restaurant. A Moroccan restaurant, yet. Shyler-deme needs a Moroccan restaurant like it needs a collective hole in the head."

He finished the wine and looked at the glass in approval. "I wonder where old Pete got this?"

Levy said, "You can still get decent wine if you're willing to pay for it. Here in the United States they've abolished the use of grapes and cereals for beverages but the Common Europe people haven't. They even still make beer over there out of grain."

"I didn't know that," Barry said. "How can they afford it?"

The mayor said dryly, "I suppose they figure that man doth not live by bread alone. You could no more get a Frenchman to give up his wine than you could a German his beer."

"Well, that's all very good. But we make our beverages synthetically and . . ."

"And they taste like it," Levy grumbled finishing his own last sip of wine appreciatively.

Barry's pocket phone buzzed and he brought it forth. He had it set for Priority Two, cutting off all calls except those of a very few persons. It must be something important. Bat Hardin's face faded in, characteristically worried, his lower lip taking a beating from his teeth.

"What spins?" Barry said.

"Listen, could you come on down to your office?"

"I'm having lunch with the mayor," Barry protested.

Bat said urgently, "I think I've got something, Barry. About you know what."

"Oh, oh." Barry took up his napkin and tossed it to the table. He said to Bat, "Coming," and deactivated the phone. He looked at Levy. "Must be some kind of a break in the murder."

"You go right ahead, my boy. I'm going to try some of this excellent cheese your chef was kind enough to send up. The man seems quite a gem."

Bat Hardin was seated in Barry's inner office. As Barry entered he was saying to Carol Ann Cusack, "Where's Jim Cotswold?"

Carol Ann said, "Why, Mr. Cotswold is on vacation."

Barry said, "What's up, Bat?"

"Just a minute. I want to check up on something." Bat looked at the secretary. "Yes, but where? I assume he left you his itinerary."

"Why, he's in Mozambique. You know Mr. Cotswold and that Poloroid-Leica of his. He wanted to get shots of animal life in nature."

"Get him for me, will you Carol Ann?"

Looking somewhat mystified, she dialed. Bat Hardin sat down in the chair behind Barry Ten Eyck's steel desk.

"Put it on this screen, please," he said.

Barry said, "What's going on? Why do you want to bother Jim?"

Jim Cotswold's angular face and upper body faded in. He was wearing a bush jacket with half a dozen pockets. Around his neck was slung a recent-design camera with a monstrously long snouted lens. He was obviously surprised. And obviously talking into his pocket phone.

"Hey," he said. "What's the big idea? I was just about to get a shot of a real lion. I mean a *real* one, right out here parading around in the bush."

Bat said, "Sorry. It's important, Jim. Let's take a look at it."

"At what?"

"The lion."

Mystified, the Second Vice-Democrat of Shyler-deme redirected his pocket TV phone screen. In the faint distance, Bat and Barry, who was now looking over Bat's shoulder, could see an African bush scene and, yes, slinking through the background was a male lion.

Jim's voice said, "Satisfied? Now, damn it, you let him get away before I could get my shots."

Bat said, "How far are you from the nearest town with a jetport, Jim?"

"A good three days by truck, dammit. What the devil do you clowns want?"

"Nothing more," Bat told him. "Sorry to bother you. Good hunting." He flicked off the set and turned back to Barry.

Barry said, "What in the devil's up?"

"He's in Mozambique, all right. And way the hell and gone out in the boondocks." Bat Hardin fished into a pocket and came forth with what at first seemed a chunk of melted copper. He handed it over to his superior.

Barry scowled down at it. Finally, he made out some lettering. "Why, it's a coin. A copper coin." He looked up at the other who was again gnawing away at his lip and scowling. "So what? Where'd you get it?"

"Harrison, down in Disposal found it, by accident, in one of the incinerators."

"Well, what of it?"

"So I checked it out with that resident who had the coin collection stolen."

Barry looked at him. Bat nodded.

Barry demanded, "You mean this is one of the stolen coins and it was found in an incinerator?"

Bat nodded again. He said, "Come on, Barry. Let's go over and see Stevens."

They entered the office of Shyler-deme's Security Chief, and Stevens looked up from his desk. Bat tossed the half melted copper coin before him and reversed a chair and sat straddled on it, his arms on the back. Barry remained standing for the present.

Stevens took up the coin and scowled at it. "What's this?"

"Part of the coin collection that was stolen yesterday," Bat said.

"Oh? I'll be darned. Where'd you get it, Hardin?"

"Pure luck. Harrison, down on the incinerators, fished it out."

Stevens grunted sourly. "Well, I don't see what good it does us. Our killer evidently ditched his loot to avoid any evidence."

Bat shook his head. "I've got a different theory."

Both Barry and Stevens were staring at him. Bat said, "He never stole the stuff."

Barry sputtered, "Are you completely around the bend?"

Bat Hardin shook his head doggedly. "The whole thing's been crazy and it was meant to look crazy. All this supposed stealing of things not worth stealing. As though some nut were at work. It's been one long misdirection and a very cute idea. Too damn cute. But our supposed burglar has been going into apartments, messing them up a bit to make them look as though they were completely ransacked, and then he'd toss a few items into the disposal chute and leave. He wouldn't be carrying a thing, in case somebody came up on him unexpectedly. He was always clean of any loot."

Stevens was scowling disbelief. "But why, for Christ's sake?"

Bat bit his lower lip nervously. "That's what I had trouble figuring out. But there's only one answer, so far as I can see. Like I said, it was misdirection. He wanted to kill poor Lawrence McCaw for some reason I don't know as yet. He must have figured out that if he just did the job, straight off, an investigation would follow. A thorough investigation. And such an investigation would reveal the fact that he had motive for killing McCaw. However, if he gobbledygooked up the whole thing and made it look like the killing was unpremeditated, that a sneak thief had been caught robbing the McCaw apartment and had killed its occupant, then nobody would look in his direction."

"Oh, Bat, this is pretty farfetched," Barry protested.

Bat looked at him. "It's the only thing that makes sense, Barry."

Barry said, "Look, you've explained absolutely nothing about how he got into the building. How he got from one floor to another without detection. How he knew the apartments he entered were empty. How he got into them. Good grief, Bat."

Bat was eyeing him levelly. "Why do you think I phoned Jim Cotswold?"

Barry blinked at him.

Bat said patiently, "Supposedly, you and I and Jim are the only three persons who can make their way around Shyler-deme, any place at all, without having to check it out with Security. Well, that narrows it down to just you and me. Jim's in the African bush."

Barry stared at him. "What the hell do you mean?"

Bat turned his eyes to Stevens, who had been looking sourly at him. Bat said, "The thing is, we *aren't* the

35

only three deme officials that can go anywhere at any time. There's one more. Our Chief of Security. In fact, he can do it much better than we can. He can also check apartments through his spy lenses to see if they are empty, before he pretends to burglarize one. He also has the means to open any door to any apartment."

"You're crazy as a coot!" Stevens blurted.

"He also admitted, when we were up in McCaw's room, that he knew the man slightly. That was a smart bit of business. If he had denied knowing him at all and somebody had stumbled on the fact that he did, the fat would have been in the fire."

Bat Hardin shook his heavy head. "No, Barry. We'll have to dig it out, but we'll eventually find that our boy, here, had a very good reason to kill Lawrence McCaw. And he had a better opportunity than anyone else in this deme. He's our man."

Barry began to say, in bewilderment, "I can't . . ."

But Stevens, his lips thinned back, had scooped a Gyro-jet pistol from a desk drawer. He snapped, "I'm getting out of here and I don't want anybody to try and stop me." He was on his feet.

"Nobody'll try to stop you," Bat said reasonably.

Stevens backed around to the door, keeping the gun at the ready. He got to the door, through it, slammed it behind him.

Bat shook his head and went over to the desk and to the phone screen. He activated it and said, "Carol Ann? Get me Chief Ben Snider, over at Administration, will you?"

Barry, still flabbergasted, couldn't see his secretary from where he stood, but he could hear her voice. "Coming up, Mr. Hardin, and if Mr. Ten Ecyk is there will you remind him we're due in the Auditorium in ten minutes for the monthly Deme-Assembly."

On the way over to the deme Auditorium, Carol Ann chattered at him excitedly.

Barry said, "It's not important. He can't get very far.

36

A man on the lam doesn't make much sense these days. He can't use the ultra-highways without using his TV phone-Credit Card to rent an electro-steamer. If he does use it, they have him. He can't buy anything without it, including food or shelter. He can't even have it on his person or the police will get a fix on him and track him down, no matter where he is. And you simply can't live in the world as it is without a credit card, Miss Cusack."

"Golly," she said, the expression incongruous from her lips.

Barry Ten Eyck said, as they approached the door of the Auditorium, "I'd like to cut this as short as possible today."

She looked at her notes. "There doesn't seem to be much besides this petition for the Moroccan restaurant. Well, except some of the older residents want to begin heating the swimming pools already this year. And we have a letter here from the occupant of Apartment 84, eightieth floor, Tower-Two, suggesting that at least one elevator be designed to have less acceleration."

He looked at her from the side of his eyes. "Why? We've had beefs before from those upper-floor people wanting *more* speed, not less."

"He's elderly and afraid of falling and claims that there are enough others in his age group to support the request."

"He might have something, at that. It's all we need, some of the oldsters breaking their legs in our high speed elevators."

The Auditorium doors were open. Barry and Carol Ann made their way down to the rostrum. As usual, there were about a thousand persons present. Ten to fifteen thousand potential voters in Shyler-deme, and only this percentage bothered to turn up to debate and vote upon their own affairs.

Barry Ten Eyck took his place, Carol Ann to one side, and banged with his gavel. He hurried through the preliminaries, waived reading of the minutes of the pre-

37

vious session and got to the several subjects for the day's discussion.

There was little talk over the heating of the swimming pool and the slower elevator and both motions passed. Barry refrained from ruling against them.

He looked at Carol Ann and she said, "The petition for a Moroccan restaurant."

Barry looked up at the thousand-odd residents of the building he managed. "Ah, yes. Any discussion?"

Down in the front row, someone began waving frantically.

Barry Ten Eyck recognized the president of the Gourmet Club, one of perhaps forty clubs that had been organized in Shyler-deme. The man's name was Samuelson, Fred or Frank, or something like that. An aggressive little type who attended all Deme-Assemblies and almost invariably spoke on every subject debated. He was thinner and more intense than you would have expected a gourmet to be.

Barry said, "Mr. Samuelson?"

Mr. Samuelson was belligerent.

He waggled his head and said, "I know how you people think and how you figure. A deme is run like a dictatorship. Sure, supposedly us residents have a big say in the way the public facilities are run, but actually you managers can overrule anything. But all I've got to say is this. Us residents have our rights and we've got our needs. And we members of the Gourmet Club say we ought to have more selection when we go out to dine. We spend our pseudo-dollars and we ought to get what we want."

"Of course," Barry nodded.

But the other was still belligerent. "We got more than fifteen hundred signatures on this petition . . ."

Barry Ten Eyck knew the way of petitions. Lord knows, he saw enough of them. Anybody with a little push could get another resident to sign a petition for just about anything. Homes for homeless pigeons, or whatever. He could hear Carol Ann Cusack, next to him, sigh.

". . . We got more than fifteen hundred signatures and we want to see this through. Now we know that as Demecrat you can overrule any project we residents vote for, but we also know that at any time we can vote for your dismissal and the owners of Shyler-deme have to remove you and put up for our approval a new Demecrat. And I warn you now, Mr. Ten Eyck, that if you overrule this petition, the Gourmet Club is going to start a campaign for your removal . . ."

Barry held up a restraining hand. "Mr. Samuelson . . ."

"I've got a right to have my say!"

Barry said, "Of course you have, but I don't think that you want to talk just for the sake of talking."

Samuelson, taken aback, shut up abruptly.

Barry said, "I've already decided to honor your request. The Moroccan restaurant will be opened. You will be pleased to know that our Head Chef, Monsieur Daunou, is well acquainted with Moroccan cuisine."

Samuelson was flabbergasted.

Barry Ten Eyck came to his feet. "You will also be interested to know, I am sure, that I am taking measures to open a Hungarian and a German—that is, Bavarian—restaurant. And I urge you members of the Gourmet Club to inform your various publications to which you subscribe, and your friends among gourmets, that Shyler-deme is also embarking on a program that will involve Russian restaurants, Swedish, Danish, Greek, Turkish and Vegetarian Hindu. And we are open to other suggestions from our residents. In short, ladies and gentlemen, in the future, Shyler-deme will have as its theme, gourmet attributes, not only in our restaurants but in foods and wines in our ultra-market and available through the automated public kitchens."

He looked at Carol Ann, who was a bit on the wide-eyed side. "If that is all, Miss Cusack?"

She nodded.

He rapped the gavel. "The Deme-Assembly is adjourned."

On the way to the door, he said to her, "I want you

to get in touch soonest with the two chefs that they let go at Victory-deme the other day, a Hungarian and a Bavarian. Sign them up. Also, I want to place some ads in the publications devoted to swapping apartments. The general idea is that Shyler-deme is now the most food-conscious deme in the United States and that we invite gourmets to take residence. Also I want you to get in touch with every one of our former residents who have moved. Let them know that we are interested in helping them expedite selling their equity in their apartments so that new tenants can move in."

Carol Ann groaned at the prospect of that amount of work. She said, "You haven't any other brain children, have you?"

"Just one more item, Miss Cusack," he said severely.

"Mrs. Cusack," she said. "Yes, Mr. Ten Eyck?"

"In the morning, when I come in, I want no more than four crises."

Part Two
Bat Hardin

As always, Bat Hardin awakened at first dawn. He yawned uphappily, ran the back of his fist over his thickish lips. He got up and threw the covers up in such wise that it would be easier for the automatic to make the bed. Sometimes the things jammed it up, although he understood the later models were just about perfect.

He pressed the button that folded the bed into the wall and made his way into the bath, still yawning. His place was not quite a mini-apartment but it was by no means large. In fact, he had precious little more space than he had enjoyed in his mobile home back when he'd worked at being a policeman in the mobile art colony of New Woodstock.

The usual washing and shaving routine over, he went over to the delivery box and dialed fresh underwear, a shirt and socks from the ultra-market down in the bowels of the building. He threw the equal numbers from the day before into the disposal chute. He could have had them laundered, of course, but rejected the idea. Storage space in an average apartment was so limited that it hardly made sense to accumulate clothing, especially with textile prices what they were these days. Pants and jackets, yes. You saved by making them last awhile. Clothes with sentimental attachments, yes; that was another thing.

He went into the kitchenette and into the routine of

41

making coffee. He could simply have dialed it on the auto-table, but that was one item where he drew the line. He liked coffee the way *he* made it, not the mass-produced product of the Restaurant Division down in the lower levels. He wondered vaguely how much coffee the automated kitchens turned out daily in Shylerdeme. Almost twenty thousand inhabitants. Some, of course, weren't coffee drinkers, but on the other hand that would be balanced by some who probably drank several cups for breakfast alone.

He grunted sour amusement. He'd have to figure it out sometime on the slipstick. Say, twenty thousand cups. What was the content of a single cup? It would run into many a gallon. Gallons, ha! It probably got into the magnitude of barrels, if not tank cars full. It would be a darned sight easier just to ask the Head Chef. An efficient type, old Pete would know down to the ounce.

The coffee ready, he dialed a straight rum on his auto-bar in the living room cum bedroom. Bat Hardin wasn't a heavy drinker by heavy drinker standards but during the Asian War he had picked up the habit of taking a slug of spirits with his coffee each morning by way of starting the body juices coursing.

He began to pour the drink into the black coffee and then stopped. He brought the small shot glass to his nose and, frowning, smelled. He tasted it and screwed up his heavy-set face into a scowl.

He muttered, "What the hell! This is *rum*?"

He turned the scowl to the auto-bar. It was programmed to deliver any of ten drinks which he selected. One of them was straight Jamaican rum, one of his few expensive indulgences. He insisted upon the imported stuff, straight from the island. The more common synthetic spirits just weren't the same thing.

He shrugged and poured the drink into his coffee and took it over to the window and stared out over the square mile of parks, woods, playgrounds and gardens that surrounded the apartment building. In the distance, one mile off, was a sister ultra-apartment house,

Victory-deme. In all, there were four demes in the pseudo-city of Phoenecia; roughly eighty thousand inhabitants, smallish as pseudo-cities went; however, large enough to offer the facilities that city dwellers desired.

A good many of the facilities city dwellers desired were less than necessary, so far as Bat Hardin was concerned. All over again, he wondered if he had made a mistake in leaving the mobile towns. He wondered where New Woodstock was by now. He had left the art colony on wheels at Mexico City and it had continued on its way down the Pan American Highway, South America its eventual goal.

Bat Hardin sighed. He had always wanted to see Peru.

Well, he had made his decision.

He finished the coffee and, not being hungry enough to eat it, threw the cup into the disposal chute and turned to that small section of his living room that he was pleased to call his study. He sat down before the typer, activated the TV library booster screen and slipped on his student's headphones. He sighed again and dialed the next lesson in the Business Management course he was taking, among others, among many others.

Studying again, after all these years, didn't come easily to Bat Hardin in his mid-thirties, but at least he had determination. Under Meritocracy, you needed it. High I.Q., determination, education ... and luck. You needed them all to get even remotely toward the top under Meritocracy.

Particularly when you got as late a start working your way up the totem pole as had Bat Hardin. He inwardly cursed, still once again, the years he had spent in the military, and then the years he had spent living on Negative Income Tax while donating his services as town police officer to the mobile towns in which he had lived.

Yes, Bat Hardin was getting a late start; however, he was under way.

43

He put in an hour at the lessons, checked the time on his TV phone screen, pulled off the headphones, stretched and headed for the closet for his jacket. He made a point of never getting to work late. Bat Hardin was on his way up—if it killed him.

Out in the hall, he had to pause a moment to let one of his neighbors go by. He was mildly surprised to see her up and around at this hour. He nodded a good morning, and received not even a flicker of a flicker in return.

He looked after her for a moment. A weird, as they called them these days. She wore a soiled pair of khaki shorts, nothing more. Not even shoes. Probably returning from the apartment of one of the others of her group. The weirds made a point of promiscuity.

What was it about youth in revolt that they almost invariably ran to the ridiculous in dress? Few of them probably realized it but the weirds were not exactly first when it came to being rebels against the status quo. Bat Hardin sometimes suspected that every generation was at least partially a lost generation. The flappers and sheiks of Scott Fitzgerald's and Hemingway's Lost Generation with their skirts above the knee and their coonskin coats weren't the first off-beats, no matter how daring they might have thought themselves, complete with hip flasks of gin. Their kids, in turn, had become the jitterbugs and zoot-suiters of the thirties and forties; and theirs had become the hippies of the fifties and sixties, complete with pot and LSD. And now, Bat thought, we have the weirds. Barefooted and often bare-breasted, and almost invariably soiled of clothing and uncombed of hair. What was there about being far-out that demanded you be dirty? If she could have raised a beard she probably would have.

Rebels without a cause. Sneering at society, but without a solution to its ills. And willing to a man to collect the free-loading Negative Income Tax. For Bat Hardin's money, they were a bunch of bums.

It was a damn shame that Barry Ten Eyck, Shyler-

deme's Demecrat, had seen fit to allow them to move
in. They pulled down a deme's standing. More conservative elements were prone to move out of a deme with
too many weirds in residence. However, he knew Ten
Eyck's motivation. You couldn't return a profit on a
deme unless you had a high percentage of occupancy.
And if nobody else would move into your building, you
had to take such off-beats as weirds and escapists.

He proceeded to the elevator banks and headed
down for the building's Administration offices.

As Vice-Demecrat of Shyler-deme, Bat Hardin was
supposedly capable of taking over the management of
any Division in the building and hence, at the present,
found himself in charge of Security. Evidently, Barry
Ten Eyck, knowing Bat had in the past been a police
officer, was in no hurry to find a new Chief of Security.
He was saving budget by doubling up officers.

He entered the outer offices and nodded to the single
Security officer who handled the six hour night shift.
Bat said, "Morning, Jeffers."

Jeffers said, "The Head Chef has been trying to get
you, Mr. Hardin."

"Pete Daunou? Oh? What's up?"

The other looked at him strangely. "You better talk
to him. It doesn't make much sense to me."

Bat Hardin went into his inner office and sat down
at his desk. His secretary, Ruth Wheeler, wasn't on the
scene as yet. He activated one of his phone screens and
said into it, "Restaurant Division, please. Pierre
Daunou."

The chef's rounded face, with its ridiculous little
French mustache, faded in. He puffed his rosy cheeks
out and popped his eyes.

"What's the crisis, Pierre?" Bat said. The kitchen division wasn't exactly from whence you expected to be
called on in Security.

"Monsieur Hardin. It is fantastic!" He popped his
eyes some more and reared back slightly and held his
breath, as though expecting the other immediately to be
astounded.

45

"Okay," Bat said. "What?"

"Twenty-five barrels of olive oil, they have been stolen."

Bat Hardin stared at him. "Twenty-five *barrels*."

"Twenty-five barrels," the chef said dramatically. "My own special Montenegrin olive oil."

"How in the hell can you steal twenty-five barrels of olive oil?"

"Listen, how in the hell can you steal twenty-five barrels of olive oil?" Bat Hardin said, looking around the storage room.

Pierre Daunou made a Gallic gesture of despair. "One does not know. It is impossible. It is ridiculous. What would one even do with it if one was not a chef for twenty thousand people?"

His assistant, who was standing next to him, grunted. "It is more than five thousand liters of the best oil. If I had five thousand liters of Montenegrin olive oil and couldn't sell it for a small fortune I would go out of business. I would soon find out where."

Bat Hardin didn't know the man, which mildly surprised him. He was reasonably well acquainted with the staff of Shyler-deme.

Pierre Daunou looked at the other in contempt. "Best of oil, ha! One knows little of olive oil if one makes such sweeping statements. For salads, yes!" He made a gesture of sweeping approval. But then his face turned indignant. "For cooking, but no. For the flavoring of, say, gazpacho, no. But, no. For such, Spanish olive oil."

His assistant was no brown-noser. He snapped, "I prefer the Italian."

"No."

"Or even the more delicate oils of Provence."

"Then you are an idiot."

They glared at each other.

Bat said, "Listen . . ."

Pierre Daunou turned his glare at him. "You too

perhaps prefer the olive oil of Italy to that of Spain for cooking gazpacho?"

Bat said, "I think the Greek is best."

They both glowered their indignation.

"Holy Smokes," Bat rasped. "Let's get off this. I don't even really know if they make olive oil in Greece and I haven't the vaguest idea of what gazpacho is. Let's get to the facts. You call me and say twenty-five barrels of olive oil have been swiped out of your storerooms. It doesn't make sense. Pilferage, yes. It always happens. Pilferage we will always have with us. But you don't pilfer twenty-five barrels of anything. What does twenty-five barrels of olive oil, Montenegrin, Spanish, or any other kind, come to? I mean in pseudo-dollars."

The Head Chef puffed out his cheeks. "Ordering in such quantity enables one to acquire the very finest Montenegrin olive oil for a paltry two and a half pseudo-dollars."

"A gallon?"

"Ha! A liter."

Bat Hardin closed his eyes in pain. "Holy Smokes." He did some quick mental arithmetic. "You mean this romp cost Shyler-deme some twelve thousand, five hundred dollars?"

The assistant said, "A bit more than that, after all."

Bat looked at him. "How do you fit into this?"

Pierre Daunou said, "This is Lester Terwilliger, my Salad Chef."

"And you order your olive oil twenty-five barrels at a time?"

The Head Chef said indignantly. "This is but the oil for salads. We buy Spanish, Portuguese, Italian, French oils for various other dishes."

"Okay," Bat said. "We've got nearly twenty thousand residents, all of whom eat three times a day, either in their own apartments, the food coming up from the public kitchens, or in one or the other of the auto-cafeterias or restaurants. I suppose to buy salad oil five thousand liters at a time isn't as far out as it sounds to me. How long have you noticed that these twenty-five barrels were missing?"

Terwilliger said, "Why, just this morning. I entered this compartment to see to attaching a new barrel to my mixing department. Pooof! No oil."

Bat stared at him, unbelievingly. They were far in the depths of the building, four floors below street level and hundreds of meters from the nearest entry. Bat said, "How long's it been here?"

"It was delivered a week . . . no, eight days ago."

"You receipted it?"

Terwilliger said, "Yes, of course. I am head of the Salad Department, responsible only to Monsieur Daunou. When I receive supplies, I report into my phone screen to the computer banks."

Bat stared around the room. "I suppose it's a routine delivery, through that door there. Who unloaded?"

"Unloading is automated, of course. The auto-electro-steamer lorry comes to the door. Mr. Pearson from down in Delivery supervised."

Bat Hardin shook his head. "You couldn't get it out. Not twenty-five barrels, without Security, Delivery and Transportation all knowing about it. It's out of the question."

Daunou made his Gallic gesture of despair. "Nevertheless one must point out that it was here and now is not."

Bat Hardin turned to go. "I'll take it up with Mr. Ten Eyck, and I'll do a double check through the building's data banks. If it happened, the computers recorded it."

"*If* it happened?" Terwilliger said indignantly. "Where is the oil, if it didn't happen?"

Bat Hardin was still scowling his worried puzzlement when he re-entered his office. Whoever had pulled this little romp had no more chance of getting away with it than he had of robbing National Banking of twelve thousand pseudo-dollars. In a cashless-checkless economy, thieving any sizable amount at all was all but impossible.

The day shift was on and Ruth Wheeler occupying her desk. She was a new acquisition, having been transferred only a couple of weeks before from a different deme also owned by Vanderfeller and Moore. The cosmocorps made a policy of shifting around its personnel for the sake of experience. She was a small woman, in her mid-twenties, very neatly proportioned in the best of secretarial tradition, but, for Bat's money, a little too aggressively out to please. Pretty enough, mind you, in a redheaded, green-eyed sort of way, but a little too *damn* efficient and pleasant.

"Good morning, Miss Wheeler," he told her, making a beeline for his own desk.

"Oh, just Ruth . . . Bat," she said.

He looked at her, a bit apologetic. "Sorry, Miss Wheeler, I'm not the type. Makes me uncomfortable. Barry Ten Eyck was born calling everybody by their first names. He can pull it off. But in my case, when I am in a position where I am either giving or taking orders, I like to keep it formal."

She made with a mock petulant flip of a shoulder, as though he was kidding and turned back to her work.

Bat said, "Listen, here's a top priority job for you. Eight days ago, twenty-five barrels of olive oil were delivered to the Restaurant Division to Lester Terwilliger, the Salad Chef. Pearson, down in Delivery, supervised and got Terwilliger's receipt. I want you to check it through all ways possible."

"Check what?"

"The oil is missing. It's more than twelve thousand pseudo-dollars worth. Find it. Check the data banks on every aspect."

She was a little on the wide-eyed side, but she said, "Right away . . . Mr. Hardin. Oh, Mr. Hardin, Mr. Ten Eyck said for you to run over there as soon as you came in."

Run on over, yet, Bat grunted inwardly. An unlikely way for Barry Ten Eyck to have said it. Especially in

49

view of the fact that he was a younger man than Bat Hardin. More experienced in the management of a deme, possibly, but he hadn't been around as much as his Vice-Demecrat and Chief of Security by a long shot.

Bat crossed the corridor, the door of the Demecrat's offices opening before him. He nodded to one or two of the staff in the outer offices and went on to Barry Ten Eyck's private domain.

Carol Ann Cusack looked up from her desk and said, "Hail the conquering Chief . . . of Security."

Bat said, "Ha, conquering yet! This chief is about to retire from the warpath and go onto the reservation."

Barry Ten Eyck looked up from some reports he had on a desk TV screen. "Something new spins?"

Bat told him about it.

Barry Ten Eyck winced. "Twelve thousand, five hundred pseudo-dollars! Wow!"

Bat said, "Don't worry. Whoever pulled this simply can't get away with it. There're ten thousand TV spy lenses concealed in this building, each one hooked up to the computers. What'd you want to see me about, Barry?"

Barry Ten Eyck brought his lanky form up more erect, and some of the easygoing quality left his face. "Did you hear Mick Mansfield's news broadcast this morning?"

Bat snorted. "The voice of Phoenecia? I seldom listen. Gossip, uninteresting accounts of everything from picnics to birthday parties and weddings, coverage of inter-deme sports. The equivalent of the country newspaper of a hundred years ago."

Barry looked at Carol Ann Cusack. "I hate to go through this again, but dial it, Miss Cusack."

"Mrs. Cusack," Carol Ann said, dialing her desk TV phone. "Mrs. Sidney Cusack."

"I hate old married ladies," Barry explained cheerfully. "I like bright young misses around an office."

"Ha. Mr. Ten Eyck, if you weren't so lazy, I suspect

you'd make a first class office wolf. Should I throw it on the wall screen?"

"Please."

She activated the wall screen, which was some six feet square and the earnest, albeit beefy face of one who was obviously a news broadcaster faded in. He was saying:

"... The Voice of Phoenecia ... And now friends, another item or two of the unfortunate type of news we've been picking up about Shyler-deme so often these days. It would seem that just everything, but everything, is happening in the realm of Demecrat Barry Ten Eyck ... Latest on the continuing riots between the children of the plain ordinary folk and those of the, ah, weirds, ha ha, as we call them, is the threat that the scraps between the kids will escalate to the point where the adults are having at it ..."

Bat Hardin turned to his superior in surprise. "Riots? *What* riots?"

"That's what I'd like to know," Barry growled. "Listen."

The newsman went on. "... Well, we all hope it won't lead to bloodshed ... There are also continuing reports of the bad feelings running between the established religions such as the Catholics and Protestants and the followers of the so-called New Temple. It would seem that several of the so-called gurus of the New Temple are demanding the right to utilize the public rooms of Shyler-deme devoted to religious services for their own rites ... Of course, in the past there has been little conflict between various denominations due to the fact that days of worship vary. The New Moslems worship on Friday, the Jewish followers on Saturday, and most Christians, ha ha, not the Seventh Day Adventists, of course, on Sunday. However, the gurus of the New Temple take a dim view of practicing their alleged new faith on any particular day and ..."

Bat said, "What in the hell's all this *so-called* and *alleged* stuff? We've never had any trouble with these

New Temple people. If they've dreamed up a new religion, so what?"

"Listen," Barry said, a weary element in his voice.

The news reporter was onto a new item. ". . . There are rumors—we'll check them out for our tomorrow's broadcast—about continuing high level pilferage going on at the Shyler-deme administration. We hate to be a continuing wet blanket but they seem to be having their troubles in our sister deme, don't they folks?"

"That's it, Miss Cusack. Kill it," Barry Ten Eyck growled.

Carol Ann deactivated the re-run news broadcast and sank back into her chair.

"What's the matter with that guy?" Bat demanded. "What was that about riots?"

"Kids in the playground," Barry said. "Some of the weird kids are dressed as far-out as their parents. No haircuts, no shoes, that sort of thing. Kids being kids, some of the others roach them about it. So. The obvious. A few black eyes, a few bloody noses."

"This is a riot? Kids have been doing that since Cleopatra barged down the Nile. When I was a kid I admittedly had a chip on my shoulder because my complexion was darker a few shades than average. Others because they were Jews or Puerto Ricans, or whatever. We used to scrap, from time to time, but nobody thought of our kid fights as riots."

"Darned if I know," Barry shrugged. "I'm going to talk to Mayor Levy about it. This sort of supposed newscast doesn't do Shyler-deme any good, and it doesn't do the whole pseudo-city of Phoenecia any good. Supposedly, the possibility of building at least one more deme is being suggested. Maybe two. Here's an item that comes more under your jurisdiction."

He handed over a lengthy sheet of paper. There was some typed material at the top, then a lengthy list of signatures. Bat estimated at least a hundred in all.

He looked at Barry Ten Eyck. "Another petition?"

"Read it."

Bat read aloud. "We, the undersigned freedom-loving and patriotic citizens of the United States and residents of Shyler-deme, protest the presence in our deme of dangerous subversives such as William Locke and demand that measures be taken to have them expelled from the pseudo-city of Phoenecia."

Bat looked up again. "Who's William Locke?"

Barry said, "I had Miss Cusack check out his dossier in the National Data Banks. Nothing remarkable. He works over at the Dodge-Myers Complex as some sort of junior engineer. Background is more or less standard for a young Meritcrat. I.Q. of 140. Educated at M.I.T. One of the top ten in his class. Unmarried. One of the original residents of Shyler-deme. Has a twin of your own apartment, Bat, in Tower-Two. Apartment 63 on the sixtieth floor. We've had no complaints about or from him, ever. Do you want more details?"

Bat said, "Criminal record?"

Barry looked uncomfortable. "A man's criminal dossier is a Number Two priority and supposedly only available to proper police authority."

Bat said, "And as Demecrat of Shyler-deme you hold a Number Two priority for access to the National Data Banks, and, for that matter, so do I, as Chief of Security."

His superior said, "Well, as a matter of fact I did check it and came up with practically a blank. A couple of traffic violations. A drunken driving charge when he was a kid, celebrating his graduation or something. Case dismissed."

"Nothing suggesting being a subversive?"

"He evidently signed a couple of peace petitions during the Asian War when he was in college. Imagine bothering to put a thing like that in a man's dossier."

"And . . ."

"And he was arrested once for participating in a demonstration against regimentation in the schools. One of those far-out things kids seem to have to get into at least once in their university days. Case dismissed again."

"And that's all?"

"Alleged to be local organizer of the Futurist Party in the pseudo-city of Phoenecia."

Bat gnawed his lower lip. "Oh, ho. What's the Futurist Party?"

"Search me," Barry said. "Miss Cusack?"

Carol Ann shook her head. "I don't know anything about politics. Who pays attention to politics any more?"

Bat said, "I'll check it out. Sounds to me like just one more of these busybody deals. There's a type of person that gravitates to causing trouble when they've got time on their hands. And there's another type of person that'll sign any petition put in front of them, usually without bothering to read it. At least this guy Locke works. I'll bet a plugged nickel that most of those who signed that petition are collecting Negative Income Tax."

Bat Hardin looked down at the petition again. "Did you notice that nobody has signed this except the petitioners? That is, it doesn't tell who circulated it. No committee or anything."

"Well, check it out, Bat," his chief said.

Bat came to his feet. "All right. As soon as I clean up this mess of Pierre Daunou and his olive oil."

He returned to his own office, folding the petition and sticking it into an inner pocket.

Ruth Wheeler looked up at him from where she had been frowning in puzzlement into her desk TV phone screen.

Bat said, "Well, Miss Wheeler, what happened to the olive oil? Some ridiculous mixup?"

She was shaking her head. "Mr. Hardin, it's got to be there."

"What do you mean?"

"Mr. Hardin, if you don't look out you're going to chew that lower lip of yours right off."

"Listen, confound it, what happened to the olive oil?"

"I checked it out from every angle. Mr. Terwilliger

requisitioned it from Central Warehouses of Vanderfeller and Moore for this area. Head Chef Daunou okayed the requisition. The twenty-five barrels were loaded at the warehouse, supervised by a Mr. Kennedy there. An automated-electro-steamer lorry brought them to Shyler-deme. Mr. Pearson of Delivery took over when the lorry entered this building's Transport Station and was passed on through by Traffic. Mr. Smith was on Traffic Control at the time. It proceeded to the stock rooms of the Restaurant Division and Mr. Terwilliger was present to supervise the unloading. The twenty-five barrels were unloaded, checked, and Mr. Terwilliger receipted the whole transaction in his TV phone screen for the computers. There has been no lorry approach to that room since, and even if there had been, it would have required someone in Delivery to have assisted in loading the oil, and then Traffic would have had to be involved in getting the lorry out of the building. The computers have no record of any such activities and they would *have* to have it if it was done, Mr. Hardin."

"Holy Smokes," Bat blurted. "Twenty-five full barrels can't simply disappear."

"No, sir."

"Listen, I'm going down there again. I'll be in the Restaurant Division, Miss Wheeler."

"Yes, sir. Oh, I know you'll figure this all out, Mr. Hardin," she gushed. "You're just the man for this sort of thing."

He looked at her sourly as he left.

However, he didn't quite make it to Head Chef Daunou's office. On the way, he passed the door to the control rooms and offices of Harry Mackley, head of the Liquor Division. He came to a halt, considered it a moment, then let the door screen pick him up. It opened and he went on in.

Mackley, the Head Bartender, was slumped in his chair, staring down at his desk. He looked up and an expression of despair came over his face.

He said, "Hello, Mr. Hardin."

"Mr. Hardin?" Bat said. "I thought it was Bat and Harry."

The other sucked in air. He was a gangly man, sparce of hair and usually of the professional bartender's traditional good humor. But something was obviously off-key now. He said glumly, "I'm afraid it's going to be Hardin and Mackley in short order."

Bat, not understanding, said, "Reason I dropped in, Harry, is that this morning I dialed Jamaican rum on my auto-bar and came up with some horrible synthetic that I could hardly get down."

"I know."

"What I meant was, could you have one of the boys in Maintenance check out my auto-bar?"

Mackley shook his head. "That's not where the trouble is."

Bat looked at him.

Mackley said, "I've been trying to cover up, but I realize now I've been a fool. It's too much to cover up."

"What in the devil are you talking about?"

"I've had to substitute a cheaper product. We don't have any more of the good rum. I've been trying to improvise, switch around. It's not too important on mixed drinks. A lot of folks think they can tell, but in actuality you put rum in coke or any other mixer except maybe water, and you can't tell the difference between the best, such as the Jamaican you like, and anything just short of the worst."

"What do you mean you don't have any more of the good rum? Why not order more?"

"Because my budget doesn't allow for it."

Bat stared at him. "Harry, have you gone completely drivel happy? Aside from an auto-bar in every apartment not occupied by teetotalers, there's a score of restaurants and nigh on to fifty bars, clubs, nightspots and such in Shyler-deme. Booze is one of our most lucrative sources of income. You've got to have the better quality stuff as well as the cheaper synthetics. People demand it, especially for a celebration, or a night on the town in the clubs."

"I know," the Head Bartender said glumly. "The complaints are beginning to come in. Rum is one of the most popular spirits there is. Makes as many different mixed drinks as the others put together."

Bat said, "Listen, maybe I ought to go out and come back in again. You've got to have good rum. So, okay, order it from Central Warehouses if you've run short of it."

Mackley sucked in air again. "Bat, the bartender is traditionally a pilferer. Maybe because in this business it's so easy. Anywhere from a drink to a bottle. Those with less conscience wouldn't dream of paying for their own guzzle, for, say a party in their own home, or for Christmas or New Year's or whatever."

Bat was still staring his lack of comprehension. "So, okay. There's pilferage in just about any field that allows for it. Most people have a bit of larceny in their blood. So what? Certainly the powers that be in Central Management of Vanderfeller and Moore have long since worked that into their computations. You mean some of the boys have pilfered so much of your better grade rum that you've run out? Forget about it. Order more."

The other shook his head. "When the pilferage amounts to twenty-five barrels, Bat, you can't just write it off."

After a long moment, Bat Hardin said, "Did you say *twenty-five* barrels?"

"That's correct, Bat. Don't ask me how. I don't know. I suppose I should have come to you immediately when I found out. But this would mean my job, Bat, and a thing like this gets on your dossier and you never get a job anywhere else again. You go onto Negative Income Tax, that is, if you stay out of jail."

Bat Hardin had closed his eyes briefly in pain. Now he opened them, grabbed a straight chair, reversed it and sat down, straddling. He put his arms on the back and said, "Okay. Undoubtedly this comes under the head of Security. Let's hear it."

Harry Mackley said gloomily, "I don't know where to start."

Bat held his peace.

Mackley took a deep breath and said, "Bat, do you know how an automated bar for a building as large as a deme works?"

"Only the general theory."

"Well, as I know you, you're not really a hard drinker. You drink, but you're not a lush."

"That's right."

"But even people who consider themselves moderate drinkers can get through more than they usually realize, living and working in a place like a deme. So how much do you drink? Count 'em."

Bat thought about it. "Well, I take a shot of good rum in my coffee in the morning, just to cut the phlegm. Then usually, when I knock off for lunch, I have a light drink to relax before eating."

The other was nodding.

Bat said, "Sometimes I have a synthetic beer with lunch, or if I'm eating with someone in one of the restaurants, especially if it's on my expense account, or his, I might have a half bottle of synthetic wine. This begins to sound like I'm a real guzzler."

"No. Go on."

"Okay. Sometimes in the afternoon something will come up where somebody offers me a drink." He grunted self-deprecation. "Come to think of it, almost every day some occasion comes up when I have one or two beers, or whatever, in the afternoon."

"Ummmm."

"Well, then I knock off in the evening and have a Martini . . ."

"Or two."

"Or maybe a pseudo-whiskey highball . . . or two, before dinner. If I'm eating alone in my apartment, I don't usually have anything with my dinner, except possibly a little brandy afterward."

"But if you're eating out, particularly with a young lady, or with a business contact, on an expense account . . ."

"Maybe wine. Damn it, I'm sounding more like a real boozer by the minute."

"Nope. You're a single man in his thirties who works hard. Go on."

"Well, in the evening I often have a couple of drinks or so. Even more if I go out on a date, or to a party. But seldom to the point that I'm hazy, and I haven't been really smashed for . . ."

"How about New Year's?"

Bat had to chuckle. "Well, then, yes."

Harry Mackley totaled it up. "Nine or ten drinks a day, if you count a half bottle of wine as only one drink. And I have a sneaking suspicion that you might take a nightcap just before going to bed. The point I'm making, Bat, is that we have pushing twenty thousand residents here in Shyler-deme. Five thousand of these don't drink at all, probably. Kids, old folks, teetotalers. Another ten thousand drink moderately. Some of them only on Christmas or such occasions. But the remaining five thousand drink as you do—or more. Can you get a glimmering of just how much booze goes through my Division?"

"Holy Smokes. I don't think of myself as a heavy drinker, but five thousand drinking at my rate would still be fifty thousand alcoholic drinks a day."

"Right. Now it's all automated. We buy our synthetic booze in bulk. That is, all the basic items, whiskey, gin, rum, vodka, brandy, ordinary wines, beer. Only the more exotic imports do we get by the five or ten gallon bottle, cordials, liqueurs, other specialized items. Our automatic bartenders are an efficiency expert's dream. Martinis, for instance. A barrel of gin, holding some fifty-five gallons; a barrel of Vermouth, the same; connected, a dispenser of green olives, containing half a ton. During the rush hour, gallons upon gallons of Martinis are whomped up and delivered in expendable glasses to your apartment, through your auto-bar, or to the auto-tables in all the auto-cafeterias, restaurants, bars and nightspots in Shy-ler-deme."

"What are you building up to, Harry?"

"That an unbelievable amount of liquor goes through this Division."

"So we come to the rum."

"Yes. Twenty-five barrels of it. They disappeared."

"How?"

"Bat, I don't know. It couldn't have happened."

"Who possibly could have pulled the deal? Obvi-ously, twenty-five barrels of rum, especially Jamaican rum, is worth plenty. It's worth swiping—always as-suming you could fence it."

"Bat, nobody could have pulled it. Not even me, and I'm head of this Division. But I'd be the nearest, I'd think. So far as selling it is concerned, I can't figure out any way of doing that. Maybe professional thieves might know, but I don't."

"There are mighty few pros any more," Bat growled. "Too many built-in ways in our present socio-economic system of clobbering them. What were the mechanics of it, Harry?"

The older man ran a weary hand through his thin-ning hair. "That's what gets me, Bat. Those barrels were stashed away in a servo-storeroom almost immedi-ately beneath here. They'd been delivered about ten days ago. Routine delivery from Central Warehouses."

"Rum has a storeroom all of its own?"

"No. Just a section. There're various other barrels kept in the same place. Various items such as tequila and mescal. Stuff that you don't use too much of."

"None of it's missing?"

"No. Just the rum. Various kinds of rum. Jamaica, Puerto Rican light, Bacardi, from Cuba. All high-grade import stuff."

Bat came to his feet with a sigh. "I suppose you have all the data on who delivered it, who receipted it, and so forth?"

"Yes, of course."

"Okay. I'll check it out." Bat hesitated. "Look, Harry, you're quite sure it was exactly twenty-five barrels of rum? Full barrels?"

"Yes, of course I'm sure. Why?"

Bat bit his under lip. "Because it's getting to be a habit."

In the morning, Bat Hardin got to his office an hour later than usual. He had spent a fruitless period in the storerooms of both the Restaurant and the Liquor Divisions and had come up with exactly nothing. He had interviewed all concerned with transporting and storing the twenty-five missing barrels of olive oil and the exactly equal number of rum. And had come up with exactly nothing. He was beginning to doubt his senses. That amount of bulk could no more disappear without a trace than he could levitate.

Ruth Wheeler looked up on his entry. "Oh, Bat," she said. "Mr. Ten Eyck is fuming at you. He's been calling every few minutes."

Bat looked at her. "Fuming? Barry?"

She said decisively, "I don't think Mr. Ten Eyck appreciates you. Why, you're his best man. He can't lay the blame for everything that goes wrong on your shoulders."

Bat said dryly, over his shoulder as he left, "If I'm his best man, I'd hate to see his worst. I seem to draw a blank on everything."

"Oh, you're much too modest," she called after him. "Don't let him impose on you."

Bat grunted and crossed the corridor. Was poor Barry beginning to get into a tizzy with all this? Actually, you could hardly blame the guy. Every wheel on the vehicle seemed to be falling off at once.

When he entered the Demecrat's office, he didn't get the impression that Barry Ten Eyck was exactly fuming, but he certainly wasn't happy.

"Where've you been, Bat? I couldn't raise you on your pocket phone."

"I had it switched to Priority One. Didn't want to be

interrupted. I was down in Restaurant and Liquor trying to trace this out." He added, sourly, "No luck whatsoever."

"Oh. Well, David Abernathy wants to see us."

"Vanderfeller's secretary? I thought Cyril Vanderfeller was over in Common Europe, or some place. Is he back in residence here?"

Barry said, "Old man Vanderfeller has more secretaries than we have petition signers, and believe me, we're fanny deep in petitions. Get this one." He handed over a lengthy sheet of white paper.

Bat took it. "Another?" he growled. It looked considerably like the one of the day before protesting the presence of subversives in Shyler-deme. It read:

"We, the undersigned, protest the presence in Shyler-deme of such fallen women . . ."

Bat looked up. "Fallen women!"

"Prostitutes," Carol Ann said demurely. "Streetwalkers, tarts, strumpets, trollops, harlots . . ."

"Okay, okay," Bat growled. He went back to the petition.

". . . As Mabel Dunnigan, who plies her degrading trade in Apartment 32 on the thirtieth floor of Tower-One. We decent women of Shyler-deme protest that our husbands and sons are subjected to her wiles. We decent men of Shyler-deme protest being solicited in the building which houses our homes."

It was signed by approximately sixty persons, most of whom had handwriting just barely legible.

Bat looked up in disgust. "Who do these people expect us to respond to? They never sign their own names. I wouldn't be surprised if this thing was circulated by the same busybodies who did up that one on William Locke, that Futurist Party guy—if he is connected with the Futurists."

Barry shrugged, standing. "It's your top to spin, Bat. What are the laws pertaining to prostitution in a deme?"

"Darned if I know," Bat said. "There's so little of it. It's like a great deal of other petty crime. Not worth the while in a cashless-checkless society where nobody can spend your money but you, where it's practically impossible to rob anybody, con them, gamble them out of their dough, or whatever." He gave a sigh. "I'll look into it."

"Well, let's go up and see high and mighty," Barry said. He looked at Carol Ann Cusack. "We'll be up in the penthouse, Miss Cusack."

"Mrs. Cusack."

He leered at her as they left.

On the way up to the hundredth floor Barry said, "On this oil and rum thing, Bat. Do you think that possibly we ought to ring in Chief Snider, over in Administration?"

Had Bat Hardin been of slightly lighter complexion, he might have flushed, his first reaction resentment. He said tightly, "I don't see what Ben Snider could do that I'm not doing. His job is Chief of Security of all Phoenecia. I'm Security Chief here in Shyler-deme. The problem has nothing to do with the inter-relations of the four different demes. It has only to do with this deme."

"Okay, okay. But if we don't come up with something soon, you might get the advice of some of the more experienced police over in Central Administration."

"I'm experienced police," Bat said tightly, keeping his voice from going hot. "I was a cop for years."

"Well, not exactly the kind of cop that handles this sort of thing."

"What kind of cop handles this sort of thing? I've never even heard of this sort of thing before and I doubt if any other cop has either."

"All right, all right," Barry said reasonably.

At the hundredth floor, which was as high as this general bank of elevators went, they switched over to the private penthouse elevator of Cyril Vanderfeller. The upper floors were largely devoted to the more swank garden and terrace apartments and to the more luxurious and expensive restaurants and entertainment

63

spots. As a rule, though not always, the higher one ascended in the deme, the more expensive became the accommodations. Few of those residents who lived in the mini-apartments on the lowest levels, ever even came as high as the hundredth floor. It was somewhat like the smallish city of yesteryear with its this side of the tracks and that side of the tracks, and ultimately Highbrow Hill, or whatever it was called locally.

Barry said to the elevator, "Penthouse, please."

"Yes, Mr. Ten Eyck," it answered.

Evidently, when Mr. Cyril Vanderfeller traveled he not only left secretaries behind but full staffs of servants in his various houses and apartments. They were met in the luxurious entrada by a Vanderfeller butler.

Bat Hardin had never met the other, and had the faintest contempt, as a man of action and hard work all his life, for those who professionally toadied to others. Had he known it, the butler had a somewhat similar and equally invalid prejudice for those of Bat's background.

Barry Ten Eyck said, "Good morning, Jenson. I understand that Mr. Abernathy wanted to see us."

"Good morning, sir. That is correct. If you will just follow me," he said sadly in that tone which is the prerogative of butlers.

Barry knew the route. He had been along it before, but he followed the black-suited servant. Bat brought up the rear.

In front of the identity screen of the secretary's office, Jenson murmured, as though apologetically, and then turned back to them. "If you will just be seated for a moment, gentlemen." He motioned toward two uncomfortable chairs against the far wall, evidently antiques of the French eighteenth century. The French, Bat decided, might have been loaded on the aristocrat level, but they seemingly hadn't given a damn how uncomfortable sitting down turned out to be.

They sat.

Bat looked at his superior. "Great. Who is this character to keep us waiting out here? I don't know about you, but I've got work to do."

Barry said, "I've got work to do, too, Bat. This guy is the secretary of one of the members of the board of Vanderfeller and Moore, the cosmocorps we work for."

"Fine. But we don't work for Cyril Vanderfeller, member of the board or not. This is the day of Meritocracy. We work under Central Management of Vanderfeller and Moore, under men who are holding down their positions because they proved their ability and right to hold them down. What the hell? This Cyril Vanderfeller might be an idiot and still be a member of the board. All you need for that is a big enough chunk of inherited stock."

"All right, all right," Barry said. "However, the old rich ultimately control even a cosmocorps. It wouldn't do for aspiring young Meritcrats such as ourselves to irritate him."

The door opened eventually and they entered.

David Abernathy came to his feet, the suave upper-echelon office worker always. He touched his Byron revival cravat, to check out the tucks, as a woman unconsciously touches her hair, and advanced to shake their hands, warmly, but not *too* warmly and not too long.

He said, "Thanks for dropping by, Ten Eyck."

"Always nice to get together, Abernathy," Barry said. "I don't believe you've met Mr. Hardin, my Vice-Demecrat, currently sub-hitting as Security Chief of Shyler-deme. Bat, David."

Abernathy shook, very democratically. Bat had the feeling you got used to, the feeling even in this day and age when the old civil rights issues were supposedly long since solved, that the other was uncomfortable with darker complexioned people. He was inwardly amused, as always. He doubted that more than one-quarter of his ancestors had come from Africa. What was there about the ultra-ultra white? Suppose a great scientist, artist, inventor or other contributor to society turned up to be one-quarter, or one-eighth, for that matter, black. You'd think the whites would call him their own. Certainly not, he was a Negro, whatever his achievements, no matter how small the percentage of Negro blood.

What in the hell was there so great about being white? Most of the great breakthroughs made by the human race had been made by those of darker skins, always assuming that the invention of the wheel, domestication of animals, agriculture, the use of metals and even such later developments as gunpowder, the use of coal, the mariner's compass, were considered basic breakthroughs greater than the atomic bomb. The whites had come late indeed into the field of human progress and a great many of their contributions had been military. That's where they really excelled—as the rest of the world found out to its dismay. The so-called Nordics had been running around in animal skins and tearing their meat off half-cooked bones when there were high civilizations in Africa and Asia.

Not that Bat Hardin gave a damn.

Abernathy said, frowning slightly, "Where is your other assistant, Ten Eyck? I wanted to talk to all three of you."

Barry said, "Jim Cotswold? He's representing us at a convention in Denver. Won't be back for a week or so."

The secretary said, "Well, we'll have to hurry. The Mick Mansfield broadcast is about on. I'd like us to catch it . . . again."

Barry Ten Eyck's eyebrows went up slightly but in his usual good-humored way he took the chair the other indicated, as did Bat Hardin.

A screen on the wall lit up with the face of the self-styled Voice of Phoenecia, the local news broadcaster.

". . . Double, double, toil and trouble, folks," Mansfield was saying, belying the words with his happy expression. "I hate myself but we'll start out with a little nasty gossip. What Demecrat is feuding with his Vice-Demecrat, currently acting Security Chief? Naughty, naughty, boys. Didn't your mothers ever teach you to love one another?" He pursed his plump lips, in mock thought. "However, I do suppose that our Demecrat has fairly good cause to suppose his Security Chief isn't doing the best work in the world . . ."

Barry Ten Eyck looked at his associate in surprise. "What the dickens, Bat?"

"What the hell, is better!"

Abernathy said, impatiently, "Listen, gentlemen."

The broadcaster said, "But now to one of these items that have been coming so often from Shyler-deme these days. It seems as though there has developed a regular phobia against the escapists. Evidently, anti-escapist residents have been chalking up signs on their apartment doors running everywhere from snide remarks to obscenities, and demanding that they leave the deme." Mick Mansfield grunted, as though in easy contempt. "Why do all these things come up in Shyler-deme? The rest of Phoenecia is so tranquil. Perhaps Mayor Levy should check into matters, with the possibility of recommendations to Vanderfeller and Moore on changes in deme management . . . Well, here's a more cheerful item, folks, but hardly from Shyler-deme. It looks as though one of the big marriages of the season is to take place in that happy, happy Lincoln-deme, and . . ."

David Abernathy flicked a switch and deactivated the screen. He said, his voice level, "I had not been aware of the fact that you two were feuding."

"Neither had I," Barry said. "Bat?"

"Feuding about what?" Bat growled.

The secretary dropped it. He said, instead. "What's all this about the escapists? I didn't know, Ten Eyck, that you made a special refuge for escapists in Shyler-deme. I—and Mr. Vanderfeller, of course—have always thought of them as rather far-out types. Almost like weirds."

Barry took a breath. "Look, Abernathy, escapists we are probably going to have with us for some time in this society we've developed in the past half century. As far as being tenants are concerned, they're good tenants. In fact, downright perfect. You never see them, but they spend just as much as anyone else in our ultra-markets and through the public kitchens. They're like hermits. They're a product of our age. The handle hung on them is well taken. They're escapists. They're withdrawing from our society. They hole up in their apartments and stay there, seldom emerging, usually living on Negative Income Tax. An apartment in a deme today makes a better retreat than any cave a hermit ever dreamed of. Your food, clothing, shelter, entertainment and everything else needed to exist—and in comfort—is readily available. The apartments are, of course, even self-cleaning. Once in a coon's age you need somebody from Maintenance Division to come in and repair something, but otherwise you need see no one. A lot of escapists are singles, either men or women, but some are couples, married or not. Very seldom do they have children, but sometimes."

"They are unnatural," Abernathy said indignantly.

"Sure. Neurotics, of course. But so are most of us, though possibly in different directions than they take. But they hurt no one. They spend their whole lives in their apartments, practically never coming out to any of the public rooms. Some are, admittedly, drunks; we get that information through the computers that handle their expenditures. Some, I imagine, are on more serious escapes from reality, such as this new euphoric, trank. However, some are students, even scholars. They keep their TV library boosters going ten or twelve or more hours a day. Some are just plain escapist hedonists. They eat as well as their income will allow, drink as well, and watch Tri-Di practically all day long. But the thing is, escapists don't *bother* anyone, which is a damn sight more than I can say for the type person who'd go to the trouble of chalking dirty remarks on their doors."

Abernathy said impatiently, "I can see the objection to them. They are outsiders, outcasts, non-conformists, malcontents, freaks. How can a decent citizen not worry about what's going on behind their closed doors? What are they doing inside there? Why don't they ever come forth and let their neighbors get to know them?"

Bat said sourly, "Maybe they don't want to know their neighbors. Maybe they've got a fairly good idea of what they're like."

"Please, Hardin, there is no call for levity. How would you like to be parents, with, say, a ten-year-old child, not knowing when these neurotics might issue forth with any sort of crime in mind?"

"If I were a parent with worries like that I'd go see a psychiatrist. An escapist is no more likely to bother young children than the next man. In fact, less so. He doesn't *want* to leave his apartment, to chase children or anything else." Bat's tone was impatient.

Barry Ten Eyck tried to head it off before the pompous secretary was antagonized. He said, "Surely, Abernathy, you didn't have us up here to discuss escapists. Particularly when there's nothing we can do about them even if we wished."

Abernathy took up a sheaf of papers, but he wanted his last word. "You could do something about them before they ever moved into a Shyler-deme apartment. You could refuse to admit them."

Barry said patiently, "How would I know a couple were escapists until after they had moved in? They look like anybody else."

Abernathy dropped it, put the sheaf of papers back down again and hit it with the back of his hand. "Mr. Vanderfeller instructed me to keep an eye on Shyler-deme's affairs while he was away."

Barry could have protested that. It was as Bat had said earlier. He, as Demecrat of the building, worked directly under Central Management of Vanderfeller and Moore. Cyril Vanderfeller was only one of the board, upon which sat various other Vanderfellers, for that matter. But Cyril Vanderfeller as an individual had nothing immediate to do with the affairs of Shyler-deme and most certainly one of his secretaries didn't. However, Barry kept his peace.

Abernathy said, "I must say, things seem to have become chaotic under your management, Ten Eyck."

Barry said evenly, "We have almost full occupancy

now, Abernathy. I've only been here two years, but during that time we've never dropped below our breakeven point and usually we show a good profit."

"A deme can drop from full occupancy to half, or less, in a matter of weeks given riots, an onslaught of such types as weirds, subversives, escapists and prostitutes, bickering between top deme officials, and above all such deterioration of staff morals that all-out pilfering becomes the rule of the day."

Barry Ten Eyck shook his head ruefully. "I'm doing the best that I can, and Mr. Hardin, here, is a good man. I'm sure he'll crack the thefts of the supplies down in the Restaurant and Liquor Divisions. The other matters are minor and will be handled as routine."

The secretary leaned back in his chair and said soothingly, "Ten Eyck, have you considered resigning?"

"Resigning?" Barry Ten Eyck could have been slapped in the face. "No. Of course not. I've worked too hard for this job to give it up."

The other nodded, as though sympathetically. "Don't misunderstand, Ten Eyck, I didn't mean for you to resign from your position as a Democrat for Vanderfeller and Moore, but simply from this position in Shyler-deme. Admittedly much, probably most, of the difficulty here is simply bad luck. Perhaps a fresh start both for you and for Shyler-deme would be the best idea. I am sure that if I made a recommendation to that effect to Central Management, with the backing of Mr. Vanderfeller, of course, such a transfer would take place."

"Who'd replace me?" Barry demanded.

David Abernathy looked at Bat. "As you say, Hardin, here, is a good man. In a surprisingly short period of time he has risen to Vice-Democrat of a deme. Under Meritocracy, promotion can be fast."

But Bat was shaking his head. "I'm an older man than Mr. Ten Eyck, but I have neither the schooling nor the experience in the field that he has. Don't think

70

I don't appreciate the offer and that I'm not ambitious. Sure, I could possibly do it, more or less. In a year or so I'd be glad to take you up. But I'm not a fool. Mr. Ten Eyck is a better man for the job than I am. If he can't handle it, I don't see why I could expect to."

"Indeed." Abernathy shrugged his shoulders superciliously. "You don't seem to be quite as ambitious as you say. However, I suggest that both of you think it over. A fresh start for Ten Eyck, a promotion for Hardin. Good morning, gentlemen."

On the way down in the elevator Barry said unhappily, "Thanks, Bat. I wouldn't like to resign under fire."

"Of course not. Particularly this kind of fire."

"How do you mean?"

"I mean something stinks. Listen, as you go through life, from time to time things that are seemingly impossible happen to you. Maybe once every few years something comes up for which there simply is no rational explanation. Something freak. Maybe you figure out a rational explanation later, maybe you don't. But the thing is that impossible occurrences don't come bang, bang, bang, right in a row. But that's what's happening now. There're too many of these screwball, ridiculous things going on for there not to be some good reason. And I'm going to find out what it is."

Barry grunted. "Maybe you're right. And how do you start?"

"First of all by going over to see that Mick Mansfield."

Barry Ten Eyck got off on the floor that housed the administration offices but Bat continued down to the lower levels and to the Transport Station of the deme. Here he dialed a two-seater electro-steamer. When it slipped up to the curb where he stood, he entered it and dialed the Administration complex of Phoenecia. It was located in the pseudo-city's Common, along with such other community buildings as the arena, the museum, the specialized stores which carried items not usually available in the ultra-markets which each deme boasted, such as antiques and the Swap Shop. The Common also boasted a golf course and race track.

He stuck his pocket phone cum credit card into the car's slot for payment and relaxed back into the cushions when it slipped into traffic. Since his destination was within the limits of Phoenecia, he remained in the automated, underground network of roads.

He came to a halt, shortly, in the terminal beneath the Administration buildings and left his small car which headed immediately for the car pool to park itself until summoned again.

Bat Hardin made his way through the maze of the building's halls on a one-man floater, until he reached his destination, the studios of Phoenecia's local news organization. It was a small outfit, quite a bit of the work done voluntarily by housewives with time on their hands, or unemployed men on NIT; a community affair. So far as Bat knew, there were only two full-time employees on the pseudo-city's payroll, Mick Mansfield and a technician.

The news broadcaster enjoyed a small office of his own. Bat stood before the door's identity screen and said, "Bat Hardin, Security Chief of Shyler-deme, to see Mr. Mansfield."

The screen said, "Mr. Mansfield is not in."

Bat said, "Where could I locate him?"

"Mr. Mansfield did not leave a message."

At this time of day? There was a small bench down the hall a bit. Bat went over and sat down and thought about it.

He took out his pocket phone and said, "Phoenecia Security, please." And then, "Security Chief Bat Hardin. Please give me the I.D. number of Mick Mansfield." When he got it, he said, "Phoenecia Security, Bat Hardin here. Please give me a cross on the pocket phone of I.D. 5M-232-8116."

A robot voice said, "Office 237, Administration Building of Phoenecia."

"That's what I thought," Bat growled.

He returned to the office which sported Mick Mansfield's name on the door. It also sported a number, 237.

Bat stood before the identity screen and said, "Bat Hardin, to see Mr. Mansfield."

The screen said, "Mr. Mansfield is not in."

Bat Hardin stood back a bit and threw his full weight into a kick. The door's lock splintered. He pushed with the flat of his hand and the door swung open. Bat Hardin passed on through, nodded at the room's one occupant, and looked down at the wreckage.

"Termites," he said, nodding again.

The room's occupant, who was obviously Mick Mansfield, the Voice of Phoenecia, came half to his feet and bleated, "You can't do that!"

Bat Hardin turned to him as though surprised. "Why not, you sonofabitch?" There was no rancor in his tone, merely question.

"I'll . . . I'll have you arrested."

"Oh? By whom? One of my friends, such as Chief Ben Snider? Possibly by one of my other friends, the Chief of Security of Victory-deme, or Hilton-deme, or Lincoln-deme? I'm sure they've been listening to your recent broadcasts and are indignant against me, ready to lynch me because of your unprejudiced news reporting."

Mick Mansfield was not a small man. In fact, he was probably a good forty pounds heavier than his visitor; however, the full forty was gathered about his waist and buttocks and there was an additional five in his jowls. He sank back into his chair.

"I demand an explanation for this cavalier intrusion into my office!" he rasped.

Bat chuckled. "I'm beginning to like you, Mick," he said. "The way you said that. Beautiful. I wish I could say things that way. Like, 'I demand an explanation of the cavalier manner in which you have been, uh, defaming me in your broadcasts.' "

"What are you talking about?"

"You know what I'm talking about, you sonofabitch. Now what's it all about?"

The other was indignant. "Mr. Hardin! I have never met you before. How could I possibly have anything against you personally? I report the news. I can't please everybody."

Bat said, "Okay. Where do you get this news? All this crud you've been running down Shyler-deme with?"

"Like every ethical newsman, I protect my sources."

"Great. I don't ask for individual names. What are your sources?"

"Why, all the good citizens of Phoenecia. I receive a hundred calls a day giving me news items. Everything ranging from a birth—to a suspiciously unsolved crime running into many thousands of dollars in the Shyler-deme service complex."

Bat stared at him. He said finally, "Okay. And now that snide crack about there being bad blood between Demecrat Ten Eyck and myself."

"I mentioned no names."

"You didn't have to, you sonofabitch."

"I don't have to take that from you, Hardin."

"That's what you think. That is, unless you'd rather have a bust in the snoot."

"You're threatening me!"

Bat had to laugh. "That I am, Mansfield. I'll take the fact that you're a newsman and that news is news. Also the fact that you have to protect your sources. However, I am not particularly fond of the way you escalate a little gang fight between kids into a riot, and such items. So I'll tell you this. You claim to have nothing against me, since you've never even met me before. Okay. But if I ever find out that you do have some motive behind all this, besides just reporting the so-called news, I'm going to come back over here, kick the door in again and give you that bust in the snoot."

He turned and strode from the room.

Mick Mansfield bleated after him, "You can't . . ."

He had managed to cool down, on the surface at least, by the time he reached Apartment 32 on the thirtieth floor of Tower-One in Shyler-deme.

He stood before the identity screen and said, "Security Chief Bat Hardin, calling on Miss Mable Dunnigan."

The screen said, "What'd'ya want?"

Bat said patiently, "To talk to you, Miss."

"I'm busy."

Bat said patiently, "Listen, Miss, obviously if I want to talk to you, sooner or later we'll talk. I'm not trying to give you a hard time."

There was a silence. Finally, the door opened.

Bat went on through and stood a few feet inside the door. Sometimes, even in this day, you'd run into types, especially women who had spent their early youth in one of the more backward sections of the South, that had all sorts of crackpot prejudices under the surface.

But seemingly Mabel Dunnigan wasn't of that breed. She was seated in a comfort chair in room's center, parked before the Tri-Di set which she had evidently turned off upon his arrival. She had an outsized glass of a nauseating pinkish color in her right hand. She made a vague gesture with it, a half invitation.

"Okay, you're part way in, come all the way. Put it down somewhere and tell me why you're roaching me this time of day. Want a drink?"

"No, thanks." Bat left the door open behind him and found himself a seat on the edge of the couch which undoubtedly doubled as a bed at night. It was a mini-apartment, indicating that she probably lived on Negative Income Tax. He fished the petition from an inner pocket and handed it over to her wordlessly.

"What in the hell is this?" she said. She was a half-pretty girl, probably in her early twenties. Half-pretty, because she was already going to pot. She must have been beautiful in her mid-teens, or possibly even her late ones. Dirty blonde, but her hair was soft and full; a beautiful neck, now getting a bit fat; a lush figure, too lush. In a few years she would be a slob. A generous mouth, startling blue eyes, a small, tilted nose. She truly must have been a beauty in her teens.

She read the petition including, evidently, every one of the names. Then she blurted again, "What in the hell is this?"

"You've read it," Bat said reasonably.

"Why these, these . . ."

"Fellow citizens of Shyler-deme?" Bat offered gently.

"Why, I could sue them."

"Who?" Bat asked. "As you'll notice, whoever circulated that petition didn't go to the trouble of indicating who they are. Are you going to sue everybody that signed it?"

"But . . . hell, I don't know a single one of these people."

"They seem to know you."

"Fallen woman. Why, that means they're calling me a whore."

"That's right," Bat agreed. "I looked it up, Miss Dunnigan. It's against the law to solicit in a deme. The law's rather vaguely worded, possibly because it's so difficult a way of making a living these days."

"Make a living? Are you nuts? Even if I wanted to, how could you make a living hustling these days?"

"That's what I wondered," Bat said, truly interested. "How could the—isn't *Johns* the word?—pay off in this checkless-cashless world of ours?"

She stared at him, half in indignation, half in complete candor.

"Look," she said, indicating the petition which she had thrown to a coffee table. "That's a lot of crud. I live on Negative Income Tax. Maybe I'm lazy or something, but, anyway, I don't ever seem to be able to locate a job. NIT is a pretty slim way of making out. So I got a few boy friends, from time to time. None of these married men, or sons of these old biddies, or anything like that. I got perfectly usual boy friends. I don't solicit them, like it says there. I meet them in the deme bars or nightclubs, or at the community dances, or one

76

of the swimming pools. Just ordinary single guys, looking for the same thing as me. A good time. Okay. We have dates. Sometimes, I admit, I put out a little, if I like him special. Okay. When I do, maybe he slips me a present from time to time."

"Such as what?" Bat said, still intrigued.

"Like this," she fingered a cheap necklace which was around her neck. "Pretty, huh? Those little ones are real opals. Sometimes they buy me a dress. Sometimes they spring for a meal in one of the nice restaurants, like the Chinese one. I'm a sucker for chow mein. Sometimes we go out on a binge, maybe to the Swank Room. If you're living on NIT, you can't have much of that life on your own. Okay, so I have dates."

Bat thought about it. In actuality, he had nothing against the girl, either personally or in his capacity as the deme's Chief of Security. It was an age in which there were few observed rules against promiscuity. In fact, marriage was rapidly becoming an anachronism. The original reasons for the institution were rapidly disappearing in the world of People's Capitalism, the Ultra-Welfare State, Meritocracy; call it what you will.

He stood, picking up the petition. He said, with a sigh, "Miss Dunnigan, it must not be pleasant to see something like this. I suggest that you be a little more, uh, discreet, with your boy friends."

She stood too as he started for the door. Her eyes ran up and down his muscular figure. Bat Hardin made a point of keeping himself in good trim, a habit dropping away from a good many in his generation.

She said, hesitantly, "Sure you wouldn't like a little drinky? You could have been nastier, Mr. . . . ."

"Hardin," Bat said, shaking his head. "Thanks just the same, Miss Dunnigan."

On his way down to the street level, his pocket phone buzzed. He took it out and said, "Bat Hardin."

Ruth Wheeler's face faded in. She said, "Bat, I've just had a call from Mr. Wonder in Transportation." Her voice sounded strange.

"Yes?"

"He reports a shortage in his lubrication supplies. Oil."

"Oh? What kind of shortage?"

"He says approximately five thousand, five hundred liters."

Bat Hardin held his breath for a long moment of silence, even as he stared into her face. Finally, he said, "Five thousand, five hundred liters. You mean twenty-five barrels?"

"Why . . . why, I suppose so. He said five thousand, five hundred liters."

Bat said, "All right. Thanks, Miss Wheeler."

She said, "Oh, Mr. Hardin. The rumors are going around about your power struggle with Mr. Ten Eyck."

"Power struggle!"

"They say you're going to take over his job, but he's fighting hard to stay in. You watch yourself . . . Bat. That's a man who likes his job and might do just about anything to keep it."

"That will be all of that sort of talk, Miss Wheeler. And I suggest you not add to any already difficult situation by passing the rumors on."

"Why . . . why, yes, sir. I just wanted to wish you luck. I'm behind you . . . Bat."

Bat Hardin checked out the location of William Locke's apartment. It was in Tower-Two on the sixtieth floor. Shortly, he stood before the door's identity screen. According to the information in the computer data banks, Locke worked a night shift and should be in at this time of day.

Bat said, "Chief of Security, Bat Hardin, calling on Mr. Locke."

The door opened.

Locke had evidently been reading on his TV phone-library booster, but had come to his feet at his visitor's entrance. He said, "Come in, Mr. Hardin. Have a chair."

He had been smoking a pipe, which mildly surprised

Bat. Over the past few decades the anti-tobacco propaganda had proven almost universally effective. That and the fact that Central Production Planning had tabooed the use of prime land for growing the weed had just about finished off the habit. Locke must have to buy imported tobaccos to indulge himself. He put the pipe down into an ashtray and looked at the Security Chief quizzically.

The apartment was a twin of Bat Hardin's, indicating that William Locke had better income than the usual unemployed living on their NIT.

Bat silently handed over the petition which had branded Locke a subversive and sat down in a straight chair, crossing his legs. He remained quiet while the other read.

Finally, Locke looked up and chuckled.

He reminded Bat of Barry Ten Eyck. About the same age, say late twenties, tall, lanky, seemingly good-natured. His face had a boyish quality. You wouldn't have picked him out as a rough and ready radical.

Bat said, "You don't seem particularly upset at being called a subversive."

"Why should I be? I am."

Bat took a nibble on his lower lip. He said, "I guess you'd better elaborate on that."

The other laughed shortly again and resumed his chair. "Think over your definition. To subvert means to overthrow established institutions or principles. There's nothing in the Revised Constitution to condemn subversion, even as amended in the patch-quilt manner in which it has been since our idealistic revolutionists first wrote it. For that matter, every time an election takes place the major party out of power tries to subvert the party in power, by definition."

"You're a member of the Futurist Party?" Bat said, unimpressed.

"Proud to be."

"Mind telling me what the Futurists stand for?"

"Changing present institutions of this country ... legally."

"Most people in this country think that they've never had it so good. Most people like the institutions we have, Locke."

"Then most people are wrong. The fact that most people think something is true doesn't make it so. The fact of the matter is that under Meritocracy our culture is falling apart."

"Go on."

"It's a socio-economic system of waste, a continuation in another form of the system that preceded it. Classical capitalism collapsed back in 1929 and it took the Second World War to pull it out of the doldrums. But when the war ended, it was no longer classical capitalism. It became, I suppose you could call it, state capitalism. The government had taken over the responsibility of keeping the economy going and that meant huge expenditures: wars, defense—so called—space projects. Billions of dollars were flushed down the drain, wasted. But eventually these no longer filled the bill. For one thing, given the complete balance of terror that existed from about 1950 on, sooner or later a spark would have flown. And the thing about war then was that everybody was to die, the billionaire as well as the slum dweller, the presidents and the kings, the senators and the prime ministers. Obviously, something besides defense had to be found on which to waste our labors and our earth's raw materials."

"Ummmm," Bat said. "The construction of the pseudo-cities."

"Largely that, and with them the laser-cut underground roads. In the past the demographers warned that by the year 2000 the population of the country would be three hundred million and we would be impossibly crowded. Nonsense. At the time, such countries as the Netherlands had a population of over three thousand inhabitants per square mile of arable land, and the United States only two hundred and fifty. Obviously there was plenty of room. The answer they came up with after the debacle of the cities which really started becoming obvious in the late sixties, was the institution of Negative Income Tax, and the guaranteeing of an apartment, house or mobile home to every citizen, financed by the Federal government. The demes, the unit of the pseudo-city, were the result. Fifteen thousand high-rise demes, scattered widely throughout the country, were sufficient to house our whole population, nor need they be clustered together in the horrible slum-cities of the past."

"So far," Bat said mildly, "you're making a pretty good case for Meritocracy. It still looks as though we've never had it so good."

"Yes, so far," Locke nodded. "The thing is that it costs anywhere from one to two hundred million pseudo-dollars to build a deme. The big corporations such as Vanderfeller and Moore put in their bids to the government which ponies up the amount, when and if they can give evidence that a deme is needed. After the deme is finished and the apartments sold, the corporation handles the operation. The residents inevitably spend almost all of their income in the deme itself, there is no need to go elsewhere, the unit is self-sufficient. The average apartment in a deme expends at least one hundred pseudo-dollars per week, not counting maintenance at about a hundred a month. That comes to half a million a week, or twenty-six million a year, probably a quarter of which is profit.

"But the thing is, Mr. Hardin, that the operating of a deme is not where the big profit resides. It is in the construction that one sees the big money. Two hundred million pseudo-dollars. Why, I imagine that right off the top, before construction ever begins, ten per cent is milked off in the way of graft. But even if it wasn't, can you imagine how much profit a cosmocorps such as Vanderfeller and Moore can make when they control, in one part of the world or the other, all the materials they need to build a deme?"

"They aren't exactly going broke," Bat said dryly.

"They aren't, indeed. The Federal government has

spent literally trillions to finance the building of the demes. For all practical purposes our economy has been kept going by it." William Locke stopped for a moment.

"So?" Bat said, slightly impatient of the long lecture. "You called it an economy of waste. So far it doesn't sound so wasteful to me. We've built reasonably good housing for our whole people."

"That's the point, Mr. Hardin. The demes have been built. They are completed."

Bat looked at him, beginning to catch the drift.

Locke said, "What do we do now to keep the economy going? What takes the place of the construction boom? Do we go back to a war-defense-space boondoggling program?"

Bat Hardin bit his under lip and shook his head. "No. Obviously, that's ridiculous."

"Yes. But I'll tell you where we do go. Back to ridiculous waste. A cosmocorps controlling a deme which can prove that the building is unsafe, substandard, antiquated due to new developments, or, for whatever other reason, no longer satisfactory, can petition the government to either completely renovate it, or tear it down and build a new one on the site. Needless to say, there is a lot of graft connected with this. There's no reason in the world why a deme shouldn't last at least fifty years—the Empire State Building did."

Bat Hardin was beginning to frown.

"But today," Locke pursued, "we're seeing buildings no more than ten years old being torn down, so that new construction can go up. The construction cosmocorps pull every trick they can dream up. They spread propaganda to make the average citizen want to live somewhere else: on the seashore, in the deserts, in the mountains, in the tropics. They want residents to move. If they can prove that a deme has fallen off to less than half occupancy, for whatever reasons, they have a strong lever to urge scrapping of the building and construction of a new one.

"There is your waste, Hardin, and that's our basic

complaint about our present socio-economic system. More than half the people are living at a much lower standard than they could enjoy if present national policy wasn't based on maintaining the status-quo and waste."

Bat Hardin stood up. "Okay," he said. "I suppose there's more, but not today. I've got other things on my hands. If your program is legal, there's no reason I can see why you shouldn't advocate any changes you like."

William Locke seemed slightly miffed. "I was about to tell you . . ."

Bat laughed in deprecation. "You're quite an agitator, Locke, but some other time." He headed for the entrance.

Outside his office door, he hesitated, thought about it a moment, then reversed his engines and entered the offices of Barry Ten Eyck. Barry wasn't there, however Carol Ann Cusack was. She was busy, but Bat said, "Mrs. Cusack, could you check something for me?"

She looked up. "I suppose so, big boy. Why don't you go on a diet?"

"Huh! I'm a svelte one hundred and ninety."

"You're one hundred and ninety, true, but you ain't svelte by a long shot. What did you want?"

"I hate critics. But a list of the staff members in each Division who have been transferred here from other Vanderfeller and Moore demes within the past month, and from where they were transferred."

"Why in the devil can't your own secretary do that?"

"Will you or won't you?"

"Oh, all right, darn it. Sit down. It won't take long."

He sat and waited it out. Finally she handed him the list, scowling her own puzzlement and evidently beginning to get a glimmering of his motivation.

Barry Ten Eyck came hurrying in, excitement in his face. "Bat!" he exclaimed. "I've just been down in Restaurant Division. Did you know that when the olive oil was being unloaded, the TV spy lens in that compartment was inoperative?"

Bat was taken aback. "Inoperative? That's impossible. I would have known about it. The only place it could have been inactivated would be . . ."

"From the Security Division offices."

Bat stared at him. And Barry stared back.

Bat said slowly, "You know something, Barry, that oil was never delivered."

Jensen, the butler, met them in the entrada of the penthouse.

Barry Ten Eyck said, "We'd like to see Mr. Abernathy, Jensen."

"Right this way, sir," Jensen said sadly. "I'm sure Mr. Abernathy will be glad to receive you."

"He'll receive us, all right," Bat growled.

They trailed the servant to Abernathy's office and waited while he went through the ceremony of addressing the door's identity screen.

The butler turned and said, "If you gentlemen will be seated."

However, Barry Ten Eyck wasn't having any. He stood before the screen and said, "It's immediate, Abernathy. We haven't the time to be impressed by sitting around waiting while you supposedly are at more important matters. Open up."

The door opened and Barry Ten Eyck and Bat Hardin entered. Abernathy was at his desk and didn't stand this time.

"I must say, Ten Eyck . . ." he began, in a huff.

"Don't bother. I told you it was important," Barry said.

He and Bat both found chairs and for a moment the two deme officials looked speculatively at the private secretary.

"Well, what is so pressingly important that it was necessary to intrude upon my time?" he demanded.

Barry said evenly, "Mr. Hardin and I have spent the past two hours discussing the series of crises that have been demoralizing Shyler-deme. We've been putting odds and ends of details together and we've come up with the obvious answer."

"It would seem to me that the obvious answer would be your resignation, Ten Eyck."

"To be replaced by somebody with less experience who could be depended upon to help the deme fall apart, eh?" Bat growled.

The secretary looked at him. "And what does that mean?"

"I'll take it, Bat," Barry Ten Eyck said. "It means that all these things that have accumulated in the past couple of weeks have one end in view, the disruption of Shyler-deme to the point where its residents will finally become so upset, so disgusted, that they'll move out like rats deserting the sinking ship."

"You don't make any sense at all, Ten Eyck!" the other snapped.

Barry ignored him and went on. "We'll skip the minor matters, the petitions, the broadcasts from your toady, Mansfield, the attempts to cause dissension between members of the deme staff, such as Mr. Hardin and myself. We'll concentrate on the deliberate sabotage. The thefts of olive oil, rum and lubricants.

"It could only be done by having persons in Transportation, Delivery, and in each of the Divisions involved, Restaurant, Liquor and, but we've already named Transportation. And there had to be one more plant, someone in Security."

"Ridiculous. What do you mean by plants?"

"Going on intuition, largely, Mr. Hardin checked out the recent changes in staff and came up with the fact that Salad Chef Terwilliger was one of these. So was Pearson from Delivery, and Smith in Transportation, Traffic Control section, and Davidson, one of Harry Mackley's bartenders, the one, by the way, in charge of rum drinks. And, surprise, surprise, Miss Ruth Wheeler, Bat's ever-loving secretary."

"Ha!" Bat grunted.

"What are you intimating?" Abernathy demanded.

"Come off it," Barry said in disgust. "None of those

twenty-five barrel requisitions were ever delivered. Always twenty-five, by the way, just to make the whole thing more impossibly confusing. They never left Central Warehouses. The lorries supposedly carrying them did, but not the alleged contents. It was all part of the scheme to disrupt us here, to foul up our operations. To get key men fired, or to resign. How high this whole thing goes in Vanderfeller and Moore upper echelons at Central Management, I don't know, and I doubt if I'll ever learn. I have no way of finding out."

Bat put in, "All five of these—saboteurs, Barry called them—were transferred from Warren-deme, in the Catskills. It seems that Warren-deme was condemned about a month ago and is slated to be torn down. Vanderfeller and Moore have a government contract to build a new ultra-deme on the same spot, one of the super-highrise deals, very expensive."

Barry said, "We're just guessing, but the obvious indication is that our five friends, including Miss Wheeler, are shipped from deme to deme, with orders to louse up the administration of them to the point where the buildings can be condemned."

"You're insane," Abernathy snapped. "This will mean your jobs, you realize."

Barry shook his head. "No, it won't, David, old man. As I say, I doubt if we'll ever find out how high this whole scheme goes. But there're a lot of people who profit by seeing new construction by Vanderfeller and Moore. Not just the very high mucky-mucks but Meritcrats all the way down the line. We're going to make some demands, Abernathy. If they're not met, then the tape that Hardin and I have cut revealing the whole scheme will go to every source we can think of where it might be effective. The press, the government, the top officials of Vanderfeller and Moore, so forth and so on."

"What are these demands?" Some of the surface indignation was falling by the wayside.

"First the resignations of all five of the saboteurs and also of Kennedy at Central Warehouses who is evidently one of their operators there. Reason for dismissal, and this to be registered on their National Data Banks dossiers, theft. Next, a signed statement by you confessing the whole scheme and that you supervised it. Next, your own resignation."

"I'd be mad to sign such a thing."

"You'll be madder if you don't," Bat Hardin growled. "This way you at least avoid criminal prosecution. Do you think for a moment that once we start bringing in police authorities on this—Federal police—that at least one of these clowns won't blow the whistle on you in hopes of getting off himself as a State witness? Ultimately, this is a Federal thing, Abernathy, and there must be a dozen senators who would love to broadcast it, some of those senators on an economy kick."

Barry Ten Eyck stood and looked down at the now shrunken private secretary. "I don't know who all is in this, Abernathy, possibly it goes as high as people like Cyril Vanderfeller himself. But I do know that from now on *you're* out of it. I'll be down in my office for the next hour. Have that confession ready. Have those people's resignations in my hands before the end of that time."

He turned to his Vice-Demecrat. "Coming, Bat?"

Bat Hardin had also risen, but now he looked at the knuckles of his right fist, reflectively.

He said, "Yeah, but not to your office. I've got a little appointment. To give somebody a bust in the snoot."

Part Three
James Cotswold

James Cotswold, 2nd Vice-Demecrat of Shyler-deme, looked up when Carol Ann Cusack entered the Administration offices. As always, she was a pleasure to behold. What did they call her type of beauty—Black Irish? Her hair was so jet as to be suspect, her eyes the darkest of blues and her well carried figure was tall but neither thin nor overly lush.

As on a score of times before, Jim Cotswold inwardly sighed. He was a bachelor but not necessarily from choice. He had just never found her—his Carol Ann Cusack. They always seemed to be already appropriated. For his money, her husband was a clown, but it wasn't his money that was involved, it was Carol Ann's.

She flicked an impersonal smile at him on the way to the inner office of Demecrat Barry Ten Eyck and said, "Morning, Mr. Cotswold."

He said, "Top of it back to you, Carol Ann. Ah, Barry isn't in."

She stopped. "Oh? What kind of an example is our lord and master setting us?"

Jim leaned back in his chair a little. "As a matter of fact, evidently a good one. He and Bat Hardin are already up and around bird-dogging the place in a patrol car. Just checking around the playgrounds, ball parks, picnic grounds and so forth. Routine. Barry says that if anything immediate comes up you can turn it over to me."

"Wizard," she said, and disappeared into the sanctum sanctorum of the Demecrat.

Jim Cotswold went back to his work. He was a man in his early forties, in good shape due to his interest in sports of the hunting, fishing, hiking, mountain-climbing variety. Angular of face, stocky of build, he failed to give the impression of aggressive ambition. However, under Meritocracy one did not achieve even the rank of 2nd Vice-Demecrat without an impressive I.Q., at least a slightly better than average education and efficiency on the job. Jim Cotswold, in view of his outside interests, might never climb to the rarified heights in his chosen field, but he would do all right for himself.

When Carol Ann re-entered he looked up again and said, "Something?"

She was frowning slightly. "I suppose this would come under the head of Security, and Mr. Hardin isn't here."

He said, "What is it? We can get Bat on the TV phone, if necessary."

She said, "Yes, well, we've just had a . . . well, I suppose you'd call it a complaint from the resident in Apartment 231 on the twenty-third floor of Tower-One. She reports no sounds of activity in the adjoining apartment, Number 233, for the past ten days."

Cotswold said sourly. "What does she do, spend her time with her ear glued to the wall? These apartments are supposedly sound-proofed."

Carol Ann sighed. "She claims that the tenant in Apartment 233, a Fredrick Green, is an escapist and she's been keeping her eye on him."

"How can you keep an eye on an escapist?" Jim Cotswold said. "They're hermits. Never emerge from their apartments except in emergency."

"Well, you know the bad blood between some of the ordinary tenants and the escapists. Some people just can't bear the thought of non-conformists in their midst. They know nothing about the escapist but they jitter over the fact that such exist—and hate them."

"Okay, okay," Cotswold said. "We could wait till Bat got back and then let him exercise his Priority Two as Security Chief to utilize the micro-spy lenses in the apartment and check it out. But we can do some preliminary investigating."

He turned to one of his desk phone screens and said into it, "Give me a report from the deme data banks on the deliveries that have been made to Fredrick Green, Apartment 233, Tower-One in the past ten days."

The robot voice from the phone screen said, "There have been no deliveries made to Apartment 233, Tower-One, in the past ten days."

"Oh, oh," Jim said. He said into the screen, "Give me a report on the number of drinks ordered on the auto-bar of Apartment 233, Tower-One during the past ten days."

The answer was the same.

"Oh, oh," Jim repeated. He said into the screen, "A report on the number of meals served from Restaurant Division through the auto-table in Apartment 233, Tower-One in the past ten days."

The answer was still the same. Jim Cotswold looked up at Carol Ann. "I don't know if this comes under the jurisdiction of Doc McCoy of the deme hospital, or Bat Hardin of Security. Unless, of course, the tenant is on vacation or something."

"Escapists don't go on vacation," Carol Ann said.

Jim Cotswold came to his feet. "I think I'll go on up there and check."

But at that moment Harry Mackley, Head Bartender of the Liquor Division, came in, his usually good-natured face—bartender style—in a vague scowl. He ran a hand through his sparse hair, as though not knowing whether or not to bring his matter up.

He said to Carol Ann, "Mr. Ten Eyck here?"

"He's making a tour of the parks with Mr. Hardin, Mr. Mackley."

Jim Cotswold said, "He left me in charge of the spread, Harry. What's up?"

Harry Mackley said, his voice puzzled, "Well, nothing, really. But something funny happened last night and I've been thinking about it ever since."

Jim looked at him, waiting.

Mackley said, unhappily, "Somebody ordered a case of Scotch."

Jim said, "Scotch? How do you mean, Scotch?"

"Scotch. Scotch whiskey."

"Don't be silly, there is no such thing as a whole case of Scotch whiskey."

Mackley shrugged.

"Look," Jim Cotswold said. "In this country, it's illegal to use grains, or even grapes, to manufacture alcoholic beverages—the land's too valuable. In Common Europe, yes. But Scotch? I haven't had a drink of Scotch in the past ten years, and then it was doled out to me in eye-dropper amounts."

"A case of Scotch," Harry Mackley said definitely.

"I didn't even know we stocked the stuff."

Mackley said, "We stock it in small quantities. The big wigs, up on the high levels, want it sometimes. It's sort of on the ostentatious side these days and most of the old rich and the top Meritcrats make a policy of avoiding living too ostentatiously, but they like to keep a bottle or two on hand for special occasions even though the stuff is worth its weight in platinum. But this is the first time I ever had a whole case ordered. Johnny Walker Black Label, at that."

"What's Johnny Walker, whatever you said?" Carol Ann said.

Mackley made the gesture of circle with thumb and second finger which indicated the superlative and said, "You wouldn't know, but it's a whiskey that's like a liqueur. I'm Head Bartender but even I never steal it. It's like ambrosia. It's . . ."

"Okay, okay," Jim said. "So what's the big deal? Some bigwig, fanny deep in psuedo-dollars, ordered up a case of Scotch, the best, so what?"

"So it wasn't a bigwig," Mackley said, the puzzlement in his voice again.

Carol Ann and Jim Cotswold looked at him.

He said, "The order came from a mini-apartment, down on the fourteenth level. The sort of place that usually orders sea-booze—when they can afford sea-booze."

"Oh, come on," Jim Cotswold said in disgust. "The type resident that has a mini-apartment is almost always on Negative Income Tax. Sure, they're usually a bunch of bums. When their monthly credit is issued to them, they throw a blast, drink up half of it in the first few days. Then the rest of the month they eat beans."

The Head Bartender said doggedly, "Once in a coon's age you get an order for a pseudo-whiskey or two from a mini-apartment resident. Big splurge sort of thing. But Scotch? Even a single drink of Scotch? Don't be silly. It's a week's income for somebody on NIT."

Both of them looked at him in lack of comprehension.

Mackley said doggedly, "I don't care what you say. This mini-apartment ordered a case of the higher priced Scotch. Not just Scotch, mind you, but one of the most expensive brands we stock."

Jim said, "What apartment?"

"Apartment 142 on the fourteenth floor, Tower-One."

"Mini-apartment, all right," Jim uttered. "That's all we've got on that floor. What's this clown's name?"

"The apartment's in the name of Harold Harrylad."

"And the case of Scotch was paid for?"

"Of course it was paid for. Do you think we would have delivered it if it wasn't paid for?"

Jim Cotswold looked blank. "It doesn't make sense."

"That's what I say."

Jim sighed. "Okay. I'll check up on it. Maybe this guy Harrylad suddenly inherited a mint, or something. Maybe he's celebrating."

Mackley said, just before leaving, "I wish something'd come up where I could celebrate drinking a case of Johnny Walker Black Label."

For a long moment, after he had gone, Carol Ann and Jim Cotswold looked at the closed door. The 2nd Vice-Demecrat said finally, "Mrs. Cusack, would you give me a balance check on the credit account of Harold Harrylad?"

She went back into the other office to her own desk and returned in about five minutes.

He looked up at her. "Well . . . ?"

"Harold Harrylad has a credit account in the National Bank of eighteen pseudo-dollars and fifty-three cents."

Jim Cotswold stood before the identity screen at the door of Apartment 233 in Tower-One and said, "Second Vice-Demecrat James Cotswold calling on Fredrick Green."

The screen didn't respond. Cotswold repeated his message, with the same result. He thought about it for a moment, then brought his pocket phone out. He flicked it open and said into the screen, "Security Division, please."

The less than handsome face of Fred Jeffers faded in. Jeffers said, "Yes, Mr. Cotswold?"

Jim said, "There seems to be some sort of an emergency here, Fred. Open the door of Apartment 233, twenty-third floor, Tower-One, for me."

"Yes, sir. You want me to raise Mr. Hardin?"

"Not yet. I'll check it out." He deactivated the phone and returned it to his pocket.

The door swung open and he looked into the room before entering. A man's home was still his castle, under the socio-economic system of Meritocracy, and deme officials went out of their way to avoid intruding on privacy. However, he took one look and entered quickly, closing the door behind him.

In the center of the room, in a comfort chair, sat someone who was obviously Fredrick Green. He was dressed solely in what would seem to be a large bath-towel which was wound about his middle in a wise reminiscent of Mahatma Gandhi, of yesteryear. His head was shaven and he was staring at his belly. His bare legs were criss-crossed under him so that he had a rather awkward resemblance to the Buddha; however, he wasn't quite that plump, though possibly he once had been. He had less than a sun-tan complexion. In fact, he looked like a sickly toad.

Jim Cotswold cleared his throat and said, "Ah, Mr. Green?"

The other's face came up with a look made of all sweet accord. "Yes?" he said gently.

Jim Cotswold cleared his throat again and said, "Look, what in the hell are you doing?"

The other said sweetly, "I commune with Lord Vishnu, in his avatar as Parasurama, who is Rama with the axe."

Cotswold stared at him. "You've been doing it for ten days, without food?"

"There is neither time nor food, for these are worldly things and mere inventions of the earthly plane, when one communes with Lord Vishnu."

"Swell," Jim muttered, "but there's starvation if you go long enough without food."

The other's eyes turned back to his somewhat flabby belly. Jim Cotswold was evidently no longer there.

He thought about it for a moment, his eyes unhappily taking in the naked man. Finally, he brought his pocket phone out again, opened it and said into the screen, "Cotswold speaking. Give me Doctor McCoy in Shyler-deme's hospital."

The face of Doctor Bert McCoy faded in, characteristically impatient. "Yes, Jim?"

"Look, Doc, I'm up in Apartment 233, in Tower-One. There's an escapist up here who's been contemplating his navel for at least the past ten days without eating."

The doctor frowned, "How do you know he hasn't been eating?"

"I checked it out with the data banks. Nothing has

95

been delivered to this apartment, either through Restaurant Division or anywhere else. How long can a man live without food?"

"Longer than ten days, but you can't go that long without water—not very likely, at least. Has he been drinking water?"

"How would I know?"

"I'll send a couple of my assistants up. We'll hospitalize him."

Jim Cotswold looked over at Fredrick Green. He said into the phone, "Make it a couple of huskies, with some equipment. He's communing with Lord Vishnu and I'm not sure he's willing to come."

"Who's Vishnu?"

"How the hell would I know? I'll wait here until your boys arrive."

Jim Cotswold stood before the identity screen on the door of Apartment 142 on the fourteenth floor of Tower-One. Offhand, he couldn't remember ever having been on this floor before. When one works in a building with 110 floors and with some five thousand apartments, one simply never gets around to being in all of them.

He said, "Second Vice-Demecrat James Cotswold calling on Harold Harrylad."

And the screen said, "Hey, read the script, the johnfuzz."

Jim Cotswold blinked at it.

The same voice said, "Shirk off, chum-pal, shirk off. We're throwin' a wassail."

Jim Cotswold sighed and said, "Look, friend, if I want to see you I'll wind up seeing you, come hell or high water. So let's cooperate."

The screen remained silent for a time lengthy enough that Jim Cotswold was beginning to speak further, but then the door opened.

It was a mini-apartment and Jim Cotswold's first impression was that it was packed to the rafters with humanity. Second count revealed that there were only nine persons present, but nine persons still packed an apartment of these dimensions. Two of them were sprawled on the couch, one was slumped in the room's sole comfort chair, others were all over the floor, some with pillows, some without. There were four women—well, girls—five men. All were in unique costume, or lack of it. Three of the men wore the currently popular—among the weirds—half beard. That is, the left side of the face was in full, untrimmed beard, the right side cleanshaven.

There was a body odor in the room composed of approximately equal amounts of sweat, vomit and . . . used sex. There was also an element, a large element, of stale drink. Johnny Walker Black Label whiskey might be the most expensive potable carried in the Liquor Division of Shyler-deme, but a whole case of it could hardly be opened in quarters this confined without the odor being described as a stench rather than a bouquet.

Most of the room's inhabitants ignored his presence. Most held a bottle, square of shape and black-labeled, in hand though some had only a glass available. They were all obviously in the final stages of intoxication, in fact, some were unconscious. There was an empty case which without doubt had once contained the bottles, in the middle of the floor, and there were two or three complete empties scattered here and there. The bottles held in hand were down to the last inch or two.

Jim Cotswold calculated. A case held twelve bottles, probably liters rather than fifths by the looks of them. Nine persons, twelve bottles. They had put away the better part of a liter and a quarter apiece, and some of them were obviously just kids, not practiced drunkards. He inwardly flinched.

He who had evidently answered the door screen was standing before Jim wavering only slightly. He seemed the oldest of those present, possibly in his early thirties and the only one cleanshaven; that is, the only one without a deliberately grown beard. He looked as though he had last shaven possibly a week before, his face was in stubble. Assuming the vacuous look was one temporarily achieved through John Barleycorn, he wasn't an unhandsome man. A good mouth, pleasant dark eyes, laugh wrinkles at their edges. His clothes, however, would have done a burlesque comedian of the past proud; they were evidently army surplus, slept in, wrinkled, baggy . . . and dirty.

He said, "Hi, *padre,* have a drink."

Cotswold said, "Are you Harold Harrylad?"

"Negative. I'm Jo-Jo."

"You're what?"

"Name, *padre.* Jo-Jo. Want a drink?" The other's hand went out shakily and lifted a half-full bottle of whiskey from a shelf behind them. He proffered it.

It was still morning and Jim Cotswold was a moderate drinker at best. However, one was not offered Black Label Johnny Walker every day in the week, or any day in the year, for that matter. He took the bottle and downed a heavy slug. It was nectar, all right. Chief Bartender Mackley hadn't exaggerated.

Jim said, "Thanks. Where's Harrylad?"

"He's over there, *padre.*"

"What's this *padre?*"

"*Padre,* Pops, Dads, take your pick, oldtimer."

Jim looked at him. "Oldtimer? I'm only forty-three."

"Tough, tough, *padre,* sooner or later, guess it creeps up on all of us." Jo-Jo took the bottle back and upended it himself.

Jim said, "Where's Harrylad?"

The other gestured with the bottle in the direction of the far corner of the mini-apartment. "Ol' Herr Hairy Harry is over thataway, *padre.*"

"Are you stuttering? I want Harold Harrylad."

"Hairy Harry's over here, come on." Weaving slightly the other led the way.

In one corner, propped up against the wall in a sprawl, was a young man, one half his face shaven, his dirty sport shirt open to the waist, an empty bottle in hand. He snored.

Jo-Jo nudged him with a bare foot. "Drunk as a fruit-cake," he announced.

Jim Cotswold stared down at the apartment's owner. A youngster. And evidently looking even younger than he was, since he had to be at least twenty to collect Negative Income Tax.

Jo-Jo looked at him owlishly. "What'd'ya want with old Hairy Harry?" he said.

Jim brought his eyes up to him. "You don't buy a case of Scotch when your credit balance is down to eighteen pseudo-dollars."

"You sure don't, chum-pal," Jo-Jo chortled. "Where'd we leave that bottle? Oughta get it before one of these others finds it. That mink over there is beginning to look around."

That mink over there looked as though she was about eighteen, if that, and wore just enough not to be pronounced nude.

Jim said, "You left it there near the door. How did, uh, Harry Harry Harry manage to buy several thousand dollars worth of whiskey on a Negative Income Tax income?"

Jo-Jo looked at him as though the deme official was inadequately equipped with reasoning ability. "Herr Hairy Harry," he said. "Get it? Big joke. Good old Hairy Harry's on the sage side. Hasn't spent any of his NIT credit for near on a year. Finally sprung big."

Jim looked at him uncomprehendingly. "Hasn't spent any of his income for a year? How did he live? NIT is just about enough to get by on as it is."

Jo-Jo said reasonably, "You ain't readin' the script, *padre*. We don't operate the way you flat folks do. You operate by the clock, we live it all the way up, all the way."

"Could you translate that?" Jim said patiently.

"Look, chum-pal," Jo-Jo said, just as patiently. "How do you live? You wake up at seven o'clock, or maybe the TV phone wakes you, if you're slept out or not. You get up and have your breakfast at seven-thirty, if you're hungry or not. Great. You go to work and show up at nine, if you feel like working or not. You knock off at twelve and eat, if you're hungry or not. Great. Then you go back and work some more. Then you go home and have a drink—if you're thirsty or not, or if you feel like you need a guzzle or not. Then maybe you look at Tri-Di for awhile, if the program's any good or not. And then you go to bed, if you're sleepy or not. Great. If you're married, maybe you make love to your mink—if you feel like sex or not. Next day, you go through the same whole routine."

"All right. How do you weirds do it? And what's it got to do with Harold Harrylad buying a case of the kind of booze only a millionaire can afford?"

"Not booze, *padre,* guzzle. Don't be a flat. And don't call us weirds. We like to think, Neo-hippies."

"All right, how do you do it?"

"Minute." Jo-Jo staggered off to retrieve his bottle before the topless eighteen-year-old located it. He returned, holding it by the neck. He pressed it into Jim's hands. "Have another guzzle on me."

Jim couldn't resist. He took another hearty swallow. It still tasted like nectar. He said, wrinkling his nose, "Is the air filtering off in this apartment?"

"No," Jo-Jo said without going further. "This is how we do it. We go to bed when we're sleepy—or if we're hot with some mink." He leered. "We get up when we don't want to sleep no more. We eat when we get hungry and we eat whatever the hell we feel like eating when we feel like eating it. None of this balanced diet crap—you know, soup, salad, meat, vegetables, dessert—at seven-thirty, noon and six o'clock sort of crud. When we feel like trank, we take trank. If we feel like throwing a wassail, we throw a wassail. We don't live by the clock. We live the way we gotta live."

"All right," Jim said. "But Harrylad buying a case . . ."

"You're still not reading the script, *padre,*" Jo-Jo said impatiently, and taking another pull at the bottle. "Pseudo-dollars don't mean nothing to nobody with us.

Suppose everybody's in my hole. Somebody gets hungry. So we dial food. Anything. Steaks, caviar . . ."

Jim winced at that.

". . . cheese, candy. Whatever anybody wants. It's on me. It's my apartment. I stick my credit card in the slot. As long as my credit account holds out. If it's all used up for that month, then we drift over to somebody else's hole, and maybe there we all get tranked up and listen to music tapes, or show some of the old classic shows on Tri-Di. Maybe we do something else." He leered. "And then, maybe we drift over to somebody else's hole. Sage, eh?"

"Suppose everybody runs out of pseudo-dollars?"

"We eat beans. Maybe we go over to the Swap Shop in the Common and flog something—if anybody's got anything to flog."

Jim said, "All right, but we still haven't explained a case of Scotch."

The other was mildly indignant. "I just told you. Old Hairy Harry accumulated enough credit to spring for the case. We all got to thinking we'd never thrown a wassail with Scotch. Somebody saw about Scotch on an old television revival show. So Harry sprung for the Scotch."

Jim was wide-eyed. "You mean he didn't spend any of his NIT for almost a year? He just sponged around all that time?"

"Why not? We just didn't get around to using up his credit. Kinda like a coincidence."

From being wide-eyed, Jim Cotswold closed his eyes altogether. He said, "And then he spent practically everything he'd saved, on this one big whiskey bust?"

"Why not?" the other said, mystified. "I simply don't read the script you flats turn out. This is *living, padre.*"

"It sure as hell is," Jim Cotswold muttered. He took the bottle from the other's hand and took another slug. "Thanks." He handed the bottle back. "Don't even bother to tell Harry Harry Harry Harry I was here. It's not important."

"Hey, don't shirk off now," Jo-Jo said hospitably.

"The wassail's just getting under way." His eyes narrowed slightly. "Hey, I got a wizard of an idea. Maybe. You look like the kind of flat that lays it up. Howabout springing for another case?" He looked about the room. "Some of these minks aren't bad and they all put out."

Jim Cotswold said, "They smell a little high to me, frankly."

"Ah, get goosed, you flat," Jo-Jo said in disgust.

Jim Cotswold made his way to the door, stepping over one of the minks in question as he went.

As he left, someone was singing, somewhat blearily, *"It's that old time religion, but it's good enough for me."*

On his way down in the elevator his pocket phone tinkled and he took it out and activated it. Carol Ann Cusack's face faded in and she said, "Mr. Cotswold, will you be back in the office soon? Mr. Ten Eyck would like to see you."

"I'm on my way now," he said.

When he entered the Demecrat's office, Bat Hardin was there as well, straddling a chair, his elbows on its back.

Barry Ten Eyck looked up and said, "What spins, Jim?"

Jim Cotswold said, "You wouldn't believe me if I told you. I've spent the last hour with escapists and weirds. Ooops, I mean Neo-hippies."

Carol Ann said from her desk, "What's a Neo-hippy?"

"That's a good question," Jim said.

Barry Ten Eyck said, even as he came to his feet, "Anything important?"

"No."

Barry said, "Well, Emmanuel Levy wants all Demecrats, Vice-Demecrats and Security Chiefs to come over to Administration."

"Oh? What does the mayor want? We just had a regular meeting last week."

"Search me," Barry said. "Coming, Bat?"

Bat Hardin stood too and the three of them filed out, Barry Ten Eyck saying over his shoulder, "Hold down the fort, Miss Cusack."

"With fervor," she said. "And I keep telling you, it's Mrs. Cusack."

They took the elevator down to the deme's lowest level and when they emerged, Bat said, "Should I summon a floater?"

Barry said, "Let's walk. If you allowed yourself, you'd never get any exercise leading this life."

They walked to the Transport Station and Bat dialed for one of the deme's Security patrol cars. He said, "Want to go up on the surface?"

"No," Barry said. "This isn't any emergency and although it's permissible for an official vehicle to go about Phoenecia on the surface, we ought to set an example. If everybody who could wrangle permission drove electro-steamers inside the pseudo-city limits, we'd soon start having traffic again."

"Good Lord forbid," Bat muttered.

When the patrol car glided up to the curb before them, they entered, Bat taking the place behind the controls and then dialing the Ad building in the pseudo-city's Common. "Where we going?" he said.

"Official escape room," Barry said.

Jim Cotswold looked at him in mild surprise. "Oh? Something hush-hush?"

"Evidently," Barry said. "Levy seemed very mysterious."

At Phoenecia's Central Terminal they let their patrol car go off to the car park and got a four-place floater. When they were all seated, Barry said into the screen, "Official escape room," and it glided off.

When they reached their destination, it was to find two strangers posted outside the door. The two were in civilian clothes but had an air of police officer about them. They looked closely at the delegation from Shyler-deme but said nothing.

Barry Ten Eyck stood before the identity screen and

said, "Ten Eyck, Hardin and Cotswold," and the door opened to admit them.

Inside, the other heads of the four demes that made up the pseudo-city of Phoenecia had already gathered, as well as Mayor Emmanuel Levy and Phoenecian Chief of Security Ben Snider. There were also half a dozen strangers present, most of whom could have been twins of the two who stood outside the door.

Mayor Levy was talking to a more individualistic looking stranger, one who carried an air of authority. When Barry Ten Eyck and his assistants entered, Levy looked over and said, "Ah, we're all here now."

He turned and spoke to the room in general. "Gentlemen, if we'll all just be seated."

The three from Shyler-deme, even as they found seats around the rectangular conference table, nodded and spoke to their fellow administrators from Lincoln-deme, Victory-deme and Hilton-deme. These present were the equivalent of the pseudo-city council under Mayor Levy and performed such administration as was necessary inter-deme wise.

The authoritative stranger, a square-jawed type in his mid-fifties, took his place at the head of the table and said, "At this point I won't introduce myself, gentlemen. First of all I'd like to ask if there is anyone present who has any reservations about the present socio-economic system of the United States, that is, Meritocracy."

Several stirred, several frowned puzzlement.

The speaker took up a sheet of paper which obviously bore their names. "Emmanual Levy?"

The chubby mayor chuckled. "I was born the son of a second-rate tailor. Today I am mayor of a pseudo-city with a salary beyond my fondest dreams when I lived in a Bronx tenement as a boy. No. I have no reservations about Meritocracy."

The stranger was evidently slightly impatient of the little talk. He said, "Ben Snider?"

"The country never had it so good."

The newcomer made the circle. He had only one negative response and that at the very last.

Victor McComas, of Hilton-deme, said slowly, "I'm only partially in favor of Meritocracy. There are aspects of the voting system, our method of selection of public officials in general, that seem less than ... democratic. And ..."

The other held up a hand and said, "That's enough, Mr. McComas. Thompson, Andersen."

Two of the other strangers, all of whom had been standing in the background, their backs to the room's walls, and in complete silence, stepped forward and stood near the Hilton-deme Demecrat.

The speaker said, "Mr. McComas, you're going on a vacation."

"What ... what ... ?" Victor McComas was astonished. "What do you mean?"

"The government is financing a vacation for you to Acapulco. Congratulations."

All of the Phoenecian administrators were staring, as shocked as their colleague.

McComas got out finally, "You mean I am under arrest?"

"Not at all, unless you wish to stretch a point and call it protective custody. There is an emergency afoot, Mr. McComas, and your presence is not required."

"But ... but how could I explain this to my wife? It's ridiculous and ..."

"Your wife may go along, Mr. McComas. You will be, ah, escorted by these two gentlemen, Mr. Andersen and Mr. Thompson. They will give you such details as are required."

Thompson and Andersen escorted a still sputtering Victor McComas from the room.

The speaker said to Mayor Levy, "This is an escape room, you said?"

Levy, still taken aback by the treatment of one of his town's Demecrats, could only make a jerky nod.

"Nevertheless," the stranger said, "we'll take double precautions. Williams!"

Who was obviously Williams came forward with a small suitcase-like burden, set it up on the center of the conference table, opened it to reveal a surface of dials and switches. He pulled out two antenna-like projections, flicked two switches, set a dial, then retreated to the place he had earlier occupied against the wall.

The speaker said in satisfaction, "The latest model scrambler, gentlemen. I doubt if there exists equipment this side of Common Europe that could bug this room—if there. And now we will come to the point."

He looked around at them, one by one. "We already knew of Mr. McComas' lack of enthusiasm for our present politico-economic system. All of your National Data Banks dossiers have been thoroughly checked on a Priority One level . . ."

There was a surprised stirring about the table and several grunts of irritation.

" . . . However, as Meritcrats there is little reason for you to agree with Mr. McComas. You are all to be considered loyal members of our society. Nor is there anything in any of your dossiers to suggest otherwise."

Bat Hardin snapped, "Listen, who in the hell are you and what's all this mystery?"

The other looked at him, checked his name on the list he had at hand. "Ah," he said, "Mr. Hardin. One would expect a bit of spirit from an awardee of the Medal of Honor." He looked about the table. "According to his dossier, during the Mekong Delta debacle Lieutenant Bat Hardin fought a delaying action which saved the remnants of his regiment."

He looked back at Bat. "In answer to your question, I am Roy Thomas, Director of the Department of Emergency Affairs, of the Inter-American Bureau of Investigation."

Barry Ten Eyck had been looking at his Vice-Demecrat half in awe, half in amusement. He had muttered under his breath, "A hero in our midst." But now he said, still low, "Department of Emergency Affairs? Never heard of it."

"Department of Dirty Tricks," Bat muttered back.

Roy Thomas said, "And to put an end to the aura of mystery, we are here seeking the most dangerous man in the United States—perhaps in the world."

Jim Cotswold said, "It'd be hard to top that. What is he, some international spy, or something?"

The Director of the Department of Emergency Affairs looked in his direction. "To the contrary, Mr., ah, Cotswold, isn't it? He is a student. Perhaps scholar is the better word."

His eyes swept the table again. "Gentlemen, Willard Saxe is a type of person little known to the layman, the man in the street. He is the present day equivalent of, let us say, Thomas Jefferson or Thomas Paine. He is the Paul Marat, as compared to Robespierre and Danton. He is Lenin's Nikolai Bukharin; Hitler's Alfred Rosenberg. He is, in short, the brains behind the party figureheads, the party theoretician."

"What party?" Mayor Emmanuel Levy blurted.

"The party which has as its goal the overthrow of Meritocracy," Roy Thomas said simply.

Larry Brooks, the Democrat of Victory-deme, said, "You mean that he is a Communist?"

Thomas said, a shade impatiently, "If he was, Mr., ah, Brooks, I would not be devoting my personal attention to him. The so-called Communists in this country were repudiated by the American people as far back as the nineteen-thirties. Whatever their position in various other parts of the world, their program was ridiculous as applied to the United States, and all but crackpots rejected them. For that matter, even in Common Eurasia the socio-economic system that prevails has little resemblance to true communism. They use the terminology, the slogans, the symbols, but in actuality their system has little resemblance to what Marx and Engels once taught."

Chief of Security Snider was frowning. "Well, what party are you talking about?"

"The Futurists, Mr. Snider."

Bat Hardin said slowly, "A splinter group. I've met exactly one in my whole life. According to him, there isn't anything illegal about the program of the Futurists."

The Thomas attention came back to him. "One of the items we can lay at the door of Willard Saxe. He is diabolically clever. He has continued to insist that the Futurist Party abide by the Revised Constitution. He intends to bring off the revolutionary changes he advocates legally, without force and violence."

All eyes were on him now, but for a moment no one spoke.

At long length, Levy said, "What is the charge against this Saxe?"

"There is none."

There was another period of silence, finally broken by the Second Vice-Demecrat of Lincoln-deme. "Then why is the Department of Emergency Affairs after him?"

"Because, as I told you, he is the most dangerous man in the United States. We must, ah, restrict him."

Barry Ten Eyck said, irritation in his voice, "Look here. From what Bat Hardin says, the Futurist Party is a tiny outfit. This Willard Saxe might be the biggest brain since Aristotle but what chance has he of getting anywhere?"

Thomas nodded. "A reasonable question. You see, Mr. Ten Eyck, in the present day world a government has many problems, many duties. Among them is to keep continually alert against the possibility of subversion, against those who would change basic institutions. Happily, such activity is on a higher level than ever before. We no longer have to depend on often stupid and brutal secret police. This is the computerized society. Three months ago, to our amazement, the computers revealed that given an aggressive, dedicated organization with a rational program, our Meritocracy could be overthrown in a period of three years, give or take three point two months."

"Overthrown to be replaced by *what*?" Jim Cotswold blurted.

Thomas looked at him and nodded again. "There are

various possible alternatives, Mr. Cotswold. Most people make the mistake of not realizing that there are various alternatives to the socio-economic system under which they live. Given proper developments, we under Meritocracy could return to an earlier form of, ah, free enterprise. We might adopt a system similar to that which prevails in Common Europe or in Common Eurasia. Given atomic catastrophe we might even go back to a form of feudalism or chattel slavery. Technocracy is another alternative, as is Syndicalism. We might adopt the watered-down version of Socialism once popular in the Scandinavian countries. We could adopt the Socialist Industrial Union government of the DeLeonists. Oh, there are various alternatives, none, of course, acceptable to we Meritcrats."

He let his eyes sweep them again, then went on. "The fact is that three things are required before a subversive movement has any chance of realizing itself. First, you must have a program that fits the circumstances prevailing. Second you must have tactics that have some chance of success. Third, you must have an organization that can propagandize your program."

Barry Ten Eyck said, "That last one is where your Willard Saxe comes a cropper, if this Futurist Party of his is as small as it must be. I've hardly even heard of it."

Thomas shook his head. "One year before the Declaration of Independence, if you had told the average American colonist that King George must go you probably would have wound up with a sock in the nose. Six months before the Bolsheviks took power, Lenin wrote that he didn't expect to live to see his revolution take place." He shook his head again. "It is not the immediate *size* of the subversive organization, Mr. Ten Eyck, it is the program, the principles. The size of the organization will come, like an avalanche, given the three requirements."

Mayor Levy said, a shade of testiness in his voice, "All this has been most fascinating, but I fail to fit it into this cloak and dagger atmosphere that you've subjected us to, Mr. Thomas. What has all this got to do with us?"

Roy Thomas exploded his bombshell.

"We have reason to believe that Willard Saxe has gone to ground here in Phoenecia."

When that had been assimilated, Jim Cotswold said, mystified, "Well, what's the big problem? Why not just get a fix on his pocket phone, I.D. number, and pick him up?"

"He has evidently abandoned his pocket phone, Mr. Cotswold."

"Abandoned his pocket phone?" Ben Snider said in disbelief. "You can't get by these days without a pocket phone. How could he buy food, or a place to stay, or transportation, or anything else?"

Roy Thomas looked at the Security Chief. "Admittedly, it isn't easy. We don't know completely how he has managed as well as he has. We first attempted to pick him up where he worked in the data banks in New Denver. But he must have been tipped off. I told you, the man is devilishly clever. Evidently keeping to the old unautomated roads, and driving an old petroleum-burning car, he took off across the country, probably calling upon fellow Futurists to supply him with fuel, food and shelter. By the time we had pursuit organized he had reached this vicinity. We suspect he might be on the way to Canada, but we're not sure of that. Perhaps he has simply gone underground and intends to continue his subversive work here in the States."

Barry Ten Eyck said slowly, "The picture isn't clear to me. From what you say the man has broken no laws. There is no charge against him. Where do you come in on this?"

"Mr. Ten Eyck, can you realize the changes that might have taken place in history if Karl Marx had been sidetracked at, say, the time he and Engels published the *Communist Manifesto* in 1848 and before he had formulated the Materialist Conception of History and the Theory of Surplus Value? Or can you picture

the authorities of the time heading off Tom Paine before he wrote *Common Sense,* not to speak of his later
pamphlets? This is the computer age, I repeat. Our
computers reveal that sixty-six percent of our population, give or take three percent, are potential rebels
against Meritocracy, given an even remotely sensible alternative program. We must find our Karl Marxes and
our Tom Paines before they are fully mature. Willard
Saxe is potentially of such stature."

Bat Hardin said, "You think he is somewhere in
Phoenecia. Okay, why not simply bring in a large crew
of your people and make an apartment-by-apartment
search, a room-by-room examination of all the public
rooms and storage areas?"

"Because we can't afford to create a martyr. When
you begin sifting through eighty thousand persons the
word goes out. Busybodies, bleeding hearts, do-gooders,
those who view with alarm, would be up in arms. In
spite of all we could do, it would hit the mass news
media. As I've already pointed out, the Futurists are
not illegal."

Emmanuel Levy said, "Then I don't see how this
Department of Emergency Affairs of yours can legally
enter into hunting down this Willard Saxe."

Roy Thomas shook his head at him, ruefully. "Long
since, in the conduct of governments we have had extra-legal agencies, Mayor Levy, whether or not the average citizen was aware of the fact. In our own country, the C.I.A. was known to operate in an atmosphere
of secrecy to promote the interests of the government of that time. In the Soviet Union was the
Chrezvychainaya Komissiva, and in England, the Dou-
ble-O Section of the Secret Service. Every nation has
some equivalent. This Willard Saxe is potentially the
greatest of dangers to our society. He must be found
and his nefarious work terminated."

Security Chief Snider said, "What is it you want
from us?"

Roy Thomas said, "We mustn't let him get his wind
up. He probably thinks his cover here is adequate. We

don't want him to go on the run again. Next time he just might make it to Canada or Mexico or some other safe refuge and we simply do not have the legal requirements to extradite him. Besides that, there are a dozen countries that would enjoy seeing the United States discomfited and would give him political asylum.

"I and my men will disappear from the scene, remaining in the background but ready to come in immediately when required. It will be your task to locate Willard Saxe, to find where and how he is hiding. Once located, we will appear and make the, ah, arrest, quietly, unobtrusively."

Jim Cotswold said, "Is this really a solution? Suppose you silence this Saxe fellow. Won't somebody else come along and take up where he left off? If sixty-six percent of our people are potential rebels against Meritocracy, they'll find a way."

"It's a good point," Roy Thomas told him. "However, remember I told you that according to the computers our socio-economic system could be overthrown in three years, given an organization with a program. Very well, but we also foresee that within a decade, only ten years, we will be so entrenched that such an overthrow will be impossible. Changes are now taking place in our government apparatus and in our people, for that matter, that will make such an overthrow out of the question."

On the way back to Shyler-deme, Barry Ten Eyck and his two assistants were unwontedly quiet.

Jim Cotswold said finally, "I don't like it."

The others maintained the silence, submerged in their own reflections.

Jim said, "What the hell's the country coming to? There's not even any charge against this Saxe guy."

"Which doesn't mean he isn't as dangerous as Thomas says," Bat growled. "You let a moron run around in a gunpowder factor with a box of matches in his hands and you're silly if you wait until he breaks the law by striking one of them."

"Evidently, Willard Saxe is no moron," Jim said unhappily.

Barry Ten Eyck said, "The question is, are we enough in favor of Meritocracy that we're willing to cooperate with Roy Thomas and his Department of Emergency Affairs?"

"In short," Jim Cotswold growled, "do we believe that the ends justify the means?"

They thought about that for awhile.

Barry Ten Eyck said, "Well, we seem to be committed. This'll have to take top priority. Both of you fellows work on it. I'll try to handle just about everything else. We have no particular reason to believe Saxe is in Shyler-deme. For that matter, Thomas never did tell us why he thought the guy was in Phoenecia."

Bat said, "The way that organization operates, if Roy Thomas says he's in Phoenecia, he's in Phoenecia. *Why* is another question."

They were all on the glum side when they entered the Demecrat's office.

Carol Ann Cusack looked up and made with an upside-down smile. "Well, the conquering heroes return. By the looks of you, you've all been fired. Couldn't happen to a nicer trio."

None of them rose to the challenge.

Bat Hardin said, "Mrs. Cusack, utilizing my Priority Two with the National Data Banks, I want you to check the dossier of every resident of Shyler-deme. I want the names, I.D. and apartment numbers of every member of the Futurist Party. I want the names, I.D. and apartment numbers of every resident who has a relative who belongs to the Futurist Party. And to the extent the information is available in the data banks, the same information on every resident who has a friend who is a member of the party."

"Guilt by association," Jim murmured unhappily.

Carol Ann was goggling at Shyler-deme's Security

Chief. "Golly," she said. "You want me to ring in several more girls to handle this?"

Barry Ten Eyck said, "No. It's all in your lap, Miss Cusack. This is very hush-hush. A fugitive is holed up in Phoenecia. We're trying to locate him but we can't afford the word to go out. Don't mention this to anyone, even your husband."

"I've never had any secrets from Sid."

"Now you have secrets from Sid," Bat Hardin growled. He looked over at Jim Cotswold. "We have the honor of having a resident here in Shyler-deme who is the head of the Futurist Party in Phoenecia. His name is William Locke and he's in Tower-Two, Apartment 603 on the sixtieth floor. I've already interviewed him once on another matter. Suppose you see him this time. Dream up some special reason. If I went to him again, he might smell a rat."

Jim Cotswold said, "What'd he have to tell you?"

"I carried a mini-recorder and taped it all. You can play it back. He seems to be a nice enough guy. But if Saxe is around, I'd think Locke would know about it."

"No," Barry Ten Eyck said. "I doubt it. The last contact Willard Saxe would make is the local head of the Futurists. He's no fool, if the picture Thomas painted is at all accurate."

"Well, it's a place we can start," Bat said, chewing away at his lower lip.

Jim Cotswold said, "There's one item that Roy Thomas didn't bring up but seems to be on the obvious side to me."

The others looked at him.

Jim said, "If he's in Phoenecia, he's almost sure to be hidden out in one of the demes. It wouldn't be practical to stay in any of the buildings in the Common, the hotel for instance. I suppose Security Chief Snider will handle that. But if he's in one of the demes, then he has to stay put in one spot."

Carol Ann said, "How do you mean?"

Jim said to her, "He's had to ditch his pocket phone, credit I.D. Otherwise they could have gotten a fix on him. That means he can't move about in a deme. God only knows how he got in at all. It couldn't have been easy. But you know how it works. He can't go from one floor to another without a computer Security check. He can't take an elevator, and the doors to the stairs are locked. Assuming he is in Shyler-deme, then he's in someone's apartment and staying put."

Barry Ten Eyck had been nodding agreement. Now he looked over at Bat. He sighed and said, "We're working on the highest of government priorities. Utilize your Priority Two and check every apartment in the deme."

Bat said, "Great. How do I know him when I see him?"

Barry looked at Carol Ann. "Get the National Data Banks dossier of Willard Saxe. Throw his photographic record on the wall screen there."

Within minutes the wall screen had been activated and they were given Tri-Di stills and motions of the fugitive Willard Saxe, portraits and full-lengths. He was a tallish blond, with a tendency to shamble in movement; there was a distant, sad, possibly melancholy aspect to his face, a vulnerable quality. Summed up, a dreamer. He didn't look like the most dangerous man in the United States or anywhere else.

It was Carol Ann who expressed that. She said, "Golly, he's handsome. He doesn't look particularly dangerous."

Barry Ten Eyck said glumly, "I'll bet neither did Karl Marx when he was sitting there in the reading room of the British Museum, researching *Das Kapital* and nursing his hemorrhoids."

Jim Cotswold said, "I don't place his face at all, but he moves like somebody I know."

Barry grunted. "He moves like Dick Wonder, down in Transportation. That's who you're thinking about."

Bat said, "How long's Dick been here?"

"Good grief," Barry said. "Don't be drivel-happy. Dick was here before I arrived, two years ago. This

Saxe was working out in New Denver only a couple of months past."

Jim Cotswold said, after Carol Ann had faded the pictures of Saxe, "There's one thing we've got. Whoever is sheltering Saxe is really close to him. He's on the run and in this society of ours there aren't many that go on the lam. It doesn't make sense. So whoever is hiding Saxe knows that it's a bad-o thing to be doing. Dangerous. It's either a devoted follower of the Futurists—not necessarily a member of the party—or possibly a girl, somebody in love with him. Although, of course, it's always possible that it's a relative, or a close friend from childhood or some such."

"It'll be easy enough to check those out," Bat said. "Carol Ann ought to have all that dope by tomorrow." He came to his feet. "I'll get on over to Security and start checking with the spy lenses every apartment in the building. Holy Smokes, what a job. Peeping Tom, peering into five thousand homes. Can you imagine some of the stuff I'm going to have to witness?"

Barry Ten Eyck smirked at him. "It's lucky you're a voyeur at heart."

Jim Cotswold said, "I have a sneaking suspicion it's not going to do you any good."

Bat looked at him. "Why not? If he's in Shylerdeme, one spy lens or the other is trained on him. Thank God for computers, at least I won't have to do the whole thing individually."

Jim said, "In this day of plastic surgery, he'd be a fool to be going around wearing that face we just saw."

Barry Ten Eyck said, "He's on the run. He doesn't have time to look up a plastic surgeon. Even if he did, he hasn't got any credit account available and plastic surgery doesn't come cheap."

"He doesn't have a credit account, but he's got a whole political party. In a political party, you've got just about every trade and profession going. Just as sure as God made little green apples, there are some competent cosmetic surgeons in the Futurist Party, and if Saxe has a brain in his head he had one of them work him over just as soon as he realized that Thomas and his outfit were after him."

Bat grumbled, "You're possibly right. However, I'll have to give it a try." He left, heading for his own offices and the screens of the TV mini-spy lenses.

Barry looked over at Carol Ann Cusack. "Anything come up while we were gone?"

"A howl from the Protestant denominations who use the Community Church."

"What kind of a howl?"

"It seems as though this new weird outfit, the Shrine of the White Goddess, wants to take over the place on Moon-Day."

Jim Cotswold and Barry Ten Eyck looked at her. "On what day?" Jim said.

"Moon-Day. Monday, evidently. It seems that the White Goddess is the goddess of the moon."

Barry Ten Eyck rubbed his right hand down over his face, in surrender. "All right, all right. So the Catholics and the other larger denominations have their own churches and so forth over in the Common, but here in Shyler-deme we have a king-size public room for the other denominations that want to use it. The New Moslems on Friday, the Jews on Saturday, various Christian outfits on Sunday. Why in the hell can't the ... what'd you call them ...?"

"The Shrine of the White Goddess."

"All right, all right. Why can't they have it on Monday?"

"Evidently, because they're pagans. The Christians and the New Moslems are up in arms. Or, at least, some of them are."

"What in the devil is a pagan? Every religion evidently figures that every other religion is pagan, or gentile, or heathen or some other unhappy name. All religions are superstitions except your own."

Carol Ann said, slightly puzzled, but definite, "No, this is *really* pagan. That is, it's a religion neither Christian, Hebrew or Mohammedan. It's the old religion."

Barry Ten Eyck said, "Why didn't I become a fiddle

player like my dear old mother wanted? What in the hell is a real pagan?"

Carol Ann said, "I didn't get much sense out of the whole thing, but from what I understand the weirds have revived a religion that goes back to the Greeks."

Jim said, "Wonderful. You mean they've got old Zeus and Pallas Athena and all the boys back into operation?"

"Well, no, not if I got a very clear picture of what Jo-Jo was trying to tell me."

"Jo-Jo," Jim Cotswold laughed. "You mean he's got off his hangover already?"

Carol Ann said patiently, "He was part of a delegation from the weirds, I guess you would call them. Golly, they looked weird enough. According to Jo-Jo the Shrine of the White Goddess goes back to before the Greeks. Or, at least, the Dorian Greeks."

"Who in the world are the Dorian Greeks as opposed to any other Greeks?" Jim Cotswold said.

She looked at him evenly. "That's a good question," she said.

"All right, all right," Barry Ten Eyck sighed. "So the weirds have a new cult that goes back before the days of Zeus and Athena and all the rest of them. So why are the Christians putting up the big beef? Why can't these White Goddess people use the Community Church on Mondays?"

"Orgies," Carol Ann said simply.

The two deme officials were intrigued.

"I wonder if they'd mind if I attended," Jim Cotswold murmured.

"Very funny," Barry said. He looked at Carol Ann. "*What* orgies?"

"Well ..." she consulted some notes. "Evidently, they want to observe certain rites. Uh, have you ever heard of Dionysus?"

"Wasn't he the god of wine, or something?" Jim said.

"Well, yes, if I've got it right. But according to the

Christians they did various other things, besides getting smashed, at his orgies."

Barry Ten Eyck took a deep breath. He said, "All right. When do these characters want to hold their first get-together?"

"Tomorrow. Monday. That is, Moon-Day."

"All right, okay it." He looked over at Carol Ann mock-fiendishly. "We'll let Jim cover it. He seems keen to attend an orgy. He can report on the orgies, or whatever. Shucks, he's a bachelor. Supposedly we have complete religious freedom in Phoenecia. Unless there's some all-out sex binge, or something, there's no reason why this White Goddess Shrine thing can't have access to the Community Church. Let Jim suffer through it."

"Amen," Carol Ann said.

"My bosom chum-pal," Jim muttered.

Jim Cotswold went over to Bat Hardin's office in Security and got the tape the other had cut of his interview with William Locke, and then returned to his own office and desk.

It was a simple mini-tape, sound alone. Jim put it in one of his desk phone screens and played it back twice. There wasn't much in it of use to him, other than some evidently standard objections that the Futurists made to Meritocracy.

He pulled it out again and recrossed the corridor. His own secretary was on leave, so he said to Pauline Nash, who was Bat's assistant, "Could you check to find it William Locke is in his apartment? He evidently works over at Dodge-Myers, but I don't know what shift."

Bat Hardin looked up from the TV screen he was scanning. "He's not in his apartment," he said. "I'm already keeping him on spy lens, on a twenty-four hour basis, or, at least, as long as he's in Shyler-deme. If Saxe contacts him here, we've got our man."

"Where is he, then?"

"Down in Sid's Saloon, the auto-bar on the second basement level. Evidently, he makes a practice of taking a drink or so there on returning from work. He's single and probably likes a bit of noise and lights before retiring to solitary existence. I know how he feels."

"Don't we all?" Jim said. "Well, I'll look him up there."

William Locke was sitting alone, at the far end of the auto-bar, his back to the Tri-Di screen which dominated the wall at the other end of the large room. A dozen weirds were seated before the screen, on the floor, and laughing thir heads off at the show which was depicting an heroic American sergeant killing off Asians by the score in the last war. As always, down through the movie era, the television era and now Tri-Di, the hero was cleanly shaven, never mussed his hair, and had a gun with an evidently unlimited cartridge magazine. The weirds thought it all uproariously funny. Probably they were high on trank, Jim Cotswold decided.

He stood above William Locke and said, "A friend pointed you out to me. Aren't you connected with the Futurist Party?"

Locke glanced up, his face friendly. "Yes, of course. Have a seat. Drink?"

Jim said, "Sure, but make this one on me. What're you having there? It looks good." He put his pocket phone I.D. card in the payment slot of the table.

"Pseudo-whiskey Manhattan. The liquor division has some imported Italian Vermouth. Might as well get our share of it before it's all gone."

"Sounds fine," Jim said. He dialed the drinks, even as he said, "My name's Jim Davis. Off and on, the past year or so, I've heard a bit here and there about you Futurists, but haven't had the opportunity to find out anything about the organization. I'm mildly interested in politics."

Locke nodded and said with an edge of deprecation, "Most of us of the common herd no longer bother. With Meritocracy and one vote per earned dollar, you have to be pretty high on the totem pole to have any effect on elections. That's one of our beefs. The powers that be are rapidly getting to the point where two percent of the population dominates government."

Jim Cotswold frowned as he pretended to think that over seriously. "Well, the theory is that the most competent in the economy are also the most competent in making governmental decisions. You wouldn't want to give a man with an I.Q. of 80 the same say in our country's affairs as one with an I.Q. of 140."

"Ummm," Locke said, "perhaps not. But that's not the whole story. The question becomes, who is to decide who are the most competent? A ruling class or clique will always *tell* you they're the most competent. Under feudalism, the aristocracy modestly admitted to being the most competent to rule, even though some of them were idiots—literally. Under classical capitalism, the entrepreneur was equally modest and by utilizing his wealth was able to dominate our political machines and had a big say in governmental affairs. By the time Galbraith's so-called Industrial State came along corporate wealth was largely in the hands of families which had inherited it, and they in turn evidently became the most competent to rule, so they in turn dominated the political parties with their sizable campaign donations and their ownership of the mass media."

The center of the table sank down to return with two chilled glasses, each containing a brownish beverage with a maraschino cherry. They took up the drinks.

"Cheers," Locke said.

"First one today—with this hand," Jim toasted in return.

Locke said, "The thing is, the theory of Meritocracy has its good points. Promotion and pay is now theoretically granted to those with the highest I.Q.s, the best educations—the most efficient, aggressive and ambitious. You win to the top through your ability. That's the theory. But the thing is this. In the lower echelons it works very well indeed, but when you get to the topmost ranks of the Meritcrats there's another matter."

"How do you mean?" Jim said, sipping his drink and simulating the keenest of interest.

"Down through the ages, Mr. Davis, man has been a practitioner of nepotism. He has been a great advocate of taking care of his own: his family, his other relatives, his friends. Meritocracy supposedly did away with that. I repeat, supposedly. The trouble is that on the lower levels it is easy enough to check out a man's capabilities. But when you get out of primary and secondary occupations and into tertiary and especially quaternary, it becomes more difficult. When you get into the quaternary occupations, then they usually decide among themselves just who is the most competent."

"You left me behind there. These different kind of occupations."

Locke said, "Primary occupations are fishing, forestry, hunting, agriculture and mining. When the country started, the overwhelming majority were engaged in them. Secondary occupations are concerned with processing the products of a primary occupation. Tertiary occupations deal with rendering services to primary and secondary occupations. And quaternary occupations are those that render services to tertiary occupations or to each other. They are the top jobs, the agencies of government, the professions, the non-profit groups and so forth.

"The thing to remember, Mr. Davis, is that Meritocracy didn't come into the world out of the blue. It's a continuation of what went on before, as every other new socio-economic system that ever came along has been. In spite of Negative Income Tax, a home guaranteed to each citizen, free medicine and all the other reforms of the past few decades, Meritocracy is no more than a continuation of capitalism, with a great deal of government control and planning. The cosmocorps are still privately owned by a comparatively small number of persons. They make a great to-do about People's Capitalism and supposedly the stock of the cosmocorps is held by the people, but in actuality most American families hold either none at all, or just a few shares. Control is still in the hands of the old rich families."

Jim Cotswold said slowly, thoughtfully and as

though he was grudgingly accepting the other's words, "Well, I guess you're right about that."

Locke nodded and took another pull at his drink. "The boards of directors of the cosmocorps consist either of the old rich, or representatives of theirs. And it is these boards that make the final decisions as to who shall be the top executives of the companies, the managers, the department heads, the heads of foundations and such. And such jobs aren't really connected with production, they're too rarified for such mundane things. They're to do with over-all policy, with the company's relationship to the government and to other governments, and the like. It is more important for a Chairman of the Board to be an excellent host, to have good contacts, to be universally liked, to be a superb public speaker, than it is to know anything about the product his cosmocorps turns out. I doubt if the President of General Motors-Ford could change a power pack in an electro-steamer."

Jim Cotswold was frowning earnestly. "Well, that makes sense too."

Locke finished his drink and reached out and dialed two more, after putting his pocket phone I.D. in the order slot.

He said, "So, theoretically a member of one of the old rich families has no vote. His income from dividends, rents and so forth, is not *earned* pseudo-dollars so he has no more vote than an unemployed citizen on NIT. However, if he is appointed by the board of directors to be president of a cosmocorps with a salary of, say, half a million a year, then suddenly he has half a million votes, as opposed to, say, my ten thousand. Others in the top echelons of the corporation owe their jobs to him, and I needn't mention how they vote in the elections."

Jim said, "So the solution, from the Futurist Party viewpoint?"

"We're of the opinion that the cosmocorps should be converted into quasi-public utilities, leaving the rest of the economy free. For a long time this nation has had such basic industries as the post office and the road system belonging to the nation as a whole. Such fields as communications, railroads and other transportation have been strongly government controlled. We think it is about time to extend this. Meritocracy has its virtues; it should not be dominated, however, by private interests which aren't necessarily those of the nation as a whole."

Jim Cotswold snorted. "Isn't that what they call creeping socialism?"

"They call it a lot of things, usually derogatory. Socialism has become a word so elastic that you've really got to dig to find out what it supposedly meant. Everything, from Hitler's National Socialism, to Roosevelt's New Deal reforms, has been hung with the label."

Jim said, "Look, this is fascinating. Can you give me something to read on the subject? I'm not sure about everything you've said, but I'd like to find out more."

"Of course, Mr. Davis. That's my job as a Futurist Party organizer. Be glad to give you some of our literature."

Jim said, "You wouldn't have anything by a ... let me see, what was his name? Uh, Willard Saxe?"

Locke looked at him silently for a moment, then, "As a matter of fact, I have two of his pamphlets up in the apartment, *Futurist Reconstruction of Society* and *The Burning Question of Industrial Unionism.*"

Jim said casually, "Somebody was telling me about this Willard Saxe. He's one of the top men in your outfit, isn't he?"

Locke said evenly, "We have no top men in our organization. We don't have any leaders. We mistrust the conception. A leader can become a mis-leader. We're a democratic organization of peers. We make a fetish of being tough about admitting members. You've got to be really well grounded in our principles before we allow you to join. We don't want numbers at the expense of clarity. We'd rather have one thousand members who really understand our program, than a hundred thousand who are only emotionally involved." He hesi-

tated. "I don't mean that we don't accept the efforts of
the poorly founded, or the newcomers who haven't had
the time to become properly orientated, but we don't
allow them to be full members. We consider them simply as sympathizers."

"Well, that makes sense," Jim nodded. "What's the
chance of getting these pamphlets you were talking
about?"

"Let's go," Locke said, coming to his feet.

Jim Cotswold had used the excuse to get into
Locke's apartment, but drew a blank. The apartment
was slightly larger than a mini-apartment, having one
extra room, but it was hardly possible that Willard
Saxe, or even a midget, could have been hidden in
Locke's quarters. Not unless he was jammed into a
closet during the full period that Jim Cotswold was
present. And the size of Shyler-deme closets, in this
size apartment, didn't lead to that conjecture.

They had spent another hour or so with Locke describing the Saxe pamphlets and giving out with another lecture on Futurist wisdom. He wasn't exactly a
fanatic, but Jim Cotswold had the feeling of being
beaten over the head with it all, and made his escape as
soon as it was consistent with his supposed interest.

The following day, after the usual morning routine
involved in helping administer Shyler-deme, he was
summoned into Barry Ten Eyck's inner office along
with Bat Hardin, who was looking a bit on the harassed
side.

Jim said to him, "Any luck on the spy lenses?"

"No," Bat said. "If he's here in Shyler-deme, he's got
one far-out hidey-hole that he's stashed away in. Either
that, or you were right about plastic surgery."

Jim said, "I'd concentrate on something other than
his face."

"Not exactly easy when you're working with our
number of apartments. You haven't got all the time in
the world."

Barry Ten Eyck looked up from his desk when they

entered. He said, "Carol Ann's got your list of everybody even remotedly connected with the Futurists."

The two took chairs and the secretary brought them duplicate lists of names, I.D. numbers and apartment numbers.

Jim Cotswold hissed dismay at the length of the list. "I thought this was a small outfit."

"It is," Barry said. "There are only two full members in Shyler-deme, William Locke and another named Bronston, Felix Bronston. Then they're ten who are more or less interested in the movement."

"They call them sympathizers," Jim said. "Evidently, it isn't as easy as all that to join the Futurist Party. They want you to be really dedicated before they'll admit you."

Bat looked up from the list and said, "You talked to Locke?"

"That's right. Played the part of somebody interested. Drew a blank."

Bat said, "Listen, Jim, it might be a good idea for you to follow this up. Locke must have some sort of a group. They must hold meetings, give talks, plan activities, that sort of thing. At such a meeting you might pick up something."

"Good idea," Jim said, going back to the list.

Barry Ten Eyck said, "It's when you get to the relatives and friends of the Futurists and their sympathizers that the list gets long. You're dealing with the relatives and friends of twelve people. Hell, it runs up into the hundreds."

"They're still our best hope," Bat said. "In fact, they're about our only hope. Always assuming that this list is complete, and it's unlikely that it is, computer National Data Banks or no."

Jim said slowly, "One thing occurs to me that might narrow it down quite a bit."

He had their attention.

He said, "If he's hiding out in somebody's apartment, it's probably a single person who is giving him shelter, or, at most, a couple. The more people in on the secret, the more chance of somebody dropping something by mistake and exposing him. Especially kids."

"That sounds reasonable," Bat said. "We'll concentrate on bachelors and couples."

Carol Ann said thoughtfully, "There's another thing. Older folk are more apt to be conservative. I'd think that an organization such as this would be composed principally of younger people. Saxe himself is on the youngish side. I'll bet if he's hiding in somebody's apartment that it's the home of some younger person."

"Well, that'd narrow it down quite a bit more," Bat said. He came to his feet. "I'll go on over to my office and start checking it out, concentrating at first, at least, on the young singles and then on young doubles from this list. I'll activate the mini-spy lenses in their apartments."

Before he got out of the room, a desk phone tingled and Carol Ann answered it. She looked up at Barry Ten Eyck, "A Priority One call, scrambled."

The Democrat's eyebrows went up. "I'll be darned. Bat, hang around for a moment. Put it on the wall screen, Miss Cusack." He flicked a switch.

The face of Roy Thomas faded in. The Director of the Department of Emergency Affairs was obviously in a state of irritation.

He said snappishly, "This is a Priority One call and supposedly secure. However, our subject was once himself employed in the National Data Banks in New Denver and undoubtedly has various associates in other key spots. Consequently, we'll be discreet in what we say. First, have you had any results? I have already checked with the other demes."

Barry Ten Eyck said reasonably, "We've had less than twenty-four hours on the job. No, thus far we've no results. We're checking out various leads."

Roy Thomas grunted. He took a breath, deeply and as though still irritated. He said, "The necessity of this project has been intensified since I talked to you. The organization we are discussing has brought out a new publication written by our subject. Evidently, in spite of his fugitive status, he is still finding time to work."

Jim said, "Another pamphlet? I've already secured two, but haven't gotten around to reading them as yet."

Bat shrugged. "One more booklet wouldn't seem to make much difference."

The director turned the impatience on Bat Hardin. "The man is developing. His first pamphlet largely pointed out the need for minor changes in the Meritocracy system, a call for reforms. Some of them actually quite reasonable, and possibly some of the demands will be met—in time. The second work he turned out showed that he had been doing a good deal of research. It came out about a year after the first, and his organization had grown considerably. It called for stronger alterations in our system. However, both of them were mild tracts compared to the pamphlet which was released yesterday. It is, frankly, dynamite. The sort of pamphlet that moves people. If you know your American history, you are aware of the fact that the actual revolution of 1776 was precipitated by a single pamphlet, Tom Paine's *Common Sense*. Our subject hasn't perhaps quite reached the culmination of his career, but he's getting closer each day that goes by. One of these days, all the parts will fit together, and he'll have the final campaign plan for his group. We can't afford for that to happen."

Bat said, "Why not confiscate this new booklet?"

Thomas snorted disgust. "And by so doing bring it to the attention of everybody in the country who can read? Our best plan is to ignore it. Keep it from being reviewed in the mass media we control. The one way to guarantee the American people will read something is to tell them they can't. Not only would the thing be published in a thousand cellars, attics and back rooms on everything from handicraft printing presses to primitive duplicating machines, but they'd undoubtedly print it abroad and smuggle it in wholesale." He snorted again. "For that matter, it's already been placed in the National Library Banks. Giving it a restrictive priority rating would, once again, focus attention on it. No, our best bet, and it's not a very good one, is to completely ignore it."

Barry Ten Eyck said, "You're quite sure our, uh, subject is in Phoenecia?"

"More so than ever. This is imperative, gentlemen. He must be found if our socio-economic system is to stand. Our subject is a bomb with a lit fuse. I'll keep in touch with your progress." The authoritative face faded.

"Our progress, ha," Bat Hardin said.

They remained silent for the nonce. The Demecrat said, finally, "Any ideas, boys?"

Jim grumbled, "No. Listen, what gets me is that this character Saxe *still* hasn't done anything illegal. Evidently, they couldn't even ban this new pamphlet on the grounds of being subversive. He still evidently keeps within legal boundaries."

"Maybe they ought to pass some new laws," Barry muttered. "Get something on the books preventing basic changes in the politico-economic system no matter what method of bringing them about is advocated."

"Great," Jim said. "And wind up a dictatorship."

Carol Ann said, "Mr. Cotswold, if you are going to attend that Shrine of the White Goddess meeting, you'll have to get along."

Jim groaned and came to his feet.

Jim Cotswold winced when he entered the Community Church. Ordinarily, the room would accommodate two thousand five hundred persons. Now it was seemingly filled to the bursting point with less than a thousand. He estimated again. There were probably less than five hundred. It was just that one weird seemed capable of taking up three times the amount of space an ordinary person might.

Jim Cotswold was mildly taken aback. He hadn't realized that there were this many weirds in the building. Weirds begot weirds. They congregated together, herded together, each trying to outdo the other in their far-out activities. If the deme ever got the reputation of being a stronghold of the movement, the more sedate residents would move out en masse. He groaned inwardly. He could just see he and Barry and Bat presiding over a deme all of whose residents were weirds.

At least half of them were barefooted, at least half of the females were topless, whether or not nature had equipped them attractively in that department. At least half of them, male and female, wore shorts, and often nothing more. At least half of the men wore the current half-beard, possibly the most ludicrous facial hair style Jim Cotswold had ever seen. At least half of them were in the age bracket eighteen to twenty-five. A few younger, a few gray beards, but teens and twenties predominated. He wondered vaguely what happened to a flapper, a zoot-suiter, a rock 'n' roller, a hippy, a weird, when they grew older. They couldn't just disappear.

He made his way down the center aisle, something like a football quarterback. Swivel-hipped, he ducked this chattering group, made way around end of that shrilling sextet, side-stepped that gesticulating trio.

At the rostrum was what was obviously the committee, or whatever they called themselves in the Shrine of the White Goddess. Two of them carried what were plainly musical instruments, but which Jim Cotswold couldn't ever remember having seen before. Then it came to him. He remembered illustrations in a book on the Trojan War he had read as a boy. What was the title of it? *The Twilight of the Heroes* or some such. At any rate, the two weirds were carrying lyres. He wondered what kind of sounds they came up with. He could see now that they wore the short, kilt-like garb usually associated with Greeks of antiquity.

Centered among them was a girl who could have stood no more than five feet. She was as cute as the proverbial button, had a moppet face consisting largely of big eyes and a big mouth, and Jim Cotswold would have laid odds that she was smiling nine-tenths of the time. She was rigged up in what was probably meant to be a Grecian gown and wore Etruscan revival sandals on her feet. Her hair was piled atop her head in what he assumed was an attempt to recreate an ancient Greek hairdo. At least she seemed reasonably clean.

Since entering the Community Church he had recognized not a single person, which didn't unduly surprise him. Shyler-deme when full could house twenty thousand persons. Jim Cotswold doubted that he knew more than two hundred, and these mostly connected with the staff.

No, he took that back, one of the younger looking weirds gathered around the girl was familiar. Then it came to him. Harold Harrylad, the young man who had accumulated his Negative Income Tax until he had enough to throw a party involving a case of ultra-expensive Scotch. The other didn't recognize him—obviously. He had accomplished whisky nirvana when Jim saw him.

They had been jabbering rather excitedly until his approach. Now they fell silent and all eyes turned to the second Vice-Demecrat. His clothes alone branded him an outsider. Hell, he decided, a clean pair of pants would have branded you an outsider in this gathering.

For some reason, he addressed the girl rather than various others who were older, or less outlandishly attired.

He said, "I'm James Costwold, the Second Vice-Demecrat of Shyler-deme. Mr. Ten Eyck thought it might be a good idea for me to check out this first meeting of yours."

"The john-fuzz, come to roach us," Harold Harrylad said in disgust. "Why don't you shirk off?"

Jim looked at him in amusement. "Finish off the Scotch, Harry Harry?"

The youngster blinked, "How come you know me, flat?"

Jim said in amusement, "A Vice-Demecrat sees all, knows all."

"Get goosed," the other sneered.

The girl said, "We have permission to hold this rite."

"Of course," Jim said. "Mr. Ten Eyck just wondered

131

if we could be of any assistance. Any additional furnishing, or whatever, you might need."

The group wandered away, except for the girl. She said, "We extend thanks to you. I am Demeter."

"You're what?"

"I am Demeter, High Priestess of this Shrine, and rejoice in the love of the Mother Goddess."

Jim said, "Oh. I thought the name of your, uh, goddess was the White Goddess."

"The White Goddess was many-titled. She was the Great Goddess, the Triple-Goddess, and was many named in her various aspects as nymph or maiden, or as nubile or mature, or as crone, elderly. Long before the coming of the Aryans, who forcefully imposed their own male gods upon the people, the whole of Europe worshipped her. Indeed she was also known in Syria and Libya."

"Well, fine," Jim said. "Actually, I haven't read much mythology since I was a . . ."

"The White Goddess is not a myth, Mr. Cotswold," the girl said brightly. "She is the mother of all and her cult, though widely suppressed by the followers of the male gods—first the Greeks and then later the Jews, Christians and Mohammedans, has never completely disappeared from ken of man."

A slightly older weird came up. Jim recognized him.

"Hello, Jo-Jo," he said.

The other scowled at him. "What're you roaching Demeter about?"

Jim said mildly, "I'm not roaching her. Just came around to see that everything's all set. She's been telling me about, the, uh, White Goddess. So you're a follower of this, uh, Shrine?"

"Nah. You're not reading the script right, *padre*. I'm just here to hear the tale. Maybe help out a little. Maybe I'll join up later. I play it sage."

"The Mother Goddess wishes to gather all to her bosom," Demeter said softly.

Jim turned back to her. He said, smiling, "With so

132

many religions already in the world, why do we need another one?"

She smiled in return. She was a quick one with a smile. "You have it the wrong way, Mr. Cotswold. Ours is the original religion, going back to Neolithic times. It is these others that are johnny-come-latelys. To the sorrow of womankind and mankind they have perverted the mother-principle religion under which all were once free and happy."

Jim Cotswold was out of his field, but he tried to keep it going. "You said the Greeks were the ones that rang in the new male gods. But I thought that under the Greeks there was a Golden Age, not a loss of freedom and happiness."

"Perhaps it was a Golden Age for men—some men, Mr. Cotswold. But the Greeks of the time of Pericles held women in subjection to the point that they were little better than slaves. And it was the Greeks, Mr. Cotswold, who brought war to the Mediterranean world."

"Now you're really readin' him the script," Jo-Jo said in approval.

"Oh, come on now," Jim protested. "War we have always had with us."

"To the contrary, Mr. Cotswold, it is a comparatively new development. Fighting we have had, yes. Even in the animal world there is conflict, especially between rival males. There were even raids and group fights in the days of the White Goddess, but it was not until the coming of such cultures as the Hittites and the Aryan Greeks that war as we now know it evolved, that is, organized warfare for political and economic reasons: thousands upon tens of thousands of highly trained men whose purpose was to kill and enslave, to loot and take over the lands of others."

"So you want to return to the old days and the old ways," he said. "Neolithic ways."

"It might surprise you to know, Mr. Cotswold, that the ethical code of Neolithic times was higher than it is today."

"Wouldn't you have a hard time proving it at this late date?"

"Aw, why don't you shirk off?" Jo-Jo muttered. "You're too ossified in the head to get it. You flats are all the same."

But Demeter was still smiling. "The White Goddess' teachings are the proof, Mr. Cotswold."

Jim said, "Oh, one thing. Some of the other groups that utilize the Community Church here have protested that you, ah, indulge in orgies in your, ah, rites."

"Oh, fer Crissakes," Jo-Jo blurted. "You *really* aren't readin' the script. You flats just can't get the scenario."

Demeter said seriously, "The term orgy is oft misused, you must understand. It is true that in our rites we eat the sacred mushroom, *psilocybe,* to acquire oneness with the White Goddess, even as did the followers of Dionysus thousands of years ago. But orgies, in the sense that the word is most often used today, are not sponsored by the Shrine of the White Goddess. As you will see, if you remain."

One of the committee approached and spoke to her in a low voice.

She turned to Jim and said, "And now I must initiate the rites."

She began to mount the rostrum and the noise in the hall largely fell away.

Just to be saying something, Jim said to Jo-Jo, "So it was the Aryans who brought modern war to the world."

Jo-Jo looked at him scornfully. "Haven't you ever read that there weren't even walls around the cities that preceded them, such as Knossos, on Crete, or Mohenjo-Daro and Harappa in the Indus valley?"

"Okay," Jim said. "Let's sit down."

He stuck it out for almost an hour, deciding, finally, that seemingly all religions propagated just about the same routine. We had to love one another, banish hate. Do good. Think beautiful thoughts. Return good for evil. And so forth and so on.

He found himself yawning and wondered when the

hallucinogenic mushrooms would be eaten and what would take place then. He decided, suddenly, the hell with it. He could get Bat Hardin's Security to activate a spy lens in the hall and check it out later. He didn't have to be present.

He said, in half apology to the weird who had been sitting next to him, "I've got an appointment. So long."

"Get goosed," Jo-Jo said from the side of his mouth.

Evidently, Jim decided wryly, as he made his way up a side aisle to an exit, he hadn't made much of an impression on Jo-Jo.

He checked with Carol Ann Cusack on his pocket phone and found that nothing in particular was demanding his attention in the administration offices, so made his way back to his apartment. Theoretically, as Second Vice-Demecrat of Shyler-deme, he was on call twenty-four hours a day. In actuality, his time was largely his own to dispose of. On an average, he found himself putting in a ten hour day, usually during the hours when Barry Ten Eyck and Bat Hardin were off, but now, of course, the Willard Saxe emergency was keeping him on the job during the same period they worked.

His apartment was somewhat larger than most bachelors were wont to maintain. As a sportsman, he disliked the ultra-small places so common in this age. He would rather put his income into roomy quarters than expend it for some of the other luxuries.

So it was that he even had a small escape sanctum, that ultimate retreat in a world where it had become difficult to retreat into solitude.

He dialed himself a drink, went over to his store of amateur films and selected a roll which he had taken in Africa on his last vacation. He took it over to the TV screen on one wall and inserted it and in doing so wondered all over again how much money he had spent in his time on photographic equipment. When he had first taken up the hobby of amateur movies, he had bought a movie projector. He had barely more than learned to operate it than the new development which allowed you to use your TV screen had come about and he hadn't been able to sell the projector for more than a tenth of what he had paid for it. Projectors were antiquated. And cameras? Ha! You hardly got one home before it was antiquated.

He sat and watched for a few minutes scenes of various wild life he had taken in East Africa on one of the reserves, but then became restless. He was nervously unhappy about the developments of the last forty-eight hours, and something he couldn't quite put his finger on was nagging him.

On the small table next to his comfort chair were the two pamphlets he had received from Locke. He flicked the TV screen off and picked one of them up. *Futurist Reconstruction of Society*. He checked the front of the booklet and found it was the second one that Willard Saxe had written, evidently more dynamic than the first, but not as much so as the one that had just been published a day or so ago. He turned to the first page, initially figuring on scanning the work, but in a few moments he had become engrossed.

When Jim Cotswold entered the office in the morning, Barry Ten Eyck and Carol Ann were already there and a weary Bat Hardin dropped in shortly later.

As usual, Barry wanted to know what spun, and they both told him, "Nothing." Bat was disgusted. Evidently, he had spent the better part of the past twenty-four hours checking out his micro-spy lenses and digging into the personal affairs of everyone even remotely connected with the Futurists.

Jim said, "One thing occurred to me, just before I came down here. How long has our friend William Locke been in Shyler-deme?"

Barry Ten Eyck's eyes narrowed slightly, as he got it immediately. He said, "You want to check that out, Miss Cusack?"

"Coming up."

Jim said, "Probably silly, but you remember that Purloined Letter bit?"

"You mean where the missing letter was right out in the open, and nobody found it because it wasn't really hidden?" Bat said.

"That's right. What better disguise could a man like Saxe have than local leader of the Futurists—right out in the open?"

Barry Ten Eyck scoffed. "According to the data banks, doesn't he work over at Dodge-Myers?"

"Ummm, but remember that he used to work in the National Data Banks. And probably so do other Futurists. Wouldn't it be possible to file a counterfeit dossier?"

"Good grief," Barry said. "I don't know if it's possible or not but, if it could be done at all, somebody who worked there would be in the best position to establish a false identity."

Carol Ann said, "He rented his apartment here from a resident who left six months ago."

Bat said slowly, "It would have been possible for him to have come here and established his identity as William Locke and then have gone back to New Denver to his job. Periodically, he could turn up here, but how much checking is done on a bachelor? He could show up weekends and so forth, and nobody would ever know he wasn't a full-time resident."

Barry Ten Eyck said, "All right. Get into the deme data banks. Find out how much food and booze and other purchases go into that apartment. Check out whether or not he actually works at Dodge-Myers. I don't have to tell you what else. Check him all ways from the middle. If his identity is phony, you'll be able to find evidence of it."

"Great," Bat said, standing.

After he was gone, Jim said to Carol Ann, "One other little item you might check for me. Could you see if there's a dictionary of weird slang in the Library Banks?"

"Of what?" she said, wrinkling up her nose.

"Weird slang, idiom. It might be listed under Neo-hippy slang, I don't know. If you find anything, put it on my desk library booster, will you?"

"No rest for the wicked," she snarled.

"What do you think you've got, Jim?" Barry said, only half interested.

"Probably nothing. I'll be in the other room."

It was only a few minutes later that Jim Cotswold's desk phone lit up and Carol Ann's face faded in.

She said, "Surprise, surprise. There are two books devoted to Neo-hippy slang."

He said, "Put them on one at a time, will you, please?"

Jim Cotswold stood before the identity screen on the door of Apartment 142 on the fourteenth floor of Tower-One and said into it, "James Cotswold, Second Vice-Demecrat of Shyler-deme, calling on Mr. Harry-lad."

The screen said sleepily, "He ain't here. Shirk off."

Jim said, "Open up, please."

The voice said, "I told you. He ain't here. Don't be a flat. We're getting some slumber."

Jim said, "I can have the door opened by Security, you know. Why go to all the bother?"

"Listen, you can't just go around breaking into apartments."

"As you just mentioned," Jim said patiently, "the owner isn't here. You're not the proprietor of this apartment."

The door opened. Inside, a half dozen or so weirds were sprawled around, most of them still asleep. Three were in the bed, cross-wise, one was in the comfort chair and the others on the floor, pillows under their heads. There was still the stale air of sweat, other body odors, booze and vomit in the room.

The one in the comfort chair was obviously he who had answered the summons of the door. He had one eye open to glare balefully at Jim Cotswold.

Jim said with a sigh, "Do you know where Harold Harrylad is?"

"Hairy Harry went off with a gang."

"Do you know where he went?"

"To some other hole. We wanted to sleep, they wanted to drink sea-booze."

"Do you know to which apartment he went?"

"No. Go on, shirk off, get spayed, we're busy."

"I can see you are," Jim said. "Do you know where Jo-Jo is?"

"No."

"Where's his apartment?"

"How would I know?" The other raised his voice. "Hey, anybody know what hole old Jo-Jo has?"

Nobody bothered to answer.

A voice came from one of the pillows, so muffled as hardly to be heard. "I saw him a little while ago in Jerry's hole. He was arguing with somebody or other. Arguing about religion, or something or other."

Jim said, "Where is Jerry's apartment?"

"Down the hall. Number, let's see, Number 148, I think. Why don't you cut out all the noise and shirk off?"

"Thanks," Jim said. He turned to leave but then turned back again. "What's Jo-Jo's name?"

The occupant of the comfort chair looked at him as though he was insane. "Wha'd'ya mean, what's his name? Don't be a flat. His name is Jo-Jo."

"What's his real name?"

"How the hell would I know what his real name is? What's wrong with Jo-Jo? Why don't you get spayed?"

Jim Cotswold made his way down the hall to Apartment 148 and stood before the screen. "James Cotswold," he said. "Calling on Jo-Jo."

"I'm busy," the door screen said.

"You'll be busier still, if you don't open this confounded door," Jim said evenly.

"Fer Crissakes, once a john-fuzz, always a john-fuzz," the door screen grumbled. "Come on in if you gotta, *padre*."

The door opened and Jim Cotswold entered. Jo-Jo was seated in the mini-apartment's sole comfort chair and had obviously been scanning the library booster screen. He looked up, his stubbly face in disgust.

Jim said, "Hi, Willard."

"The name's Jo-Jo," the other said.

"The name is Willard Saxe," Jim Cotswold said.

The other looked at him for a long moment, ruefully. "Oh," he said. "Now that you mention it, so it is. Evidently, I underestimated you, Mr. Cotswold."

"Yes," Jim said. "And in a way, I'm sorry."

The weird guise was now dispensed with, as was the terminology, but suddenly there was a small Gyro-jet pistol in the other's hand.

Jim shook his head and smiled deprecation. "You couldn't use it, and unless you're willing to use a shooter, it doesn't do you any good."

"How do you know I couldn't use it?" Saxe said, bringing a tough rasp into his voice.

"Because I've read two of your pamphlets, Mr. Saxe, and it isn't in you to kill a man in cold blood. On top of that, if you did, Roy Thomas would, at long last, have a legitimate charge against you, one that would even enable him to extradite you if you left this country."

"You're right, of course," Willard Saxe said in disgust. He tossed the gun aside. "How in the hell did you locate me?"

Jim Cotswold lowered himself on the couch and said, "A lot of little things. For one, although your plastic surgery job is excellent, such mannerisms as your walk are still with you and I recognized it, although that didn't come to me for a time. Another thing that was in the back of my mind was that by merging yourself into the undisciplined ranks of the weirds, you were able to eat and sleep without having a credit card of your own. They drift about like herds, sleeping here one day, somewhere else the next. This apartment belongs to one called Jerry, evidently, but he isn't here now, and evidently doesn't give a damn if you stick around, days on end, probably. Possibly he doesn't even know you are here.

"But that wasn't the big thing. You know, a good many people have little slang words or phrases of their own, sometimes using them unconsciously. "Yours is, *you ain't reading the script*. It came to me, in a vague sort of way, that I hadn't heard anybody else among the weirds ever use that term. And then, last night, I read your *Futurist Reconstruction of Society* and in one tongue-in-check passage—by the way I congratulate you on your humorous style . . ."

"Thanks," Saxe said dryly. "Go on."

"In one passage you used the phrase, '*the Meritcrats just aren't reading the correct script.*' That clued me. I checked a slang dictionary and found that the term isn't part of Neo-hippy idiom."

Saxe nodded wearily. "I underestimated you, Mr. Cotswold."

Jim said, "It was a good try. You must have set it up some time ago, when you first considered the possibility that the Department of Emergency Affairs might try to crack down on you in some extra-legal manner. You arrived here and got in touch with some associate, possibly Locke. He met you outside the deme and loaned you his pocket phone I.D. card. With it, you were able to enter the building and the elevators and go to his apartment, since our Security checks a pocket phone, but unless you attempt to buy something, or some service, using the fingerprint screen is not required. Once in his apartment, another associate carried his pocket phone back down to him so that he too could now enter. From there on I don't know the details, but obviously don't have to. You submerged yourself into the ranks of the weirds. You were able to move around with them, within reason, since they go about in unruly packs. A spy lens has its work cut out with a milling mob of weirds. You were probably even able to borrow a pocket phone, from time to time. You couldn't use it to buy anything, of course, but you could get about the building with it. There must be between five hundred and a thousand weirds in this deme; the line where one becomes a complete weird is on the elusive side. I imagine some of those in Shyler-deme are sympathetic to the Futurist cause. They probably ponied up the extra food and other requirements."

"All right," Saxe said. "You've made a few mistakes, but they aren't important." He leaned forward. "Mr. Cotswold, the work I am embarked upon is most necessary."

"I don't doubt that. At least in your eyes," Jim said sourly. "However, Roy Thomas brands you the most dangerous man in the United States."

"Yes," the other snorted. "Most dangerous to Roy Thomas and the group he represents. But does this group represent the best interests of the majority of the people of our country?"

"We who agree with him think so."

"Cotswold, let me tell you something. A big change took place in the United States about the middle of the Twentieth Century. For the first time in the history of the race we reached an era where man no longer had to work to secure subsistence. Technology had brought us to the point where we could produce an abundance with a minimum of labor. Your father and mine *had* to work for their daily bread, unless they were born into the ranks of the wealthy. No more. The average citizen today can simply go on what amounts to an endless dole, from cradle to the grave, if he so wishes."

Jim Cotswold said glumly, "And an increasing number so wish. A whole new generation has already grown up ignoring what we used to think were the basic virtues."

Willard Saxe nodded very seriously. "And under Meritocracy the trend will intensify."

Jim scowled at him. "How do you mean?"

"I mean that the highest ranking Meritcrats and the old rich who own the cosmocorps do not wish changes in the status quo. Changes could jeopardize their privileges. They refuse to increase the amount of NIT for a double reason. If it was increased, then a larger percentage of the population would shun the more menial jobs, such as being servants, and there are still such jobs even in our computerized, automated, ultramated society. Secondly, larger incomes might lead to greater numbers being able to go further through school and in other wise educate themselves, and an educated people are a dangerous people. Don't look to your poor and downtrodden for the rebel in society, Mr. Cotswold. The poverty-stricken have no time for revolt, they are almost invariably stupid, the elements of which mobs are made perhaps, but not devoted reformers or social pioneers."

Jim said, unhappily, "Go back away there. If there's not enough work in the country for most of the people on NIT, what would you have them doing, even if you did increase NIT?"

"Mr. Cotswold," Saxe said urgently, "man has reached one of the goals that has been before him since his infancy. We have the ability to make this world of ours a paradise now. Instead, what are we doing?" He made a gesture that encompassed the room, but was obviously meant to extend beyond. "We live like ants in demes. We eat mass-produced food and drink beverages that come out of laboratories and factories rather than from vineyards. We wear artificial textiles that have little real beauty and are deliberately manufactured to be disposed of after a few days of wear. Ours is an artificial, unhappy society. Our adults as well as our children spend a disgusting percentage of the day staring at violence on their Tri-Di sets. And now the government is even ignoring, if not sponsoring, the use of trank, a happiness drug, to keep the rank and file content.

"Mr. Cotswold, now that we've solved the problem of producing abundance, we must return to the old things that used to bring man satisfaction. We should return to the arts, the handicrafts, the love of the countryside, the pleasures in nature. Here we are keeping ourselves cooped up in a few thousand demes scattered about the country. It's madness. Why, just take one thing, the forests. When the white man first landed in America, he promptly began cutting down some of the most beautiful forests on earth. He cut them down for lumber to build his homes, for firewood, for furniture. He cut them down to clear the land for his agriculture, later to manufacture paper. But now, Mr. Cotswold, we no longer use lumber for building materials, furniture, nor certainly for heat. Paper we use in moderation with the coming of modern media. We could embark upon a gigantic reforestation of our country which could make it one vast national park, save for those areas most suited to agriculture. All New England, for instance, could be a national park."

Jim said, "So, instead of taking in each other's washing, we'd take in each other's paintings, eh?"

The other chuckled ruefully, and began to come to his feet. "I'm being foolish. Obviously, I can't convert you to my way of thinking in half an hour. We might as well go. I suppose you'll want to turn me over to Roy Thomas's bully boys."

Cotswold didn't stir, as yet. He said, "Thomas told us that, given a dynamic organization such as the Futurists, the computers report Meritocracy could be overthrown within three years. But he's of the opinion that if the authorities can stave this off for ten years, they'll be so entrenched that no revolt would be possible."

Willard Saxe said bitterly, "And he's right. Past police states never had it so good. What spirit is left in our people will have been submerged in a sea of freeloading, Tri-Di shows, and trank. And the police will have their spy lenses and bugging down to the point where everything that anybody says or does will be computer monitored. But, as I say, I can't convert you in half an hour, Cotswold. Let's go."

Jim Cotswold stood at last, feeling infinitely weary. He said, "You'd better get underway, Saxe. To Canada, or wherever. If I was able to find you, Barry

Ten Eyck and Bat Hardin will be able to do so, too. And maybe they won't feel the way I do."

Willard Saxe looked at him for a long silent period. Finally, he said, "And how do you feel?"

Jim Cotswold said, with self-depreciation, "You see, I subscribe to the statement once made by S. G. Tallentrye, but which is usually attributed to Voltaire. *'I disapprove of what you say, but I will defend to the death your right to say it.'* "

Part Four
Carol Ann Cusack

By the time Carol Ann Cusack had gotten back from her brisk constitutional in the parks which surrounded Shyler-deme, Sidney Cusack was up and shambling about the apartment. He looked at her blearily even as he dialed a cup of coffee on the auto-table in the little alcove that doubled as kitchen and dining room. Why they still called them kitchens was a question; less than half the apartments in the deme contained any kind of stove.

Carol Ann said commiseratively, "How are you feeling, dear?"

He grinned at her in self-deprecation. "Lousy as a louse. However I discovered a great truth which shall undoubtedly be useful the rest of my life. You should never mix liquor and trank."

The table sank in the middle, came back up again with the steaming coffee. He reached for it shakily and carried it into the living room.

"Where've you been, doll, jogging around the woods again? One of these days you're going to meet some crackpot out there, this early in the morning, when there's nobody else around, and he'll knock you over the head."

"I doubt it," she said, turning the sides of her wide warm mouth down. "The Security TV spy lenses are operative on a twenty-four hour a day basis. Anything

147

offbeat picked up is flashed to whoever's on duty. If necessary, a Human Relations officer comes zipping up in a patrol car. I don't believe there's been a successful mugging in the history of Phoenecia."

"There can always be a first time." He shakily sipped at the coffee.

Carol Ann went over to the auto-table and dialed her own breakfast. Scrambled eggs, synthetic bacon, toast, margarine, marmalade, coffee. She made a practice of taking a good breakfast. Watch the calories, if you must, at lunch and dinner, but start the day with a substantial meal.

She said casually, her glossy brows slightly quizzical, "You came in late, dear."

He looked over at her impatiently. "I was discussing a deal with Larry Tinker and Bert Allen."

"Over drinks and trank?"

"Oh, come off it Carol," he said irritably.

"Sorry," she said, sitting down to the small table. "But why is it always a deal you're working on—never a job?"

He was slightly indignant. "You know how hard I've tried to get a job, doll. There just aren't any jobs any more these days. You're lucky to have one. Why, half the people in this country must be on Negative Income Tax."

"It's partly luck, perhaps, but luck averages out. Just about everybody gets just about the same amount, over the years. You've got to be able to grab it when it comes along."

Her food arrived and she darted a look at the time and began to eat.

"What is that supposed to mean?" he demanded, as though being put upon.

She sighed. "Oh, golly, Sid, you're too hard to please in looking for work. You don't take your chances when they come along. Any kind of a job at all is better than just sitting around day in and out collecting your NIT. Under Meritocracy the thing to do is get in anywhere,

148

anywhere you can find an opening, and then prove your value."

"With my half-assed education? I've got two strikes against me before I start."

"I'm sorry, Sid. I seem always to be after you. I know you had bad luck in your school. So much illness and all. But ... well, for that matter, you could be taking courses now. Studying here at home through the TV schools, since you're not working anyway; preparing yourself for one of the positions that do open up from time to time."

"Ha," he grumbled. "Such as what? Besides, I'm no kid any longer, Carol. I'm past the age of taking lessons. I've just got to wait around until the breaks come."

Carol Ann finished her coffee, put down her cup. She said, "Look, dear, I'm in pretty good with the Head Chef. He has some twenty persons in his Division. There's a more than usual turnover in the Restaurant Division. Cooks and other food workers seem to be temperamental. They're always quitting and going off to another job."

"So?"

"So you could take some quick courses in food handling. Prepare yourself. I'll drop a word to Pierre Daunou. Perhaps Mr. Ten Eyck will do the same—as a favor to me. Then the next time there's an opening ..."

"Women's work," Sidney Cusack said in disgust.

Carol Ann said, "Why, that's ridiculous, darling. All the great chefs are men. Why, more than half of the kitchen staff are men."

"I say cooking is women's work. Those guys who go into it are all limp-wristed types. Besides, I haven't studied being a chef. I've got no background in the field. If I got a job, it'd be the lowest one in the division. I'd be peeling carrots, or something."

She said wearily, "In an automated kitchen, Sid, nobody peels carrots, or anything else. There's no more

149

drudgery. It's more like office work than anything else."

"Well, there's another thing. I'd start at the very bottom of the totem pole. I wouldn't get much more than I collect on Negative Income Tax. And you're secretary to the Demecrat in this deme. You'd be making at least twice as much as me."

"Well, golly, dear, you've got to start somewhere. You're not making anything at all now. I admit it must be hard on a man like yourself to have his wife making a larger salary, but how much pride can you take in remaining on NIT?"

He dialed himself another coffee. "My chance will come along. But I doubt if it will be here in Phoenecia."

"How do you mean, dear?"

"I mean they're down on me here. I've had a run of bad luck and now they've all got a mistaken idea. That Dodge-Myers job fell through when I got, uh, sick and ... well, anyway, I'm all but blacklisted in these parts."

The pace of his words sped up and his tone became urgent. "Look, doll, why don't we do this? You ditch your job and I'll apply for a mobile home and electro-steamer to pull it. We'll abandon this apartment, or sell the equity in it, if we can, and we'll go out West and join one of the mobile towns or cities. See the country. Then somewhere we'll get a chance for both of us to get jobs—sooner or later."

Carol Ann checked the time again and finished off the meal. She wasn't hungry enough to eat the dishes and threw them into the disposal chute.

She looked at him, keeping impatience from expression and tone. She said, "Poor Sid. Admittedly, you're eligible to apply for a mobile home. You've never applied for any kind of home. This apartment is in my name. But the thing is, dear, that the moment you do, from then on the National Bank automatically deducts, each month, from your Negative Income Tax credit, until the home is paid for. You don't even manage to get by on your full NIT. How could you possibly make out if there was a sizable deduction from it each month?"

"But we'd both be getting NIT and living out there in the West, or down in Mexico. It's cheaper than it is here in a high-rise deme. There aren't so many things to spend your money on in a mobile town. It's the real life, doll." He was talking himself into a high state of enthusiasm.

She said gently, "Darling, don't you see you're kidding yourself? You like deme life. You like all the facilities. You like to eat out in the restaurants, have drinks in the bars, associate with all your friends, take in the live theatre. All that would be gone in a mobile town, particularly down in Mexico. And we'd no longer have my income. We'd both be on NIT, right on the edge of the poverty level."

She came to her feet. "I'm going to have to run."

His slightly puffy but handsome face was in just short of a pout. However, he said, "Uh, Carol, what's the chances of ordering some trank for me?"

She looked at him, her unusually dark blue eyes registering surprise.

He said urgently, "I've used up all my Credit Balance for this month and . . ."

"Already?"

"Well, yes. I've got to carry my share of the load in a bar, or wherever. You can't get a reputation as a deadbeat. If you do, you'll never get a break if some deal jells. You have to be in good with the boys. Last night, Larry and Bert picked up the tab. I ought to at least spring for some trank, today."

She went over to the apartment's delivery box, fishing her pocket phone cum credit I.D. card from her purse. She said worriedly, "Sid, you shouldn't be taking trank during the day hours—if ever."

He didn't answer that.

She put the pocket phone in the appropriate slot and dialed the ultra-market down in the bowels of the high-rise building. She dialed pharmacy and gave her order verbally, at the same time placing her right thumb print on the delivery box's identity screen.

She didn't wait for the delivery but took up her small, flat pocket phone, which when closed looked remarkably like a cigarette case, and returned it to her bag.

She said, "I have to hurry, darling. Will I see you for lunch?"

"Well, I don't know. I've got a couple of important things cooking, doll."

"Well, try to make it if you can, dear."

She perked her face up for his kiss, refraining from showing annoyance at his breath. He must have been drinking that cheap sea-booze the night before.

When she arrived at Administration, Jim Cotswold was already at his desk in the outer office, although she was early.

He looked up when she came in and said, "Early to bed, early to rise doesn't do much for those milkmen guys."

"Huuup," she snorted. "You're out of date. The last milkman died of old age, years ago. It's all automated now. Besides, I thought it went: all work and no play makes jack."

She paused at his desk for a moment and said, "How was the convention?"

He shrugged. "The usual. You ought to attend one, one of these days, Carol. You get a lot of new ideas rubbing up against other pros. Barry wouldn't mind you attending."

"He seldom goes himself," she said. "Too busy, he says. Personally, I think they bore him."

"They're fun. Lots of laughs, lots of drinks. You renew friendships, meet Demecrats and division chiefs from all over the country. Did you know there was a deme down in Arizona, sitting off all by itself in the middle of nowhere, devoted completely to nudists?"

"Golly, what a theme," Carol Ann laughed. "Don't

tell me their delegate to the convention came in a fig leaf."

"I still say you ought to take one in. It'd give you a needed break."

She shook her head. "I couldn't go without Sid and non-employees of demes aren't encouraged."

Cotswold shrugged again. "Why don't you dump that clown and take up with Barry Ten Eyck? He's hot for you."

She said evenly, "I thought you were a friend of mine, Mr. Cotswold. It so happens that I love my husband."

He said, "Sorry. It's your business."

"Yes." It wasn't in her to hold rancor. She said, in different tone, "What was particularly new?"

"Oh, the same old stuff. New architecture, new gadgets. Bechtel and Kaiser presented a new idea that's going to wow them, variable-size apartments."

"Variable? How do you mean?"

He leaned back in his chair. "They lay the deme out in such a way that you can increase the size of your apartment, or decrease it, according to your needs. Suppose a young couple takes an apartment with four rooms. They get prosperous and decide they can afford an escape sanctum. Next to them is a fellow whose wife just died and he's all alone and doesn't want the expense of maintaining such a large place. Bing, bing, a couple of buttons are pushed and their apartment takes over one room of his. Then suppose they have a child and want still another room. Assuming that there's one available from the other side, or from the single they already got one from, they take it over. Or if there's an empty mini-apartment next to them they might take the whole thing over."

She said, "They're getting quite a sizable place."

"Sure, but that comes into it, too. When they get older and retire and the kids go off and get married, they decide they don't need so much space and turn one or more rooms over to any neighbors who might.

Or, for that matter, alter one or more of them into mini-apartments and sell the equity."

Carol Ann was interested. "How is it adjusted with the government, and your payments on your apartment?"

"The government refinances your loan, either upward or downward."

Barry Ten Eyck entered briskly, briefcase under his arm.

"Morning, all you beaming happy people," he said purposely overdoing it. "See you're back, Jim. Come on into the office and give me some ulcers describing how our competitors are antiquating good old Shylerdeme."

"You'll acquire half a dozen of them," his Second Vice-Demecrat said, coming to his feet to follow.

The three of them filed into the Demecrat's private office and found chairs, Barry Ten Eyck and Carol Ann Cusack behind their respective desks. Carol Ann took a quick check of her auto-secretary phone screen to see if there was anything immediate that had accumulated since her last shift. There didn't seem to be anything urgent.

"There's one little item that will eventually chill you, old chum-pal," Cotswold said. "It looks as though that bill allowing the construction of demes and even pseudo-cities in such countries as Mexico, Guatemala and Costa Rica is going to pass."

"Good grief," Barry said. "It'll start a new fad. Residents will be swarming south of the border like lemmings. But how are they going to keep from antagonizing the locals by having what would amount to American colonies all over their countries?"

"They're going to allow the natives to buy apartments. The won't be exclusively American. Americans, of course, get the government loan, just as up here, the others have to pay up in cash, or get local loans from their own sources."

Barry said, "The idea of the construction of the pseudo-cities was to keep the American industrial

154

boom going. And the idea of Negative Income Tax was to keep consumer buying booming. This will send a lot of the boom abroad."

Jim shook his head. "They took care of that. The bill provides that all materials used in construction must come from the States, or from sources owned by American-incorporated cosmocorps. And three quarters of all materials and commodities used for serving the demes have to come from the States."

Barry shook his head. "Well, what else came up that's going to result in losing residents?"

"All the latest-design demes have larger mini-apartments. Same price, but larger. In fact, it's stretching a point to call some of them mini-apartments any more."

"How can they be the same price, if they're larger?"

"Old chum-pal, ultra-mation marches on. Mid-West Construction is spending half a billion this year on new plants. They figure they're going to have the amount of labor to build a deme. By the way, they also figure that their new buildings will be so ultra-mated that they'll be able to cut the staffs by one third."

Barry Ten Eyck winced exaggeratedly. "This deme of ours is only nine years old and already it's antiquated. Miss Cusack, how many apartments were vacated this past week?"

"Mrs. Cusack," she said, checking a phone screen. "One hundred and twelve."

He groaned but said, "That's not as bad as it might be. How many of the vacancies were filled?"

"Forty-eight."

"And that's not as good as it might be."

Carol Ann said, "The trouble is, Mr. Ten Eyck, that it's the better grade apartments that are being vacated. Our new tenants are usually weird types moving into the mini-apartments. Most of them are on NIT, evidently, and the more of that type we get the more the element holding down jobs and leading normal lives moves out. It's something like the cities in the old days. The more relief families that moved in from the South and Puerto Rico, the more the middle class and the higher-paid workers moved into the suburbs. It eventually got to the point that nobody who could avoid it remained in the cities."

"You're telling me nothing new, Miss Cusack."

Jim said, "Did you hear the news this morning?"

The other two looked at him expectantly.

"More agitation to raise the amount of Negative Income Tax. The argument being, of course, that it would keep up the expansion of the production of commodities."

Barry shook his head wearily. "It's a vicious circle. Already we have a large element that goes from the cradle to the grave without working. And what's more they don't want to work. They plan their schooling so that they'll wind up with abilities that are unuseful in any industry, they deliberately choose parts of the country in which to live where jobs are unavailable. Theoretically, you're supposed to take a job if one is available and you're on the Negative Income Tax, but in actuality there are a score of ways to get out of it. Or, if you finally do find yourself working, to get yourself fired so you can go back on NIT."

Cotswold nodded agreement. "The only thing that keeps as many of us working as are is that NIT is just above the poverty level—as they define poverty these days. If you increased it, another large percentage of the population would decide that there wasn't any point in working."

Carol Ann said soothingly. "It doesn't apply to everyone, Mr. Ten Eyck. It doesn't apply to you, for instance."

"All right, all right. It doesn't apply to me. I'm ambitious to get ahead in this Meritocracy of ours. And I doubt if it applies to either of you two. However, it applies to one hell of a large percentage of the working population that hold down the less desirable jobs, the more tedious ones, and they still exist in spite of all of our automation and technology."

A screen buzzed and Carol Ann checked it and looked up. "Mr. Hardin, Mr. Ten Eyck."

Barry flicked a switch on one of his own screens and said, "Morning, Bat, what's spinning?"

Bat Hardin's heavy face filled the screen. "Minor crisis. Want to hear about it?"

"No," Barry sighed, "but come on over. Jim is fouling up my day telling me about new developments at the convention." Barry flicked off the screen.

Bat came in moments later, his face in habitual worry.

"Unlax, Bat," Barry told his Vice-Demecrat. "You said it was only a minor crisis."

Bat said his good mornings to Carol and Jim Cotswold and sank down into a chair. "Big fight up in Tower-Two, eighteenth floor. Well, not really as big as all that, but I'm afraid we're going to have to expel some tenants before we're through."

"Oh, swell. We aren't losing them fast enough, we have to kick some out," Jim Cotswold said.

"What happened?" Barry said.

"Big party some of the weirds threw. The usual, objectionable type. Lots of sea-booze, lots of trank, lots of noise, lots of promiscuity, probably. It evidently started out fairly small but then more and more of the crackpots drifted in. The apartment was only a two-roomer. The party began to spill out into the hall and into a mini-apartment across the way. Loud music, loud voices. The usual weird get-together."

"So?" Barry said wearily.

"So some of the inhabitants of the neighboring apartments came out and gave them an argument. It erupted into a fist fight and some of the complaining residents took a beating. They went back to their own quarters and called Security. I wasn't on. Fred Jeffers was. He sent a couple of the boys up to quell the thing and they did. However, those that were hurt put in a beef. They named the three weirds that did the fighting. Charged them with assault."

"All right, what conclusions have you come to, Bat?"

"We're going to have to expel them or it'll result in

157

more desirable elements leaving. Actually, we don't want them anyway. Troublemakers."

"All right. I assume we have sufficient evidence of that to kick them out. Miss Cusack, get their names and apartment numbers."

"Mrs. Cusack," she said. She looked over at Bat Hardin.

He seemed embarrassed and chewed momentarily on his lower lip.

"Well, what are their names, Mr. Hardin? I'm recording it."

Bat Hardin took a rueful breath. "Bert Allen, Larry Tinker and . . . Sidney Cusack."

Her face was flushed. Carol Ann Cusack came to her feet. She snapped, "Mr. Hardin, my husband is not a weird."

"Sorry. I'm just passing on what the Human Relations officers reported. I'm sure everybody concerned will have a fair hearing." Bat Hardin's voice was apologetic, but firm.

Carol Ann turned abruptly and without a further word marched from the room.

The three of them looked after her expressionlessly.

"Couldn't you have handled that more diplomatically, Bat?" Barry said.

"No, I couldn't. She works here in this office. Sooner or later she'd have to know." Bat Hardin sighed. "I don't have to tell either of you the fellow's a slob. He beat the bajauz out of a man fifteen years older than him, evidently using hand combat methods he picked up during his hitch in the military. He was drunk, of course, and probably on trank as well, but that doesn't excuse anything. He could have seriously hurt the guy."

Barry Ten Eyck said, "She's the best woman on the staff. She's loyal. If he goes, she'll go."

Jim Cotswold said, "She's not only a top worker, but she's pleasant to have around. Damn nice girl."

His two assistants looked at Barry Ten Eyck for his decision.

He stirred unhappily in his chair.

"Bat, talk to the guy. Look here, you wouldn't have a job for him in Security, would you?"

"I wouldn't have him in Security," Bat said flatly, "military experience or no military experience. But you're the boss."

"No. You're right, of course. Talk to him. Within reason, give him hell. As for the other two, kick them out as quickly as you can push it through." He looked at the others in despair. "What is it that makes a weird?"

Jim Cotswold said sourly, "It's not really a new breed. We've always had the equivalent with us. You've got two kinds of people. The one kind has to work, an inner drive. They want to produce, create, be of use to the society in which they live. The others don't want to work. In past societies they were usually, but not always, driven to it. The Roman lumpen proletariat, the mob, were an example. Finally, keeping them in bread and circuses pulled the Empire down."

Barry Ten Eyck sighed. "Yeah, well. Handle it, Bat, as best you can. Meanwhile, Carol Ann is far from stupid. Eventually she'll get fed up with the guy."

When Carol Ann got back to the apartment, Sid had finished shaving and cleaning up but still hadn't dressed.

He said, surprised at seeing her, "What're you doing off the job, doll? Did laughing boy fire you?"

She said emptily, "What happened last night?"

His tone was defensive, but he looked away from meeting her eyes. "I told you I took a little too much trank and sea-booze."

"Security reported it. A more than usually all-out weird party . . ."

"Hey, they got some nerve, calling my friends weirds."

". . . which finally ended in a free for all with the

159

neighbors. It's not just your friends who have been branded weirds, Sid. You are too. Bat Hardin thinks you and your chum-pals Larry Tinker and Bert Allen should be expelled from Shyler-deme."

"They can't do that. Both Larry and Bert own their mini-apartments."

She said, her voice tired, "Yes, they can, Sid. The rules pertaining to a deme allow a Demecrat arbitrarily to expel any resident. It can be appealed to the Central Management of whatever cosmocorps controls the deme, but in a case like this there's small chance that they'd reverse the decision of a Demecrat with as good a record as Barry Ten Eyck, especially when these friends of yours live in mini-apartments on NIT."

Sid Cusack was indignant. "Well, what happens to their equity in their apartments?"

"It's wiped out by the government, who ponied it up in the first place. Or, if the apartment was bought outright, the government refunds the present estimated value of it."

"It's not fair."

"Be that as it may, dear, that's the way it's done. Your friends can go elsewhere and get different apartments, or buy mobile homes."

"Well, how does laughing boy feel about it?"

"When I left, the impression I got was that Mr. Ten Eyck was in favor of tossing all three of you out."

Sid Cusack thought about it, his face dark. "The sonofabitch would never kick me out. He wouldn't want to lose you. They know when they've got a good thing. Actually, you know as much about running a deme as Ten Eyck, Hardin and Cotswold put together. You ought to be at least a Second Vice-Demecrat."

Carol Ann sighed again. "Among other things, I haven't a degree in deme management from a university, dear."

"Well, they'll never take a chance losing you. Good deme staff personnel doesn't grow on trees."

She took a deep breath. "Sid, face reality. You've simply got to stop living this almost weird life you do and get yourself a job. It can't go on this way. And, golly, dear, just look how well we'd be fixed if we were both working. A couple of years of saving part of our income and I could take the time off to have a baby."

"A *baby!* In this day and age?"

"It's the reason why most people get married, isn't it?" she said trying to hold back the testiness in her tone.

"And add to the population explosion?"

"Don't be ridiculous, dear. There is no population explosion any more. The birth rate has been going down since shortly after the Hitler War. And I only suggested one baby, though actually I've always wanted at least two. Population isn't exactly exploding if a man and wife have only one descendent."

Sid said, "We're getting away from the point. One of these days I'll come up with some deal that'll make a lot more pseudo-dollars than any kind of half-assed job I could find."

Carol Ann said, "Some day when?"

He said abruptly, "Maybe today, doll. While you were gone I got a call from Holly Owyler. He wants me to come and see him."

"Who is Holly Owyler?"

"Who's Holly Owyler? I can see you don't know the ins and outs of Shyler-deme as well as you think you do, doll. He dropped by at the party for a few minutes last night. Holly Owyler owns one of the swankiest apartments in the deme, up on the hundred and fifth floor.

"There are five thousand apartments in Shyler-deme, Sid. I can't possibly keep track of all the residents, particularly since they come and go. What does he want with you?"

"That I'll have to find out. Uh, look, doll, how about advancing me the pseudo-dollars for a new suit? When my NIT comes in, I'll buy you something to balance it out."

She said, "But you just bought one last week."

"It's getting crumby and I have to keep up appear-

161

ances if I'm going to get along with anyone as high as Owyler."

"Golly, I'm not made of credit, dear."

He waited her out.

"Oh, all right. Dial it." She went over to the delivery box and put her pocket phone, credit card in the slot, her thumb print on the identity screen.

He had evidently already looked up in the catalog screen the clothing he wanted and dialed it rapidly. By the time it arrived, she had taken a chair and was slumped in it, looking at him emptily. There was a slight sheen in his eyes as he dressed. He had probably already taken a trank—even at this time of day.

She said, "Good heavens, what kind of material is that?"

"Donegal tweed, doll. You want to give a good impression, you need the best."

She let out her breath. "Imported, eh? Sid, we're simply not in the bracket to buy imported tweeds for you and then toss them into the disposal chute after a week or two."

"Oh, I wouldn't throw an outfit like this away, doll."

She looked about the small apartment. "Well, we certainly don't have the room to store a great deal in the way of clothing."

He grinned at her puckishly. "How do I look, doll?"

She had to grunt amusement. "Like a million pseudo-dollars, darling. Good luck with your Mr. Owyler."

"You see if there isn't some way to get around Ten Eyck, eh? He can't be serious about kicking me out of Shyler-deme."

"I'll try, dear."

"Well, gimme a kiss to send me on my way."

Sidney Cusack had never been above the hundredth floor of Shyler-deme before. These apartment areas were doubly checked by Security to see that outsiders were unable to intrude, and such public facilities as restaurants and night clubs were so expensive as to exclude any but the well-to-do.

On the hundredth floor, when he crossed from the elevator bank in which he had ridden to this point to the other bank across the way which contained elevators for the balance of the journey, his pocket phone tinkled as he stepped inside.

He took it out and flicked it open, activating it.

The screen didn't light up but a robot voice said, "What is your destination, please?"

Sid Cusack said, "The apartment of Holly Owyler, hundred and fifth floor, Terrace Apartment B."

"Thank you." The elevator began to ascend.

When it stopped, he stepped out and looked up and down the hall. He shrugged and started to the right.

There was a screen across from the elevator bank. "Mr. Cusack," it said, "I.D. Number 15-LM-163-200. This is Security. Your destination, which has been authorized by Mr. Owyler, is Terrace Apartment B. You are heading in the wrong direction."

Sid Cusack grunted and reversed himself. He muttered, "I'd hate to try to burglarize one of these apartments."

He found the Owyler place finally and stood before the identity screen. "Sidney Cusack," he said. "To see Mr. Owyler."

In a few moments the doors opened to reveal Holly Owyler coming down a luxurious hall toward him, a hand outstretched in a ready welcome.

Owyler was a hefty, powerful man with a fleshy, sallow face. He was just about exactly half-bald, with no hair growing forward of a line which could have been drawn across the top of his head from one ear to the other. He had inordinately shaggy eyebrows and heavy lips. He was dressed informally but in clothes that only the rich can afford; style evidently meant little to him; however, his shirt was open at the throat.

"Mr. Cusack," he said in a voice indicating he was greeting a long-time friend.

Sid shook, somewhat taken aback. "Just Sid," he said.

"Of course, of course, and Holly. Come on in, chum-pal." Owyler put an arm over Sid Cusack's shoulder as he led the way down the corridor. "We're all back in the escape-sanctum."

Sid Cusack didn't have the vaguest idea to whom the other was referring, but he let what would develop. He had never been in as ostentatious a home as this. The place reeked with high living and wealth.

Holly Owyler was chuckling. "Sid," he said, "I must say I admired the manner in which you handled the situation last night. Bang, bang, bang, with the edges of your hands. That clown didn't have a chance. He's lucky you didn't break his neck."

Sid Cusack said modestly, "Well, uh, Holly, I pulled my punches."

"Where in the world did you pick up that technique?"

"I took some courses in the army. I kind of liked it, so I used to work out with the instructors, even after the regular lessons were over."

"Marvelous, Sid, marvelous. I certainly envy your ability to take care of yourself. Ah, here we are . . ."

The door automatically opened before them and they stepped through. And into a room that at first seemed jampacked with humanity. Sid Cusack's initial quick impression was that some sort of meeting must be going on, but then he realized that the majority were either sitting around card tables or gathered about a crap table and a roulette layout. Most seemed to have glasses in hand or ready at elbow. Most seemed at least middle-aged. All were obviously of the better-to-do elements that resided in the deme. Sid Cusack recognized not a single one. That wasn't too unbelievable when it was realized that such prosperous elements as these didn't associate with citizens on Sid Cusack's level, seldom, if ever, coming into those sections of Shyler-deme in which Sid lived, ate, or entertained himself. He was suddenly glad for his Donegal tweed suit, considerably more expensive than that he usually wore.

Holly Owyler beamed. "Nice layout, eh?"

Sid Cusack was staring about him in utter surprise. "They're all gambling."

"Of course. It's a gambling club. We're meeting here in my place today."

"But gambling is illegal."

"Don't be ridiculous, my boy. This is a private club. Everybody here is a member. And so are you now."

"But it's still illegal. It's against the law to do anybody out of his pseudo-dollar credits by gambling, even if it was possible to figure out some way of doing it."

Holly Owyler put his hands in his pockets, rocked back and forth on heels and toes and chuckled. "My boy, my boy. You can do just about anything in a private club. Suppose, for instance, you started up a judo club in this deme. You could work a fellow club member over in such style that you broke both of his arms and a leg, but could the authorities touch you? Could they charge you with assault and battery? Certainly not. You might even kill your companion, your opponent, and the worst that would happen would probably be a manslaughter charge which would eventually be dismissed."

Those who were playing had not looked up on the entrance of Holly Owyler and the newcomer. The play was obviously on the highly intense and expensive level. Sid Cusack could now see that there was a blackjack game also in progress. The other tables seemed devoted to poker. There were three of these.

He said, in bewilderment, "But what're they gambling for, matches? There is no money any more. This is a cashless-checkless economy. Everything is handled through your credit card, through the computers in the National Bank. What good is gambling without money? It's kid stuff."

Holly Owyler chuckled happily again. "If I've had to explain how we've got around that once, I've done it a hundred times. It wasn't easy to figure out but where there's a will, Sid, there's a dozen ways. And one of man's strongest wills is to gamble. Did you know they trace dice back to stone-age cavemen?"

"No," Sid said. "What in the hell could they gamble for in those days? They didn't have money or anything like it, did they?"

"Who knows?" Owyler chuckled. "Maybe women, maybe favorite weapons, or something. But they gambled and now so do we in the socio-economic system of Meritocracy, the Ultra-Welfare State or whatever you wanta call it. They thought they plugged up the loopholes, but we've found a way."

The younger man was intrigued. "But how?"

"Well, sir, this is what we do. A club member goes to our club banker, Marty Cantine, over there at the desk, and establishes a credit of, say, one thousand pseudo-dollars. He is then allowed to draw on it in the way of chips. He plays. Roulette, craps, poker, blackjack. Obviously, he either wins or loses."

"Sure, but how does he get the money he wins into his credit account? The computers would stymie it."

"He doesn't. We don't play immediately for money, but what money will buy."

Sid Cusack looked at him, uncomprehendingly.

Owyler chuckled happily. "Suppose you win and your credit with Marty, who is currently our banker, goes up to two thousand pseudo-dollars, and you decide you would like a new fur coat for the little woman. You tell Marty. He checks the records and finds that, say, Frank Samuelson, who makes a habit of trying to fill inside straights, is about fifteen hundred pseudo-dollars in the hole. Great. Marty gets you and Frank together and Frank buys the fur coat and hands it over to you. Say the coat costs a thousand. His account with Marty is credited with that amount, and yours debited."

"I'll be damned," Sid said in awe. "Suppose you don't want a coat, or anything else, for the time being?"

"Then you simply let it accumulate until something comes up that you do wish. Very simple, my boy. No laws broke, nobody hurt. And avid gamblers, such as we admittedly are, enjoy themselves."

Sid Cusack looked about the room some more. He said, "How do you pay the, wha'd'ya call 'em, croupiers?"

Holly Owyler was a compulsive chuckler, hardly being able to get out a sentence without one. He chuckled and said, "We don't. Remember, this is a club. We take turns at the stick on either the crap table or roulette table. At the blackjack table the players switch around handling the bank. Evens out the odds. If a player gets a blackjack, it's his turn to take the bank. Some of the boys get a kick out of acting as croupier. Ned Haines over there on the roulette wheel. He'd rather be on that side of the table than playing, so, hell, we let him do it. And Jake, over on the crap table. "What's your weakness, Sid?"

"Well, poker, I guess. Stud poker. I played quite a bit in the army. We had to play for matches, or candy, stuff like that, but we played. Had to kill time somehow."

"Okay, Sid, come on over here and I'll fix you up with Marty Cantine."

The younger man hesitated. Then, "Uh, well, sure."

Marty Cantine, seated behind a desk, was a small, wizened type with a mouth full of overly large and crooked teeth, an anachronism in this day. Sid Cusack decided the man must be afraid of Dental Surgeons. Before him was the screen of a private mini-computer. He looked up at their approach.

Owyler was saying, "In a club this size you find all types. Marty is a frustrated banker. Inherited too much money to ever have to really work, so he takes it out being club treasurer."

They stood before the desk and Owyler said, "Marty, meet Sid. Sidney Cusack, Martin Cantine. Sid and I met last night and hit it off right from the beginning, Marty. He's a boy that likes the action, so I thought I'd invite him to join up."

Cantine stuck out a thin hand to be shaken. "Why

not? The more the merrier. How much should I put you down for, Sid?"

Sid Cusack looked blank. "Well, what's the usual?"

"It's up to you. Why don't you start with five hundred? You can always get more."

"Five hundred!"

"If that's not enough . . ." the club's banker said.

"Oh. No, well that's enough to start with, surely." Cusack gave a nervous laugh.

Holly Owyler chuckled.

Cantine said, "Now if you'll just let me have your credit card. Formality, to prove you're currently solvent. That's a laugh, eh?"

Sid Cusack flushed, then patted his pocket. "I swear to God, I must have forgot to put it in my pocket when I changed suits this morning."

Holly Owyler said, "Nothing, nothing. Forget about it, Sid. I vouch for him, Marty." He said to Sid Cusack, "You oughten to be that vague, boy. It's against the law not to have your pocket phone on you. Suppose Uncle Sam wanted to get in touch with you?"

Marty Cantine shrugged and said something into the mini-computer screen. He said to Sid, "How many chips do you want from your balance now?"

Sid looked at Holly Owyler.

The jovial worthy chuckled and said, "If you're going to be playing stud, you'd better take the whole five hundred."

Sid cleared his throat. "Well, okay."

The banker counted out the chips from a rack to his left. "These are twenties, these are tens, these fives." It didn't seem to amount to many chips in the Cusack eyes.

Holly Owyler took him by the arm. "Over here. I'll introduce you to some of the boys."

The *boys* at the stud table all out-aged Sid Cusack by at least ten years. They were stolid in their unsmiling game. Nobody bothered to shake hands. The extent of acknowledgement of the introduction was a curt nod of the head. There were six of them and one empty chair. Sid Cusack put his chips down before it and sat himself. He looked up at Holly Owyler who was beaming.

"I'll have to amble around and check things out," Owyler said. "This is my day to host the games. Ned Haines has it tomorrow. Apartment 106, in Tower-Two. I'll see you get cleared through with Security, if you want to show up."

Sid said hesitantly, "Does every member have to take his turn entertaining?"

Holly Owyler patted him on the shoulder, "No, no. We got it split up among six of us who're especially keen, got lots of time on our hands, and with the escape sanctums big enough to hold us all." He winked hugely. "This is a private club and we don't feel like we're treading on anybody's toes but it's still a good idea to hold the meetings in escape sanctums. We don't want anybody prying into our private affairs."

The player with the deck said, "Let's play cards."

"See you later, Sid," Owyler said, strolling off.

The ante was five dollars. The first deal, Sid Cusack got eights, back to back. Two of the others folded. A queen high bet a ten dollar chip.

When it got around to Sid, he raised it ten, clearing his throat and saying, "My first hand. I feel lucky."

Nobody answered that. Their faces remained in the traditional lack of expression of the poker player. Two more dropped out. They might look as though between them they owned all the pseudo-dollars in the world but they didn't throw any of them away, evidently. At least, not at poker.

Nobody picked up anything with the following card. The queen was still high. He passed it to Sid who bet another ten chips. The queen stayed, the third player dropped out.

Sid Cusack caught another eight. With a pair showing, he was now high. He bet a twenty. Queen folded.

Sid raked in the pot. Without making it obvious, he hoped, he very nonchalantly counted his take. He drew in a short breath. He had netted exactly a hundred dollars.

When Carol Ann returned to the apartment that late afternoon, it was to find Sid bent over the library booster of the TV phone, which was in itself mildly surprising. Sid Cusack was ordinarily more apt to be watching a historical war show on the Tri-Di. He had a predilection for vicarious violence.

She tossed her bag to the couch and went over to the auto-bar and dialed herself the one long pseudo-whiskey highball which she liked to take for relaxation immediately upon return from the office.

Sid looked up, almost as though impatient at being interrupted and said, "Hi, doll. You're kind of late, aren't you?"

She picked up the drink as soon as it was delivered and went over to the comfort chair and sank into it. "Everything and its cousin came up today, beginning about noon. I didn't even have time for lunch. We got a petition signed by over two thousand residents demanding a reduction in the maintenance fee. Barry Ten Eyck's been arguing with their committee all day. I had to sit in, of course."

"Hey, that's good. It'd apply to us too. How much would we save?"

"Fifty pseudo-dollars a month if it went through. The trouble is, dear, that we're skating too near the edge of the breakeven point for this deme as it is. A reduction of an average of fifty dollars per apartment for all five thousand apartments would come to a quarter of a million a month, or three million a year. I doubt if Barry could do it and still make a profit for Vanderfeller and Moore."

"Well, that's no worry of yours, doll. And laughing boy has some nerve keeping you overtime almost every day. What does he think you are, a slave?"

The sheen was there in his eyes again. He had probably taken a trank pill since noon, she realized.

She took another pull at her drink and said, "That's

the trouble with being top management, darling. In theory, the Democrat and his two assistants work an eight-hour day. In actuality, it's something like being a ship's captain. You're on duty all the time."

"Well, that's their job, and they get paid for it but plenty. But your salary isn't enough to put up with that treatment."

Carol Ann sighed. "A Democrat's secretary is his right arm, darling. If he works sixteen hours, so do I. It couldn't be any other way. And always remember, a Democrat's secretary is very handy for promotion when there's a vacancy."

He said sourly, "Like you said, you don't have a degree in deme management."

"Which brings us to something I wanted to tell you about. I'm going to start studying for one, Sid. Right here in the apartment on the TV booster screen, of course."

"What! I swear to God, doll, we hardly have any time for ourselves as it is. We haven't been out to a nightspot since Friday."

"It's Meritocracy, darling. If you drop behind in upgrading yourself, you look around one day and find that you're dropping out, period." She finished her drink.

He got up in disgust and headed for the bathroom. "I think I'll get myself a trank."

She stood too, preparatory to taking her glass to the disposal chute. She said softly, "I think you've already had a trank, dear."

"So what? I'm a big boy, I can stand two in a row." He turned and went into the bathroom, half slamming the door behind him.

On her way past the chair in which he had been seated, she idly looked down into the library booster screen, wondering what he was reading. The book was, *The World's Greatest Gambling Systems,* by Leo Guild and the chapter was devoted to poker and entitled "The Odds System."

Frowning puzzlement, she dropped her glass into the disposal chute and returned to her chair.

When he came back, his eyes sparkling now, his humor restored, she said, "How did you make out with Mr. Owyler?"

He grinned happily. "Can't tell you, doll, but I've come up with something at last that's going to make us both rich. I've just got to figure it real carefully, get all the angles down pat. What'd you think if I told you I ran up over three hundred pseudo-dollars today?"

"I'd say, *how?*"

He grinned slyly and touched the end of his nose with his forefinger. "Can't tell you yet, but one of these days you're going to be in for a big fat surprise, doll. A big fat surprise."

She sighed. "Another one of your deals?"

"You won't be so upstage about my deals, honey, when it starts raining pseudo-dollars."

"I'm afraid you're overdoing that trank, darling."

"Have you ever tried it?"

"Well, no."

"Then you oughten to knock it. What's the old wheeze about all censors being illiterates?"

She tried to suppress her impatience. "It's a long history, man's search for a happiness drug. If and when he ever finds it, I suspect it will be the end of man—at least as we know him."

He didn't know what she was talking about. Sid Cusack said definitely, "It's already been found, Carol. It's trank. LSD, mescaline, marijuana, all the rest of them, were just the preliminaries. Trank gives you everything, takes away nothing. It's even legal. Why? Because there's no bad effects. It isn't habit forming, no hangover, even kids and old folks can take it, you never have to increase the dosage and it's dirt cheap."

"In fact, I'm beginning to think the government subsidizes it," Carol Ann muttered.

"If they don't, they ought to. It keeps everybody happy, which isn't the easiest thing in the world if you're living on NIT. I still say you ought to give it a trial, doll."

"No thanks," she said. "I'll achieve my happiness, such as it is, through my own efforts, not through a pill."

Three days later, when Carol Ann returned to the apartment, it was to find Sid not at home. She decided that he was probably having a swim in one of the pools down in the lower levels and shrugged out of her jacket. She went to the small closet in the bedroom to hang it up. It was a favorite jacket, an import from Common Europe, and one of the few articles of clothing that she had cleaned when required rather than disposing of it.

She was taken aback to note three men's suits hanging there, suits she had never seen before. She made space for the jacket and returned to the living room for her highball and to await Sid.

Three suits at once, and a fourth that Sid was wearing?

Theirs was somewhat larger than a mini-apartment but still small by the standards of yesteryear. When the building boom had begun, the all-out effort to supply decent housing for everyone in the country, the first demes to go up stressed efficiency in size, for the sake of packing in as many residents as possible. But now that the boom was falling off, the housing shortage a thing of the past, the new demes being built were beginning to feature more space. It had become a status symbol to have several rooms in your apartment. It was one of the headaches with which her boss, Barry Ten Eyck, had to contend. Residents of Shyler-deme would move for the sake of a larger apartment.

However, even these new places didn't waste space in the manner of fifty years before. One no longer accumulated large stocks of clothing; one used it and disposed of it; automation of production and the new synthetic textiles made clothing so inexpensive that it didn't make sense to launder or clean. Nor, with the advent of the National Library Banks, hooked up to your TV screen, did it make sense to accumulate books, records or tapes of music. Every bit of music, from folk to opera, was in the banks. So were all the movies and TV shows ever cut, for that matter.

Sid, beaming happily, came in just as her drink was being delivered.

She started to ask him about the suits, but he spoke first, holding up a small box in his hand.

"Doll," he said. "Remember when we had to sell your engagement ring, over in the Swap Shop in the Common, back before you got this job and we were always so broke?"

She said, "Of course, darling, but you needn't worry about that. Everybody has their emergencies. You'll buy me another some day when you get on your feet."

He grinned at her. "Here it is." He flicked open the box. A ring gleamed there.

She stared at it. "But that's not the same ring. Where . . ."

"Of course not," he crowed. "The Swap Shop has long since sold your first one. But this is better."

She took it, completely dumbfounded. "But, dear, where could you have possibly gotten it? And, Sid, those suits in the closet. Three of them, and they're of the best quality."

He was obviously delighted with himself. "I told you it'd be raining pseudo-dollars for us, doll. And it's just the beginning."

"But . . . but how . . .?"

"Ask me no questions, I'll tell you no lies," he grinned. "Actually, I, uh, did a favor for a friend and he insisted on my buying six hundred dollars worth of things on his credit account. Anything I wanted to select. Maybe I put too much of it into the clothes, but the kind of people I'm associating with these days, doll, I have to keep up my front."

"*What* kind of people?"

He touched the end of his nose confidentially. "Rich people, doll, people so rich the pseudo-dollars drip off them unnoticed."

Carol Ann Cusack dropped into the Security office the following day, just before lunch.

Bat Hardin looked up at her and smiled, "Hi, Mrs. Cusack. What spins, as Barry would say?"

She was frowning. She hesitated, as though wondering how to put it, or even if she wanted to put it at all. Finally, she said, "Mr. Hardin, how much gambling goes on here in Shyler-deme?"

"Gambling?" He leaned back. "Not a great deal. Not here or anywhere else in the United States. It's not very practical without a currency. It's one crime, if you can call it a crime, that took a nosedive when the National Bank took over with the Universal Credit Card. Anybody so hot for gambling that they've got to have it can always go over to the Bahamas, of course. The so-called government there has legalized gambling and controls it itself. You can play with your International Credit Card. Every gambling device has a payment slot. You make your bet and are either debited or credited with the amount you lose or win."

"I don't mean in the Bahamas or Malta or any of the other wide-open places around the world. I mean right here in Shyler-deme."

He said, "Real gambling, like I said, isn't very practical. I understand there's a card club of some sort or other up in the higher floors. But I imagine they play for fun, or perhaps prizes, or some such. I wouldn't know."

He flicked a switch on one of his phone screens and said something into it which she didn't catch. He looked down into the screen for a moment, then up at her as though he had just validated something.

"It's not one of our regular organized clubs, that is, organized and controlled by the deme. Very private and restricted. Probably a chance for some of the boys to get together periodically and get a bit boozed up, away from their wives. Fellow named Holly Owyler seems to be president, or whatever they call him."

"Owyler!"

175

"Yeah, that's right. Why?" He frowned at her. "Listen, is something up?"

She looked confused. "No, no I guess not. I was simply curious. Forget about it, Mr. Hardin. Thanks." She turned to leave.

He looked after her thoughtfully for a long moment. After awhile he began to gnaw his under lip. Finally, and hesitantly, he flicked a switch and said, "Give me the I.D. Number of Holly Owyler and his apartment number as well."

Sid Cusack was sitting in his comfort chair, staring unseeingly and unhappily at the far wall of the room when the identity screen on the door hummed. He jerked and his eyes went to it.

The face there was the toothy one of Marty Cantine.

Sid Cusack hesitated for a long agonized moment. He could simply ignore it. The visitor had no way of knowing that Sid was at home. He could ignore it and Cantine could only go away.

But it wasn't that. He couldn't avoid the other indefinitely. He activated the door and came to his feet, forcing a smile to his face. He didn't realize it but the smile was on the sickly side.

Cantine came in, followed by another gambling club member. The name vaguely came back to Sid Cusack. Ned Haines, the one whose big weakness was roulette and who liked the game so well that he usually took the stick as a volunteer. He was evidently one of the club's most avid members since he was always present at the meetings. Sid hadn't run into him much since Sid Cusack was strictly a stud poker man.

Sid said, "Come on in, gentlemen. Could I dial you a drink?"

They shook hands. Both sets of eyes went around the apartment. The eyebrows of Ned Haines went up slightly. Cusack got the impression that the other had never seen an apartment this austere.

"Too early, Sid," Marty Cantine said. "We'll make it

brief. Came down for a quick spot of business. Sorry to intrude on you."

"Not at all, not at all," Sid said. "Have a chair, gentlemen."

Cantine said, "Haven't seen you at the meetings for the past few days." He found a seat on the couch and Haines took a place beside him.

"I haven't been feeling too well."

Cantine said, "In that case we'll wind it up briskly and leave you to your recuperation. Now, let's see . . ." He consulted a note. "You're down about seven hundred pseudo-dollars, and Mr. Haines, here, has got a nice surplus."

Sid Cusack cleared his throat unhappily.

Cantine went on. "Mr. Haines has decided to take a little trip to Switzerland. He has some international credits there that he figures he might as well use up. We can arrange the tickets for the Supersonic through the Transport Division right here in Shyler-deme. If you'll just order them. Let's see, the round-trip ticket comes to four hundred and twelve pseudo-dollars. We'll debit that to Ned's account and credit it to yours."

Sid said unhappily, "How . . . how do you mean?"

Marty Cantine laughed gently, as though his host was joking. "You know how it works, Sid. You're down seven hundred and Ned, here, has a surplus in the club bank of over two thousand. He's calling on you to buy his tickets for his Common Europe trip."

Sid Cusack looked at them blankly. He swallowed.

Cantine scowled. "Look here, this has all been explained to you. In fact, last week you hit a pleasant winning streak, wanted a few things and had Jake Foster, a member who was behind, order them from his credit account with the National Bank. So now, it's your turn. You're running behind."

Sid Cusack said, "Look, gentlemen, this is very embarrassing. I happen to have run into some unusual expenses, all in a row, and my credit account is, uh, short." He licked his lips unconsciously.

Ned Haines said unbelievingly, "So short that you can't afford four hundred pseudo-dollars?"

"I . . . I'm afraid so."

Marty Cantine's face was impassive. "Mr. Cusack, when you joined the club you opened an account for five hundred pseudo-dollars. For awhile, your luck was excellent. But then, a few days ago, you were rather badly hit, so I understand. But, sir, a club member's account is . . . is, well, his bond."

Sid Cusack spread his hands. "I'm sorry. It's just . . ."

His two visitors stood.

Marty Cantine said sharply, "I'll take it up with Mr. Owyler, who sponsored you. Shall we leave, Ned? We'll get your tickets through one of the other members who are down on their club balance."

Ned Haines, as though embarrassed for the younger man, said, "Of course."

Sid followed after them, stammering an attempt at apology. Neither spoke further.

When they were gone, he said aloud, "Oh, Christ."

He thought desperately. He could take the suits over to the Swap Shop on the Common, and Carol Ann's ring, for that matter. But he had no illusions. At the Swap Shop they could legally buy anything from you from used clothing to old masterpieces, and credit you with the amount. But who wanted used clothing these days? And he knew very well that a piece of jewelry would sell for only a fraction of what you paid for it. Markup on jewelry was fantastic and if the Swap Shop proprietors wanted to make any kind of profit at all when they resold the ring, they'd probably only pay him a quarter of the original retail price. He simply had nothing to sell that would raise anything like better than four hundred pseudo-dollars.

It wasn't too long before the TV screen hummed.

He could have avoided that call too, of course. But what was the point? Sooner or later he had to face this whole situation. Oh, Christ, it had been the best contact he had ever made in his life. If things had gone right, almost anything might have resulted from meeting these money-heavy aristocrats. He had always had a belief that if you ran around with rich people sooner or later some of it would rub off on you.

The face in the screen, needless to say, was that of Holly Owyler.

Owyler seemed unbelieving. He said, coming immediately to the point, "Cusack, I've just had Marty Cantine on the phone. I suppose you know what he had to say."

"Well, yes, I suppose so. Look, Holly, I can explain this."

"I hope so. I certainly hope so. See here, Cusack, could you come up to my apartment soonest?"

"I suppose so."

"Very well, I'll be expecting you." Holly Owyler wasn't chuckling right at present. His face faded.

Sid Cusack said, "Oh, Christ." He wondered briefly, if he could get the required amount from Carol Ann. No, no he couldn't. He was already far, far into Carol, whose instincts were all on the frugal side.

Holly Owyler met him personally at the door of the large Terrace Apartment on the hundred and fifth floor. He said coldly, "Come on in, Cusack."

Sid Cusack said, "Look, Holly, this is all a misunderstanding."

"I'm sure. Come on back to the escape sanctum."

The Holly Owyler escape room was considerably different than when they were having a meeting of the gambling club. Evidently, they moved the ordinary furniture out, during such sessions, to make room for the card tables and the layouts of roulette and craps. Now it was done up in a swank such as Sid Cusack had never witnessed save, possibly, on Tri-Di shows.

Owyler said, "Sit down, Cusack."

He sat himself. He didn't offer Sid Cusack a drink. Instead, he stared at him.

He said, finally, "I should have known, when you got your first five hundred pseudo-dollars credit from Marty that you were a deadbeat. You claimed that you

179

didn't have your credit card, TV phone on you. That's nonsense. You couldn't have got up here to my apartment without it. Security checks out everybody's identity who comes up to these floors. You would have had to identify yourself through them to get here."

Sid said, "Look, I'm sorry . . ."

"That doesn't do us much good, does it? You're a welcher, Cusack."

"Look, what can I do? I swear to God, I want to make it up."

The other thought about it. "I suppose you're on NIT, eh?"

"That's right," Sid Cusack said in embarrassment.

"NIT is just barely enough to get by on. You can no more save anything on NIT than you can fly."

"My wife works. She pays quite a bit of the expenses."

"I'll bet she does," Owyler said grimly. He thought some more.

He said finally, "There's just one thing, Cusack . . . Sid. In fact, not only can you make this up but possibly there'll be a bit of a good thing in it for you, in the future."

Sid Cusack leaned forward, hopefully. "I'd do anything to make this up to you, Holly."

The older man pursed his lips. "I'll tell you something, Sid. This club has more ramifications than you might first think. You see, you're not the first member who's welched. Never like this before, maybe, but even some of the wealthiest members we've got on the rolls sometimes get soreheaded. They get teed-off and refuse to pay up. Of course, this being a non-profit operation that means that all the rest of us members take a beating, especially if the amount involved is large."

"Yeah, I understand," Sid Cusack said. He didn't.

Holly Owyler said, "You can see the position we're in. If one member was allowed to get away with it, before we were through there'd be so many doing it that the club would have to fold. Nobody wants to honestly carry their part of the load and see somebody else welch."

"Well . . . well, what can you do about it?"

Holly Owyler chuckled a bit. "We can lean on them a little. Make an example, in a way."

Sid Cusack stared back at him, still uncomprehending.

Owyler said, reasonably, "Money is the most serious thing in the world, Sid. If you let others do you out of yours, you're a damn fool. This club is for fun, but the money is dead serious, and none of its loyal members will put up with being cheated."

"I see." He didn't.

Holly Owyler came to the point quickly then. "So we have a little muscle on our payroll, to take care of types that welch."

"Muscle?"

"I admired the way you handled yourself at the party the other night, Sid. And now it occurs to me that you might cooperate with us, using your skills. In fact, this very night two of our other boys are going to, ah, lean on a welcher a little and throw a bit of the fear of God into him."

"You mean you'd beat up a fellow resident of Shyler-deme? Jesus, you can't do that. Bat Hardin, down in Security, would be after you in minutes. The guy would put in a complaint and we'd all be in jail before the night was out. Not only me, and these other two *boys* you were talking about, but you and God only knows how many others of the club members. You can't put the slug on people in this day and age."

Holly Owyler chuckled. "You don't know how it works, Sid. We don't ever use muscle on fellow residents of Shyler-deme. As you say, that would be silly. But you see, there's another club over in Victory-deme, with much the same problems. We cooperate with them. Now this is the story. They've had some trouble with this character, more than the seven hundred you're into us for. A helluva lot more. He thinks he's tough, see? He thinks he was taken—how silly can you get?—and won't pay off. All right, the fellas over there have him fingered, but good . . ."

"Fingered?" Sid said.

Owyler chuckled. He got up and went over to the auto-bar and dialed. "Pseudo-whisky for you, isn't it? Or would you rather have a trank?"

"Whiskey," Sid said.

The older man came back with the drinks.

"You don't look at the old revived TV shows enough, Sid," he said. "What I mean is, they've got a complete rundown on this welcher. Every evening he goes out into the park around Victory-deme and has a drink or two at one of the places with a sidewalk cafe deal. Every evening he sits at the same table, off to one side. Likes to watch the kids, or something. Anyway, you and the other two boys come along and pick him up and work him into an electro-steamer and take him out into the country."

Sid Cusack was wide-eyed. "And then . . .?"

"And then you put the fear of God into him. He's never seen you three. You don't even live in the same deme he does. You work him over pretty good. You let him know he pays off or the next time is the last time. You make it pretty clear if he goes to Security, it's just a matter of time before you're back to finish him for good."

"Finish him for good? I swear to God, Holly . . ."

"Oh, don't be a clown, Sid. All you're doing is scaring the pants off him. The bastard's a welcher, isn't he?"

"So am I," Sid Cusack said lowly.

"Don't be silly, you're on the team now."

Sid Cusack breathed out, as though exhausted.

Owyler chuckled. "Now we get to the good news."

"*Good* news?" Sid Cusack snorted in despair.

"Sure. The thing is, Sid, there're angles to this gambling club deal. A hell of a lot of money goes through this club. It's non-profit, of course, but there's expenses. How do you think we get the equipment? How do you think we get the mini-computer Marty Cantine has to have to keep track of all the accounts and the chips and all?"

"I didn't think about it."

"Well, it's a non-profit operation but the fact is that the roulette wheel and the crap table take in a percentage. Okay, we use it to keep the club going. We got expenses, they take care of them. Everybody is happy. One of the expenses is having a couple of muscle boys we can depend on to lean on welchers. Most club members don't even know this takes place. But it's all part of keeping an efficient club going. So okay, you cooperate with us, Sid, and we take care of little items like the seven hundred you're into the club for. Besides that, every time you have a little assignment, we give out with a little right off the top."

"How do you mean?"

The gambling club head chuckled. "It's simple enough. Suppose after this little job tonight, we want to show our appreciation by letting you have a couple hundred pseudo-dollars. Fine, the profits made on the roulette wheel and crap table automatically go into the bank, of course. So I just tip Marty to record to your account the two hundred. You can either play with it, or in the usual way, spend it—through some club member who's down on his account."

Sid thought about it. He said, "These guys you'd call on me to help work over are all welchers, eh?"

"Of course. And always reside in some other deme. You don't know them and you don't care, and they don't know you. You don't even know the particular circumstances. You don't even know the name of the welcher. The boys in the deme where he lives just tell you where and at what time you pick him up."

Sid thought about it some more. "Well ... if they're welchers you've got a right . . ."

"Of course."

"Well, this thing tonight. How do I get about it?"

Holly Owyler came to his feet. "The other two boys that are going on this job with you will come by your

183

apartment and pick you up. You'll soon get the hang of it."

Sid stood, frowning unhappily, and let the other escort him toward the door. "Do they have gambling clubs in all three of the other demes in this pseudo-city?"

"Sure. Why not? And we cooperate with all of them. If they need a little muscle, we help them out. If we need some, they send over a couple of their boys."

It was the following day that Holly Owyler was slightly surprised to hear the hum of the identity screen on his apartment door. In the Security that particularly applied to these rarified floors of Shyler-deme, you received advance notice before anyone came to your apartment. You had to okay the visitor before he was even allowed to enter an elevator.

He activated the screen and didn't recognize the dark, heavy face of the other.

Owyler said, "Who the hell is it?"

"Bat Hardin, Chief of Security of Shyler-deme."

"Oh. Oh, yes, of course. Come in, Mr. Hardin."

Holly Owyler got up from the comfort chair in his living room and headed for the door. He ran a hand over the bald area of his head thoughtfully but by the time he had gotten down the hall to the door there was the characteristic good-natured smile on his face.

Bat Hardin came through the door and the older man greeted him with outstretched hand and chuckle. "Surprised we've never met, Mr. Hardin. I've heard about you."

"It's a big place," Bat said. "When you've got five thousand apartments, you never actually meet more than a fraction of the residents."

"Of course not, of course not. Come on in and have a drink."

Bat Hardin followed him to the living room and took the proffered chair while the other went to an elaborate auto-bar. It was obviously one of the newer models, not the standard supplied by Shyler-deme.

"What'll it be?" Owyler said hospitably.

"Rum's fine," Bat said, equally at ease. "Rum and water."

The other brought the drinks, sat himself down as well and lifted his glass. "Cheers."

Bat gestured with his own glass. "Health," he said and took a sip.

"So," Owyler said, "pleasure to meet you, Bat, but I'm sure you didn't come up just for a cordial drink."

Bat put his glass down on a cocktail table next to the comfort chair.

"No. Actually, a bit of routine, Mr. Owyler . . ."

"Holly."

"Thanks. You're president, or whatever the title is, of a club here in Shyler-deme that isn't registered with the building administration."

"That's right. It's a very restricted club, Bat. If it was a regular deme club we'd have to let in all comers."

"That's correct. No rules against having a private club. But could you tell me a bit about the nature of this one?"

"No reason why not. We play cards."

Bat nodded. "For what kind of stakes?"

"No stakes. Just for amusement."

"I see. What kind of card games?"

"Oh, poker, bridge, sometimes blackjack."

"I used to play a bit of poker during my military days in the Asian War. They still had money then, over in those countries. There isn't much fun, unless there's something to bet on. And, of course, gambling is illegal in the States."

Owyler chuckled ruefully. "Well, in a way we get around that 'something to bet on' thing. You see, we issue free chips to each member, the same number to each. At the end of the month, we check up on everybody's standing. The man who won most is guest of honor at a party we throw. The man who is at the bottom has to pay the tab. He also has to buy a silver cup for the big winner. So, in a way, I guess you can say we are gambling—but it's just for fun, of course."

Bat Hardin laughed easily, took up his drink again and sipped. "No profit involved in any way, eh?"

"Course not. Our membership is highly respectable. Actually, money means nothing to any of them. Mostly old rich or retired top-ranking Meritcrats."

"I see. You're president. Would you mind telling me the names of the rest of your officers?"

"Why not? We're on the informal side, but we have a few club duties that have to be performed: arranging for whose apartment is going to be used for a meeting, arranging for banquets and parties, keeping track of the scores so we can figure out who's low man and who is high. At present, Martin Cantine is our treasurer, Ned Haines our secretary, Jacob Foster, Benjamin Horowitz and Michael Duncan entertainment committee members. That's all the officials we have."

"How long do you hold office?" Bat said idly.

"Oh, theoretically a year, but it's awfully informal. Most of the members would just as readily let somebody else do the work, so anybody who's willing can take on the job. Don't know how long it's been since we held an election."

"You sometimes hold your meetings in this apartment?"

"Usually once a week I'm the host. I'm retired, nothing else to do with my time."

"Where else do you hold them?"

"In the apartments of the other members who have places suitable and who're bachelors."

Bat Hardin looked down at the names of the officers, which he had jotted down. "Do you ever hold them in the apartments of Cantine, Haines, Foster, Horowitz or Duncan?"

Owyler's eyes narrowed infinitesimally beneath his shaggy brows. "Why, yes. They're bachelors, too. That's one of the reasons they consent to act as club officers. They've all got time on their hands, and no families to get in the way." He added, "See here, what's this all about? I don't mind cooperating with you people in Security. You do a good job here in Shyler-deme, but doesn't this begin to come under the head of not being your business?"

"I'm not sure," Bat Hardin said, his voice agreeable enough. "Frankly, Mr. Owyler, I'm somewhat surprised at the layout you have here."

"Why?"

"Because I checked your dossier in the National Data Banks yesterday, Mr. Owyler, ah, Holly, that is."

"My dossier! You're not allowed to pry into my private dossier!" The other was indignant. "I'll complain to Central Management of Vanderfeller and Moore! I'm a respectable tenant of this deme and have my rights to privacy."

Bat looked at him speculatively. "Don't misunderstand, Mr. Owyler, ah, Holly. As Security Chief in a deme I can exercise a Priority Two in the National Data Banks and check into such items as Medical Records, Criminal Records and other such data usually restricted to physicians and the police. However, Mr. Ten Eyck, our Demecrat, makes a point of avoiding prying into such private information. I only exercised Priority Three, open to almost anybody."

Holly Owyler was keeping relief from his face. He said stiffly, "Well, and why are you surprised at my layout here, as you call it?"

"Because your dossier ... Holly ... indicates that you are on NIT."

"What of it?"

Bat Hardin looked about the lavish living room. "I doubt if you could even pay your maintenance to Shyler-deme for an apartment like this with Negative Income Tax."

"Don't be silly, Hardin. I obviously don't have to."

Bat looked at him politely. "If you have no other income than ..."

Owyler grunted contempt. "See here, Hardin. I am retired."

"Your dossier doesn't indicate that you've ever worked."

"I haven't had to. My parents left me adequately fixed."

"How could you be collecting Negative Income Tax if you had income from other sources? You'd be paying tax, not collecting from the government."

"See here, young man. I can legally collect the small amount involved in NIT and I see no reason why I should not. I have no income in the taxable sense of the word."

Bat looked at him, waiting for him to go on.

"The fact of the matter is, though it is none of your business, that my parents left me various art objects. Both were avid collectors. Periodically, I sell one or two either through the local Swap Shop, in the Phoenecia Common, or through some larger dealer in Greater Washington, or wherever. The proceeds are not taxable under present laws."

Bat Hardin took his lower lip in his teeth, unhappily. He said, "I see. The deme records show you as full owner of this apartment . . . Holly . . ."

"Mr. Owyler, please."

"Of course. But you didn't originally purchase it. It's original value was one hundred and fifty thousand pseudo-dollars. You are able to raise such sums selling the collected art of your parents?"

"Once again, that's none of your business, Hardin. However, I'll tell you that this apartment was a gift to me."

"A gift!"

Holly Owyler sneered. "The friends I associate with daily, Hardin, are hardly in your financial bracket. One of them decided to leave the country and retire to Switzerland, fed up with so-called Meritocracy. He undoubtedly could have sold this apartment but simply didn't wish to be bothered. I made the mistake of admiring it once. I like the view. So nothing would do but that he sign it over to me." The gambling club head snorted. "He even insisted on paying the gift tax."

Bat Hardin stood. "All right, Mr. Owyler. Thanks for your time. Sorry to have bothered you."

"Not at all. Not at all," the other said, though ungraciously. "Undoubtedly you have your duties and even such unpleasant ones as these have to be handled. Good day, Hardin."

Back in his office, Bat Hardin sat for a long time staring away into space . . .

Finally, he looked over at his new secretary. "Miss Nash, I want you to do some research for me. You'll have to start with the dossier of Mr. Holly Owyler. Get the names of his father and mother and check their dossiers. They are evidently dead but that makes no difference, of course. The material will remain until hell freezes over, in the National Data Banks. I want to know what their estates were when they died. I want to know what kind of field his father was in. How much money he made. I also want the dossiers on ..." he looked down at his list of names and read off the other officers of the gambling club.

"I can exercise only Priority Three, sir. Do you wish to exercise your own priority rights to go further?"

"Priority Three is all I want for the present. Privacy is a very important basic right, Miss Nash, and should be invaded only as a last resort."

"Yes, sir. I'll get right at it."

He said, "There is no particular hurry. It's probably all a false alarm."

But Bat Hardin was wrong. There was a particular hurry.

That night the officers of the gambling club, so-called, held an emergency executive meeting. Over the drinks, Holly Owyler gave them the details of the visit by Bat Hardin. None of them were excitable types. They had been through emergencies before.

Finally, Jake Foster said, "Any of us know anything about this Bat Hardin joker? Can we get any kind of leverage on him?"

Nobody seemed to know him.

Ned Haines said, "I've seen him around once or twice, he's that husky nigger."

Horowitz looked over at him. "What the hell do you call me when I'm not around, that fat kike?"

"Oh, the hell with it, shut up, Ben," Owyler growled. "That's all we need, a nice argument when all the chips are down."

Marty Cantine said, "Why d'ya think all the chips are down, Holly? Seems to me you handled it pretty good."

"Then that's what you think. This sonofabitch Hardin is smelling a rat. He's not sure, yet, but he's got a kind of intuitive something."

"When in the hell is an intuitive something?" Jake Foster growled.

Owyler snorted at him. "You call yourself a gambler and you ask that? He's not happy. He instinctively feels something smells. He only partly bought the story about the club. Oh, sure, I left it open. He knew we had some little angles where we were really gambling. I let him know that on purpose. He probably figured we had little deals where one guy could pay off to another a bit. He just hasn't got the whole picture yet, but he's going to start prying."

Haines said, "We run a pretty tight operation. The marks love to have some way of gambling. Hell, half of them would cry into their pillows for months if anything happened to the club they think they got."

Horowitz said, "Sure, we've screened them from hell and gone. We don't let anybody in unless they're real suckers, really hooked on cards, roulette or whatever. We're pretty safe. None of them is going to put in a beef. They don't *want* anything to happen to the club. Not even those that've really been burnt. That's the last thing in the world they want. But thing is, we can't afford any really close investigation."

"What the hell!" Duncan said. "I got no record at all."

Owyler looked at him wearily. "Crap. It's all according to what you mean by record. How in the hell you gonna prove your source of income once that bastard Hardin really gets to probing? He's only half curious now, but he's the type that'll pry around and he can't help turning up something."

"Such as what?"

"Such as something he already turned up today. I got this apartment in my own name. It was *given* to me. But how many things as expensive as this are outright given to anybody? He took all your names. What's it gonna look like when he finds that all the apartments we have were given to us?"

"Oh, Jesus," Horowitz said, "did you have to give him our names?"

Owyler looked at him in contempt. "Do you think if I hadn't he couldn't have found out soonest? Don't be a clown."

Marty Cantine said, "Look, why are we stalling? Something's got to be done about this guy before he gets any further."

"Yeah," Owyler said disgustedly. "How many other characters do we know might be in on his suspicions? His secretary? His boss, Ten Eyck? He doesn't operate in any vacuum. You want I should get some of the boys from Victory-deme to lower on him? Swell. The fat would be in the fire before morning."

"Oh, fer Crissakes, Holly," Horowitz protested. "We aren't stupid."

Ned Haines said, "How come you never say Holy Moses, or something like that?"

"Listen, you Catholic bastard, I'll say whatever I please."

Owyler chuckled, "Boys, boys," he said. "Ice it down. I'm beginning to see some light. You know our new boy, Cusack?"

They looked at him.

"His wife is secretary to the Demecrat himself. He's a clown on the make but she evidently figures his crap doesn't stink. And guess what? The Cusack apartment is on the same floor as Hardin's. He doesn't have to check it out with Security if he wants to pay a little call on Hardin. He can make a little visit without anybody at all knowing about it."

In the morning, after the usual get-together between Barry Ten Eyck and his two assistants, Barry looked over at his Vice-Demecrat.

"Why so pensive this morning, Bat, What spins?"

Bat Hardin frowned. "A something came up that I'm not sure about."

Jim Cotswold said, "Well, what is it?"

Bat looked over at him. "I'm not sure I ought to say anything as yet. If I'm wrong, it might antagonize a good many of our better-to-do residents. If they put up a howl to Central Management, it might mean heads would roll. If you and Barry know nothing about it, they can't fault you."

Barry laughed good naturedly. "So you're willing to throw yourself to the lions but are protecting us, eh? Stout fella."

Bat grinned ruefully as he came to his feet preparatory to leaving. "It's probably nothing. I'll be able to tell you about it tomorrow, one way or the other."

It was only minutes later that Carol Ann Cusack came into the Security Chief's office. As Ten Eyck's secretary, she had been present at the meeting of the three top Shyler-deme executives, of course. Now she looked worried.

She said, "Mr. Hardin. That matter you just mentioned. Has it something to do with Mr. Owyler and that card club of his?"

Bat looked at her carefully. "Why do you ask, Mrs. Cusack?"

She said unhappily, "Golly, I don't know if I should tell you or not."

He continued to look at her, but said nothing more for the moment.

It came out in a gush. "It's Sidney, my husband. I

think that you know that he's been having hard luck, that he can't find a job."

Bat nodded. "I didn't even know he was looking, but go on."

"Not long ago he mentioned that he had made friends with Mr. Owyler and hoped to make some sort of a deal with him. A business deal, I assumed. A few days later, he evidently had pseudo-dollars to spend.

"How many?"

"I don't know. He was rather secretive, but at least several hundred."

Bat puckered up his heavy lips in a silent whistle. "You think possibly he got them gambling?"

"I don't know. But then, a few days ago he seemed to be more morose. Something was roaching him. He's usually on the happier side, bad luck and all."

Bat said, "Carol Ann, this is none of my business. But you're an ambitious, hard-working young woman. That boy is bad news. Why don't you . . . ditch him?"

There was a pathetic something behind her eyes. "I happen to love the man, Bat. Possibly he's not the best husband in the world. I know he's weak. He needs a chance, a good chance, that's all. I'm sure. And I love him."

He sighed. "I guess that's as good a reason as any. Maybe I'll have some news for you later. I'll let you know anything that pertains to your husband as soon as it's practical."

"All right, Mr. Hardin. Thanks." She turned and left.

After a moment he looked over at his secretary. "Any material on those names I gave you?"

She was puzzled. "One rather strange thing, Mr. Hardin. They are all on NIT."

Bat scowled surprise.

"But all of them have very swank apartments on the top floors," she added.

Bat Hardin made a hissing sound through his teeth. He thought about it.

Finally, he took his pocket phone cum I.D. card

from his jacket. He put it in a slot on one of his desk TV phones and said, "Bat Hardin, Security Chief of Shyler-deme. Priority Two. I want the Criminal Records of the following men and also a complete listing of all property held in their names." He gave the necessary information.

He looked over at his secretary again. "This material will be coming in shortly, Miss Nash. Take it down on your auto-secretary."

"Yes, sir."

Bat Hardin got up to make his routine rounds of the morning.

That evening, when Carol Ann returned from the office, Sid was waiting for her, nervously. He had made her usual relaxing highball and handed it to her. She looked at him questioningly.

He said, "Look, doll, do you know whether or not Bat Hardin is prying into Mr. Owyler's, uh, card club?"

She frowned, taking the drink. "Why do you ask, Sid?"

"I can't tell you now. Is he? It's important . . . to me."

"Why, as a matter of fact he is."

"How do you know?"

She took a gulp of her drink, then a deep breath. "I was worried about you, dear. I didn't know where you were getting all that money. I thought maybe it was from gambling and asked Mr. Hardin if that was possible."

"So that's what set him off," Sid groaned.

"I don't know what you mean by that, but I think he's checking up on your Mr. Owyler."

"How many others has he discussed it with?"

"Why . . . why nobody except his secretary, Pauline Nash, I suppose. She would have to know. But he hasn't brought it up with Mr. Ten Eyck or Jim Cotswold. He evidently wanted some definite information. Where are you going, Sid?"

"I've got to see somebody."

Later that evening, Sid Cusack approached the door of Bat Hardin's apartment. He darted a quick glance up and down the hall, saw it was empty and brought a Gyro-jet handgun from beneath his left shoulder. With a practiced motion, he jacked a cartridge into the breech, then returned the gun to its rig, checking that it was set right in the holster for a quick draw.

He stood before the door's identity screen and activated it. It opened and he entered. Bat Hardin was getting up from his comfort chair to greet his visitor. He had a drink in his hand.

He said, "Why, hello. Sidney, isn't it? Sid Cusack, Carol Ann's husband."

"That's right," Sid said tightly.

"Well, come on in. Have a drink. I'm glad you dropped by, I have a few things to ask you about."

Sid said tightly, "I haven't any answers for your questions, Hardin. I came around to get you to come to a . . . conference."

Bat looked at him. "At the request of Holly Owyler, undoubtedly. No thanks, Cusack. I might be stupid, but not that stupid. Your pal Owyler is about to have the boom lowered on him. I suggest we sit around for a little and see if we can get you out from under—for your wife's sake, not yours."

"Let's go, Hardin."

Bat grunted amusement. "Do you think you're big enough to take me?"

Sid Cusack said bluntly, "Maybe, maybe not, but I haven't got the time to find out. Besides, I want you to walk out of here, not have to be carried. It'd be too conspicuous."

"So where are we supposedly going?"

"Down to the transport station. There's an electro-steamer waiting for us there with Mr. Owyler and some of the others—and Miss Nash. She's going along."

"Miss *Nash!* How did you get hold of her?"

Sid Cusack said, "She thought she was meeting you. Something to do with the job."

Bat Hardin began heading for the other, angrily. But

then there was a gun in Sid Cusack's hand. Bat came to a quick halt.

"Are you completely around the bend, Cusack, pulling a shooter?"

"This is an important conference, Hardin. They want you to attend, real bad."

Bat Hardin turned deliberately and resumed his chair. "Okay, listen. I'll come peacefully but only on condition that you sit down for a minute and we'll go over a few things."

Sid Cusack thought about it. "All right, but don't try any tricks, Hardin. I've had military training too. I know how to use this thing." He sat down on the couch, the gun trained steadily. "Start talking."

Bat said evenly, "They took you for a patsy, Cusack. I don't know the details but I can make a good guess. You were broke, but they let you get into them for a few hundred pseudo-dollars. They even probably let you win a bit at first. Then they demanded their money. When you didn't have it, they sucked you into their organization. You're expendable, but you probably don't know it. They've got you primed now, so you're even ready for murder."

"Murder! Don't be crazy."

"When you're willing to point a gun at somebody, Cusack, you're willing to shoot him. And why do you think they want me to attend this so-called conference?"

"I don't know. Maybe they want to make a deal with you."

Bat laughed sourly. "They want to kill me, Cusack. Me and Miss Nash, because we're wise to them and before tomorrow was out they'd all be under arrest."

"Don't be silly, it's just a non-profit gambling club."

Bat laughed again. "You almost make me believe you think that."

"Well, it is. I ought to know. Half the most prosperous men in this deme belong."

"I'm sure they do. What do they play besides cards?"

Sid Cusack hesitated. "Roulette and craps."

"Very profitable percentage on both and I'll bet the stakes are high. But that isn't the only source of the big income. Owyler and his gang are really on the take, but they're not foolish enough to scare the big marks away by crooked wheels, or by taking advantage of the average man in the so-called club. What they do is occasionally set up one of the big suckers for a real fall. Did you know that Owyler and Cantine both have yachts down in Florida, supposedly given to them by millionaire friends?"

Sid Cusack was scoffing disbelief. "They're rich themselves."

"Like hell they are. Every one of those club officials are collecting Negative Income Tax. Their only source of income beyond that is milking the sucker. They've even worked out a method of getting pseudo-dollars transferrred to their credit accounts. They'll get deeply into one of the victims, probably using marked cards or rigged dice, and have him buy one of them an expensive painting or other art object to pay off. Then they flog it at the Swap Shop, or through some dealer in one of the larger cities. Seemingly, no law broken."

Sid Cusack was irritated but he jiggled the gun. "All right, I listened to what you had to say. Now let's go."

Bat said, "Actually, you're beginning to believe me. Listen, Cusack, all six of those men have lengthy criminal records, run up when they were younger and before the institution of the Universal Credit Card made crime almost impossible. Owyler has two counts of murder against him although he beat the romp both times. Haines has spent two terms in the pen—back in the days when they still had penitentiaries."

"Let's go, Hardin. You can tell them about it when you see them."

"Can't you see? They figure that Miss Nash and I are the only two persons who know about the whole operation. They *have* to finish us off. But then, Cusack, there's one more person who knows and they realize that, too."

Sid Cusack was scowling. "That's how much you know about it, Hardin. You and this Nash dame are the only two."

"And Carol Ann."

Cusack was staring at him.

Bat said softly, "They'll have to finish her off too ... Sid."

Cusack was staring at him.

"They'll probably keep you on their hook for further dirty work. They have you where they want you. But Carol Ann will have to go. If you give them any trouble, you too. They probably have in mind taking us out into the countryside and faking an electro-steamer accident on one of the unautomated mountain backroads. But Carol Ann will have to go because she'll smell a rat and report to Barry Ten Eyck."

Sid Cusack had come to his feet while the other talked. Now, wearily, he tossed the gun to the couch. "Okay," he said. "I couldn't have done it anyway. If what you say is true, and everything stacks up, then the only thing they can do—if they want to remain in business—is kill you. You're right."

Bat Hardin looked into his face for a long moment, then turned to a drawer, opened it and brought forth a Gyro-jet pistol of his own. He threw the magazine and checked it, slugged it back into the gun's butt with the heel of his hand and jacked a cartridge into the barrel.

He said, "How many of them are there, down in the electro-steamer?"

"Owyler, Haines, Foster, Cantine, Duncan, Horowitz and two muscle boys they use for trouble-shooters—the way they were using me."

"The whole gang, eh?"

"Not exactly. It comes to me that the clubs in the other demes aren't really independent. It's probably a big organization. I don't know who the top man might be."

"We'll find out," Bat said grimly. He gestured with his head at the gun Cusack had thrown away. "Can you really use that?"

Cusack looked at him in some surprise but said, "I was a member of the pistol team of my regiment."

"Okay. Pick it up and let's go. We're rescuing Pauline Nash."

Sid Cusack swooped the gun up, jammed it into his shoulder rig. "How about some of the rest of your security men?"

Bat snorted. "I don't think a single one of them has ever been shot at in his life. Besides, we don't have time. And, besides, you've got to do a bit of redeeming ... Sid."

"Right, Bat," Sid Cusack said. "Let's go. They'll think I'm bringing you in, as instructed."

Bat Hardin was saying, "So that about winds it up. Haines and Foster were game—and stupid. They shot it out. It was Haines that nicked Sid. Not too bad, though. Owyler and the others had their hands up before we hardly got our shooters out."

Barry Ten Eyck said to Sid Cusack, who was sitting side by side with an anxious Carol Ann on an office divan, "How bad is that, Sid?"

Sid brushed it aside, albeit a bit ostentaciously. "Like Bat said, just a nick. I'll have this bandage off in a week."

Jim Cotswold said, "What about the other demes?"

Bat said, "I turned it all over to Chief of Security Snider and Mayor Levy. They'll wind it up before the day is through."

Carol Ann said, "Golly, what'll happen to this Holly Owyler and the others?"

Bat looked over at her. "It's a Federal romp. Messing around with getting pseudo-dollars away from people illegally." He grunted amusement. "We've got two or three club members who are willing to testify. Probably ones who had been burned more than usual. But, you know, ninety-nine percent of them are indignant. They can't bear the idea of the club folding up, crooked or not. You know what one of them said? He said, 'Hell, I knew it was crooked, but it was the only place I know of where you could gamble.'"

Barry Ten Eyck had to laugh. "How compulsive can you get?"

Bat said, in a more serious vein, "Now this is what I suggest. I'm going to take Sid, here, under my wing. Break him in as a basic Human Relations officer. Give him a course of studies, work him in on the job. I'll make a cop out of him if it kills me—or, more likely, him. If I ever see that shine of eye that indicates trank, I'll . . ."

But Barry Ten Eyck was shaking his head.

" 'Fraid not, Bat," he said. "It's not the way it spins."

All eyes were upon him, all, except Sid Cusack's, indignant.

Carol Ann said, "But . . . but, Mr. Ten Eyck . . . it's . . . it's his chance."

Barry Ten Eyck didn't even bother to look at her. He said to Bat Hardin, "You're no longer our Security Chief, so you won't be able to sponser Sid Cusack, as such."

Bat was flabbergasted. "But, Holy Smokes, how come? Listen, I figure I've been doing a pretty good job. And the way this deme is going, doubling up as your Vice-Demecrat and your Security Chief helps out on the staff budget."

"Ummm," Barry Ten Eyck said. "But the thing is this. I just got a call from Mayor Levy over in Administration. Vanderfeller and Moore are completing a new pseudo-city down in Guatemala. It seems that I speak Spanish. It seems that I'm being transferred from this moth-eaten, crumbling, nine-year-old deme to one of the ultra-new ones down there. It also seems that instead of transferring someone else here, that everybody on the staff is being bounced upward."

They were goggling him.

"So, Bat, you're no longer Security Chief. You're the Demecrat of this rapidly deteriorating building, and the Lord take mercy on your soul. Jim, you're the new Vice-Demecrat, God help you. Miss Cusack . . . ah, that is, Mrs. Cusack, you are now among the ranks of the mighty, Second Vice-Demecrat of Shyler-deme."

"But ... but, golly, Mr. Ten Eyck, I don't even have a degree for ..."

He grinned at her. "They're waiving that, temporarily. Good deme management is in short supply. And you've been recommended from hell and gone. You'll have to study after hours—if there are any after hours, I was never able to find any."

He looked at Sid Cusack who had been stricken dumb by the last ten minutes' developments.

"I assume the job on security is still open. Bat Hardin's boss now. You'll be starting in at the bottom of the totem pole, and your wife's pretty near the top. It'll take guts to be able to accept that, but it should give you incentive to work and to study."

Barry Ten Eyck got up, yawning mightily.

"It's been a busy day, folks. I suggest we all knock off, nobody telling nobody where we're going, and adjourn to the Swank Room, up on the highest level and get smashed, smashed, smashed ..."

Four voices said, simultaneously, "I second the motion."

ABOUT THE AUTHOR

Born in California fifty years ago of stock going back to Gold Rush times, MACK REYNOLDS has made his living as a free-lance writer since 1950, specializing in science fiction. He has published some thirty books and book-length serials and over five hundred novelettes, short stories and articles. In addition, he has co-edited several books, including *The Science Fiction Carnival* (with Fredric Brown), a collection that has been reprinted many times in several languages. Due to a life-long interest in socioeconomics, he has specialized in his extrapolations into the future on themes based upon political economy. Coming to the conclusion that every science fiction writer should have a specialty and deal with a field in which he is knowledgeable, Mack Reynolds has decided to concentrate on the year 2000 and for some time has attempted to write "realistic" science fiction dealing with the problems that will confront us at that time. So successful has he been that organizations such as EIDOS, the Theoretical Research "think tank" specializing on the world of tomorrow, has asked him to become a member. Realizing that books alone are inadequate for research, Mr. Reynolds in the 1950s began a campaign of seeking out material for his stories all over the world and, since, has lived in or traveled through more than seventy-five countries in every continent but Antarctica. A true adventurer, he once crossed the Sahara to Timbuktu and on the way was captured by the Tuareg (The Forgotten of Allah, and the so-called Apaches of the Sahara). Another time in the tropical jungles of Mexico he was bitten by a vampire bat and had to be treated for rabies. During his travels, Mack Reynolds has been in more than half a dozen wars, revolutions and military revolts, ranging from being shot at by the Huks in the Philippines to being bombed by anti-Castro Cubans. During World War II, after graduating from the Army Marine Officers' Cadet School and then the Transportation Corps Marine Officers' that is, Mrs. Cusack, you are now among the ranks of the mighty, Second Vice-Demecrat of Shyler-deme."

"But ... but, golly, Mr. Ten Eyck, I don't even have a degree for ..."

He grinned at her. "They're waiving that, temporarily. Good deme management is in short supply. And you've been recommended from hell and gone. You'll have to study after hours—if there are any after hours, I was never able to find any."

He looked at Sid Cusack who had been stricken dumb by the last ten minutes' developments.

"I assume the job on security is still open. Bat Hardin's boss now. You'll be starting in at the bottom of the totem pole, and your wife's pretty near the top. It'll take guts to be able to accept that, but it should give you incentive to work and to study."

Barry Ten Eyck got up, yawning mightily.

"It's been a busy day, folks. I suggest we all knock off, nobody telling nobody where we're going, and adjourn to the Swank Room, up on the highest level and get smashed, smashed, smashed ..."

Four voices said, simultaneously, "I second the motion."

ABOUT THE AUTHOR

Born in California fifty years ago of stock going back to Gold Rush times, MACK REYNOLDS has made his living as a free-lance writer since 1950, specializing in science fiction. He has published some thirty books and book-length serials and over five hundred novelettes, short stories and articles. In addition, he has co-edited several books, including *The Science Fiction Carnival* (with Fredric Brown), a collection that has been reprinted many times in several languages. Due to a life-long interest in socioeconomics, he has specialized in his extrapolations into the future on themes based upon political economy. Coming to the conclusion that every science fiction writer should have a specialty and deal with a field in which he is knowledgeable, Mack Reynolds has decided to concentrate on the year 2000 and for some time has attempted to write "realistic" science fiction dealing with the problems that will confront us at that time. So successful has he been that organizations such as EIDOS, the Theoretical Research "think tank" specializing on the world of tomorrow, has asked him to become a member. Realizing that books alone are inadequate for research, Mr. Reynolds in the 1950s began a campaign of seeking out material for his stories all over the world and, since, has lived in or traveled through more than seventy-five countries in every continent but Antarctica. A true adventurer, he once crossed the Sahara to Timbuktu and on the way was captured by the Tuareg (The Forgotten of Allah, and the so-called Apaches of the Sahara). Another time in the tropical jungles of Mexico he was bitten by a vampire bat and had to be treated for rabies. During his travels, Mack Reynolds has been in more than half a dozen wars, revolutions and military revolts, ranging from being shot at by the Huks in the Philippines to being bombed by anti-Castro Cubans. During World War II, after graduating from the Army Marine Officers' Cadet School and then the Transportation Corps Marine Officers'

School, he became a second officer (navigator) on army transport class ships and served in the South Pacific. Later he was offered a soldier of fortune position by Chiang Kai-shek. He says he has been in more jails than he can count off-hand "but never for a dishonorable reason." Although not at present affiliated with any political group, he has written books and stories extrapolating on what the future would look like if the Technocrats, Anarchists, various varieties of Socialists, Fascists and other reactionary groups were to realize their dreams. Besides all of the science fiction magazines (especially *Astounding*, later renamed *Analog Science Fact and Science Fiction*, to which he contributed on a frequent basis), his stories and articles have appeared in publications ranging from *Playboy* to *The New York Times*. Today, *persona non gratis* in Morocco, Algeria, Syria, Libya, Egypt, Jordan and Saudi Arabia, he makes his home in San Miguel de Allende, Mexico.